Protecting his Secrets

Guarding Royalty 3

Elouise East

Contents

Author note	V
1. Nick	1
2. Malachi	11
3. Nick	22
4. Malachi	32
5. Nick	42
6. Malachi	53
7. Nick	63
8. Malachi	74
9. Nick	84
10. Malachi	95
11. Nick	106
12. Dominic	117
13. Malachi	120
14. Nick	131

15. Malachi   141

16. Nick   151

17. Malachi   162

18. Nick   172

19. Owen   183

20. Malachi   186

21. Nick   196

22. Felix   207

23. Malachi   209

24. Nick   219

25. Malachi   229

26. Brett   241

27. Nick   244

28. Malachi   255

29. Nick   266

30. Malachi   277

31. Nick   288

Protecting Jason   297

Protecting his Life   299

Books by Elouise East   301

About Elouise East   304

Author note

If you would like to see any potential triggers for this book and any other books I've written, please go to this link on my website: https://elouiseeast.com/triggers

1

Nick

Nick Tennant studied his surroundings, his brain instinctively mapping the area, the exit points and the people lounging within the area of Club Royal, the best-kept secret of the United Kingdom. Club Royal was a BDSM club owned by the royal family. Yes, the royal family owned, ran and attended a BDSM club. It was something that had shocked Nick when he'd first been told about it—after he'd signed an NDA when he'd begun to work for the Sutcliffes—but once he'd seen how it worked, who the Sutcliffes were behind closed doors, and how they cared for others, it was just another tick in the they were "amazing" column.

Not that the public would know about it. There were rumours, of course, but no one had ever corroborated those rumours. After all, who could take on the crown and expect to win? Keeping Club Royal a secret was essential, not only for the royal family but for the members who attended, too. It wasn't all rich people who could afford an exclusive membership. It was for anyone who wanted to join and who would abide by the rules.

Laughter brought his attention back to his group of friends.

"I can't believe you're still telling that story, George," Kieren said, pursing his lips. "Find new material, for god's sake!"

Prince George held up his hands with a laugh. "It's a good story. Only when it becomes a not good story will I stop using it."

As a bodyguard to the king, Nick had expected to be ignored and brushed aside by the royal family when he'd first started working for them, but the warmth and camaraderie between the royals and their guards and staff were unexpected. Never in his wildest dreams had he expected to sit amongst royals and guards alike while celebrating the birthday of a guard who had become a member of the royal family. Kieren had been Prince Patrick's bodyguard for years, and then, almost two years ago, they fell in love. As with all relationships that involved the royal family, it wasn't without its issues, and with the treasonous activities of other members of the royal family, it had made things harder, but everyone had got through it.

Well, not everyone.

The usual wave of tightening across his chest, reducing his ability to breathe fully, hit him with the memories of those who hadn't made it through, not least of which were three guards he had worked closely with for many years: Selena, Jared and Simon. Fuck, Simon. Simon had been their boss, a role now taken by Dominic, and he had been the nicest guy on the planet. He hadn't deserved to be shot and killed during an assassination attempt, but fate had other plans. Simon, Jared and Selena had lost their lives that day, and Landon, Viola and Nick had been injured. It had been a shitstorm from the moment they had left the event and one that stayed with them every day.

Breathing through the wave, Nick's chest eased with each passing second, until he could inhale fully again. It was something he'd needed to learn during his physiotherapy appointments.

Whenever his grief consumed him, he had to breathe, even when he hadn't thought he could.

"You good?" Brett asked, leaning closer to be heard over the conversation.

Nick nodded and smiled the smile he knew people wanted to see. The happy joker of the pack. "You know me. Unless I'm tired, I'm good."

Brett snorted. "Yeah, god help anyone who disturbs or stops you from sleeping. I have no idea how you will ever manage when you find a partner."

"Drug them?" Brett glared at him, and Nick laughed and raised his hands, palms forward. "It was a joke!"

"Uh-huh. One in poor taste."

Nick sighed dramatically. "Fine." Those jokes right on the edge of crossing a line were ones that had got him into trouble before now, but they were also the ones that everyone loved him to make. And he was nothing if not a crowd-pleaser. "I can't believe Kieren wouldn't let me plan his party." He huffed. He loved organising parties for people.

"I think after throwing out ideas for a 'voyeur party,' a 'skinny dipping party,' and a... what was it?" Brett tapped his chin, pretending to think.

"The porn party was an inspired idea," Nick argued, shaking his finger in the air. Brett stared at him, the green and brown swirls changing depending on his mood, and Nick sighed. "You're such a buzzkill."

"And you are like a monkey on a leash," Brett muttered. "Ready to cause havoc the moment you're let loose."

Nick threw his head back and laughed, the image of a Nick-shaped monkey traipsing around Windsor Castle something he couldn't let go. "I need an illustration of that."

"An illustration of what?" Felix asked from Brett's other side.

"Me as a monkey," Nick said, laughing again. "So much opportunity."

Brett shook his head. "How did I ever agree to having you on my team?" he grumbled.

"Because I'm awesome."

Nick's gaze landed on the king and his partners, Kean and Kendal, as they stood, heading for the entrance they used to keep them away from the regular patrons. Although Nick wasn't working that night—Colt and Landon were—he couldn't help his need to ensure they were all right. As if he could do much about it if they weren't. He shook his head.

There was still one aspect of that fateful day that plagued him, and probably always would. His brain understood that he'd been injured and, therefore, unable to assist as he usually would, but his heart couldn't let go of the feeling of letting King Andrew down. He should've been able to do more, help more, save more people. But he didn't. And that would stay with him for the rest of his life.

Swallowing down the nausea, he refocused on his friends. One by one, throughout the evening, they disappeared as couples, triads, or singles wanting to find someone, and Nick stayed right where he was. He wasn't in the mood for company, so while Brett and Felix chatted beside him, Nick's thoughts drifted to the one person who was never far from them—Malachi Sanders.

Malachi was a reporter—mainly written work, but he occasionally appeared on camera, too—and he was a thorn in Nick's side. His comments about the royal family left a lot to be desired, and he found himself wanting to strangle him more than once. The media was a fickle business, enjoying the drama and downfall of people more than the building up of them, and Nick hated it. Seeing false headlines about his friends was something he would never get used to, but it came with the territory. How Andrew and the rest of the Sutcliffes ignored it was beyond him.

If it had been his supposed truths plastered across the front pages, he doubted he would be so chilled about it.

"Hey, I'm heading out," he said to Brett and Felix. "I'll see you tomorrow."

Brett frowned at him but nodded. "Take it easy."

"See you," Felix said.

Nick headed through the double doors, away from the conversation room, as Prince Douglas called it, and back into the foyer. He stopped by the front desk and placed his thumb on the sensor.

"Heading home?" Clarice asked. Clarice was the one person who kept Club Royal running as well as it did. She was the one person who could keep anyone out without remorse, and if anyone crossed her, they were done for. She was also the nicest person when it came to the royal family and their staff.

"Yeah. I need sleep," he lied with a smile.

Clarice chuckled. "I've heard about you and sleep, so yes, you better get home."

Nick threw his hands in the air. "Does everyone know I'm grumpy when I don't sleep enough?"

Clarice raised her eyebrows. "Yes. It's an important piece of information."

Nick laughed and waved. "Take care."

"You, too."

He headed down the lift to the parking garage beneath the club and slipped into his car. When the door slammed shut, he rested his head back and closed his eyes. His calf ached, as it often did when he'd been on it for too long. It never impeded his work because he could push the ache aside, but it was a niggle that would forever remind him of what happened.

Another reminder was the front page news the day after the event:

BODYGUARDS EFFED UP!

As if they weren't grieving enough with the loss of their colleagues and friends, they had to have their faces rubbed in the fact that they hadn't protected the king as they should have. Yes, he'd survived, but it was a close call. One Nick promised to never allow to happen again.

Exhaling a huff of air, he started his car and headed home, which was a modest one-bedroom apartment close to Windsor Hospital. His home fit him perfectly, designed with shades of nature—greens, browns, beiges and the occasional blue—to soothe his down-to-earth personality. Though he was an air sign, Aquarius—yes, he knew his zodiac sign thanks to his sister's influence—his mind called more to the earth signs, and he'd honoured his need to think outside a box someone tried to put him in. Just because someone said he should be a certain way, doesn't mean another way wouldn't suit him better. He had his parents to thank for that way of thinking. They'd hated being put into boxes by their parents and had made sure they didn't expect the same from their kids.

He parked the car, entered the building and took the lift to the fourth floor. When the doors opened, he grinned and shook his head.

"Rye, what are you doing?" he asked his brother, who sat on the floor in front of his door.

Rye glanced at him and stood. "Finally! Where were you?"

"Out. What are you doing here? I wasn't expecting you."

"Do I have to announce myself every time I want to come and see you?" Rye asked.

Nick raised his eyebrows and leaned against the wall, making no move to enter his home until his little brother answered some questions. "No, but I would've been here quicker had I known. Now answer my question."

Rye deflated and crossed his arms over his chest, his black hair falling across his forehead as he stared at the floor. "My date went badly. I left after the starter."

Nick's heart broke for him. Rye was an amazing guy, who kept putting himself out there to find that special someone, but every woman he chose was only after sex and every man was an asshole, to put it not so nicely. One day, he'd find the man or woman for him, but Nick wished it was sooner. He deserved it.

Nick unlocked his door and let his brother in first, locking the door behind them. He threw his keys on the table by the door and kicked off his shoes, placing them in the shoe cupboard. "Do you want a drink?"

"Whiskey?"

"How about tea, coffee or hot chocolate?"

Rye was old enough to drink, but Nick didn't encourage it. Too many people had been taken advantage of when they were drunk, their sister included, and so they had always tempered how much they drank whenever they went anywhere. Well, Nick did. He wasn't sure if his brothers and sister did so anymore. But after Eliza had nearly become another statistic of rape, Nick made sure he was mostly firing on all cylinders while he was out with friends.

"Hot chocolate, please," Rye answered. "Marshmallows?"

Nick smiled. "Of course."

He set to work, making hot chocolate using chocolate powder and hot milk, plus an extra square of actual chocolate that, once melted, made it taste that much better, and then marshmallows sprinkled on top. Once it was ready, he joined Rye in the living room where he was curled up on the sofa with his head resting on his arms.

"Here we go," Nick said. "The best cure for a broken heart."

"My heart's not broken." Rye rolled his eyes and reached for the mug.

"Well, in that case..." Nick took the drink way before Rye could take it.

"Hey!" Rye snatched it back, barely keeping everything inside the cup. Though Nick's carpet was brown, so it wouldn't make much of a difference.

Nick settled beside him, tucking one leg beneath him, and leaned his elbow on the back of the sofa, the mug resting carefully on his knee. "Is it just that he was an awful guy, or is something else bothering you?"

The fifteen-year age gap between them wasn't an issue. They were as close as if they'd been born as twins—or he supposed quads because he was as close with all three of his siblings, but there was something between him and Rye that just worked. If Nick was being honest, he could see Rye was at the same crossroads in his life that Nick had been at his age. It was as if Rye was a younger version of him, and he could see where Rye was going and what mistakes he would make along the way. But it didn't matter. Mistakes were there to be made, and if he warned him away too much from a certain path, Rye was stubborn enough to do it, anyway. Better that he found out for himself, even though he would get hurt before the hurt got better.

Rye sighed and stared at his mug, swirling one marshmallow through the others as he spoke. "I'm just sick of the duds. I'm tired of playing the waiting game. I have a job I love, a family I get on with and friends I enjoy hanging out with, but I want someone to share it all with. Is that too much to ask?"

"Not at all. I don't have an answer for you, Rye. As you can see, I'm hardly living my dream."

Rye scoffed. "You have everything you love except a partner, too."

"Exactly my point. If I knew the answer, you'd be the first I'd tell, but I don't have a clue."

"Life sucks and then you die," Rye muttered.

"Don't say that," Nick said. "Life doesn't suck. Only one part of it does, and not for the right reasons." He waggled his eyebrows.

Rye let out a burst of laughter, which was what Nick had hoped for. They drank their rapidly cooling hot chocolates, and Nick asked if Rye wanted to stay for a movie.

"Nah. I'm going to go home and sleep it off. Tomorrow is another day, and the sooner it gets here, the better."

Nick hugged him tightly before he left, making sure it was the best hug ever, because he always wanted to have his hugs remembered if there was ever a time he didn't come back to them. Simon's, Selena's and Jared's deaths had made it more than clear that there was always a chance the same would happen to him. So from that moment, he had given "goodbye" hugs to every member of his family every time he left them. It was a morbid thought, but no more than making a will in the event of his death or writing down exactly what songs or poems he wanted at his funeral.

When he locked the door behind his brother, he exhaled and scrubbed his hands over his face. With nothing he could do to help, he paced, looking at the problem from every available angle. But no. It was Rye's life, and he had to live it himself. Nick's protection could only go so far, and putting them all in bubble wrap wasn't an option, unfortunately.

He climbed into the shower and washed away the day before dragging on some pyjama bottoms and a T-shirt. Venturing into the living room, he grabbed the remote, pulled the fluffy throw from the back of the sofa over his legs and scrolled through the endless list of movies and TV shows. It would probably take him longer to choose something than it would to watch it, but decisions were hard sometimes. When it came to his life, anyway. He could make decisions with his job in milliseconds, but that was it.

Rye had hit the nail on the head when he'd said everything in his life was perfect except for finding a partner. It was the same for Nick. Thinking back to Club Royal, he wasn't averse to the kinks and lifestyles he saw there. He loved watching, which might make him a voyeur, but he didn't get off on it. He wasn't into bondage. The pet play was cute, but again it did nothing for him except think they were adorable. He couldn't see himself being a handler. He loved the community aspect of the club and that was the main reason he went—if he excluded that he had to be there whenever he was on duty and the king went.

He had no idea what he wanted. He only knew when he met someone and they didn't click. The only person he had a remote interest in—and nothing romantic at all—was Malachi Sanders. That reporter was a thorn in his side, and one day, Nick wouldn't be able to hold back his opinion of the lying asshole. He didn't begrudge anyone trying to pay their bills, but that man took it to a whole other level of mean.

What confused Nick, though, was that Malachi didn't seem to be the same person he was in person. Whenever he'd overheard the man talking, he was polite, well-spoken and kind. It didn't mesh with the tone of his writing, but who was Nick to argue?

As the chosen film wore on, Nick found his thoughts reaching for the enigma that was Malachi regularly, as it had done for many months. If Nick couldn't have someone to share his life with, he could use that space to fixate on something else. What else did he have?

2

Malachi

Malachi Sanders strained his neck over the crowd of reporters following Prince Consort Kendal as they entered Windsor Hospital. Luckily for him, the royal family had allowed only two reporters to enter with them, and one of them was him. So, when the bodyguard called Nick waved him and another reporter forward, he squeezed his way through to the grumbles of the many surrounding him. He followed them at a sedate pace, not wanting to seem as excited as he was.

The Sutcliffes allowed a select few reporters to accompany them, depending on the event type, and they were fair about who they chose. Every credible reporter—no matter the tone of their reports—was allowed to accompany them. For example, there were two reporters for this event because it was based at a hospital, and the royal family didn't want to overwhelm the patients in attendance. At other events, such as dinners, more reporters could be selected. But each reporter would get the chance again when the other reporters had received their chance. Fair, but it took far too long for his turn to come around each time.

It had taken him by surprise when he'd received his first invitation to join them because they hated him—and Malachi couldn't argue with them. The tone of his reports was argumentative and aggressive, and he hated every minute of writing them. So why did he? Because he had no choice. Being the reporter for Windsor Chronicle came with certain contractual obligations, and since he hadn't worked his way through his five-year contract with them yet, he still had to abide by the original terms. No amount of negotiation had worked to get the terms changed, so Malachi was stuck.

Having to write each report in a negative light took a little more of his soul each time, but there was light at the end of the tunnel. As long as Tucker didn't go back on his word, Malachi would be free of the old contract in a year, and a new, better-tasting one would take its place.

Refocusing on the corridor they walked down, Malachi forced himself to listen to what the hospital administrator was saying to the king's partner.

"—the blood donor unit within the hospital is busy, but we need more donors all the time. As you can understand, blood is essential for many parts of the hospital, from transfusions to surgeries to accidents. There is always a need for it."

"How much blood do you go through each week?" Kendal asked as they entered the blood department.

"Well, we need around five thousand donations each day to keep up with demand over the entire NHS."

"Wow, that's...a lot," Kendal said. "I'm assuming you get what you need."

The administrator waved his hand back and forward. "Most of the time, yes. We're always asking for more donors to come forward because every day there are reasons current donors can't donate. It could be because someone got pregnant or their iron levels were too low. They could have a cold or the flu. They might've had a recent tattoo or a dental procedure. There are many reasons someone might not donate, which is why we ask for new donors as often as possible."

"I never thought of that."

Malachi studied the room. It seemed like any other hospital room, except there were several beds towards the back of the room and lots of chairs at the front. Hot and cold drinks and biscuits sat on a table to the side, where people sat to wait before they could leave. Malachi hadn't donated blood before, but with everything the administrator said, maybe he should start.

The conversation continued, and Malachi made a few notes, wincing with every stab at the royal family he knew he was going to make. It broke his heart every time he saw their expressions tighten with his words, and it was one reason he created an alter-ego.

"Does anyone have any questions?" Kendal asked, glancing at him and the second reporter, Stan Willows.

"Do you donate blood?" Malachi asked.

Kendal smiled at him. "Not currently. My iron levels have been too low, and I've been working to get them higher so I can start. But I know Kean does, and Andrew does occasionally."

"Why does the king not donate regularly?" Malachi asked.

There it was. The slight tightening of Kendal's eyes, and it broke another piece of Malachi's soul. "With his age and health in mind, his physicians believed it was better to reduce the number of donations he did each year."

"Is the king ill?" he asked, cutting the other reporter off again.

Kendal laughed, the gentle sound reaching his ears like soft music. "Not in the slightest." They glanced at his companion. "Stan, do you have any questions?"

As Stan spoke, Malachi wrote down some thoughts about how his report was going to go. A tingling shot down his spine and bumps raced across his forearms, the hairs lifting and lowering as the shiver made itself known. He glanced around and met Nick's gaze. His brown eyes narrowed at him, and Malachi froze, not wanting to startle the bodyguard into chasing him away. Because that's what it felt like. He was the prey, and Nick was the predator.

"Shall we move on?"

The question drew everyone's attention, and the administrator waved towards the door. Everyone followed suit, and Malachi dropped to the back of the group, not wanting to get more attention than he already had. He'd already decided what the report would focus on—the king's health—but he also had an idea for the corresponding report he would write. He would have to wait to see what the backlash was on his report and, undoubtedly, the one Adelaide Thompson would submit, but he believed he could counteract most of the damage they would cause.

Adelaide was a fox in a chicken house, and she made everyone else look like child's play, even Malachi, so whenever she wrote something about the royal family, his alter-ego counteracted it with a separate report, taking each of her points and giving alternative points of view. She hated Kai Ruffers with a passion, and every time she mentioned him, Malachi stood a little straighter. Because Kai Ruffers was the only way he could live with himself.

"You're not making any friends being like this, you know?"

Malachi didn't need to glance to the side; he already knew who it was. "I'm not here to make friends," he said, staring ahead.

"You might get more chances if you were."

He feigned ignorance, pouting his lips. "I get enough content without needing chances." Playing the role got harder every day.

"Well, I suppose if you can fall asleep at night with everything you write, you must be used to sleeping in dog shit." With that,

Nick dropped back again, and Malachi swallowed against the words and tears that wanted to escape. No one understood. But that wasn't their fault.

After spending an hour touring certain areas of the hospital, they were led back to the exit. Kendal held out their hand and shook Stan's hand before offering it to Malachi—a move that shocked him.

"Thank you for being here. I hope you can help to bring some light to the need for more blood donors with your articles. It really is a worthy and essential cause," Kendal said.

Malachi understood the undercurrents of their words, but he would only be able to help with one column, and not the one the royal family knew about. Instead, he asked one more question.

"Do you have any plans for Prince Consort Kean's birthday?"

Kendal chuckled. "We're spending time with our families. That's a celebration right there."

Malachi couldn't help but commend Kendal's way with words, and how they diverted the attention when they needed to. It was taught to most royals, Malachi knew that, but Kendal seemed to have taken it to a whole other level.

"It truly is," Malachi agreed. "Thank you for the opportunity today."

"You're welcome."

He headed for the exit, Stan having already left, but felt the hairs on his neck prickling again. Glancing over his shoulder, he caught Nick's gaze once more. Under normal circumstances, he wouldn't have minded being studied like a specimen in a petri dish, but right then, that feeling of being the sole focus of someone was unnerving. Malachi ducked his head and left, exhaling heavily.

"Did you get whatever trash you're going to write about them now?" a voice said beside him as he finished writing his last notes.

He lifted his gaze to Stan's. "Everyone is entitled to write what they want, Stan. You know that." Though his stomach agreed with Stan. If he didn't work his way into an early grave with stomach or sleep issues before his contract ended, he'd be surprised.

"Of course they are, but even you can give them a break some days, surely."

"I write the story I see, Stan." Meaning, he wrote the stories Tucker wanted him to.

Stan huffed, shook his head and left, and Malachi swallowed down bile. *I'm right there with you, Stan. One day, you'll all see.*

Heavy with the burden of keeping secrets, he headed down the street, having not bothered with his car as he lived close by. His phone rang as he walked off his melancholy, and he pulled it from his pocket, grinning at the screen.

"Hola, Abuela," he said.

"Ah, Kai. Anyone who said you couldn't learn languages was wrong," his grandmother, Sally, said with a chuckle.

Malachi returned the laugh. "That's all I can manage. You're the one learning languages like you're five years old."

He could almost hear his grandmother's shrug as she brushed off his compliments. "What else do I have to spend my time on? Languages are there to be learnt. Spanish is a lovely sounding one."

"It is. I just wish I could do it justice."

"That you try is all I can ask. Are you still coming for dinner?"

Malachi wandered down the path to his front door. "I am. I just need to finish this article, and then I'll be over. Is everyone else joining us?"

He had an older brother and three younger sisters, who occasionally made time in their hectic—cough, cough—schedules to join them at their grandmother's house for dinner. They had their own lives, but Malachi could never understand why they wanted to distance themselves when Sally and their mother, Emily, were the best and most down-to-earth people he knew. But each to their own.

"Vanessa and Christine said they might make it, but Ben and Zara should be here. Are you being unkind to the royal family again?"

Malachi sighed, taking his shoes off just inside the door. "I'm doing my job, Grandma. That's all." Sally fell silent, and Malachi squirmed. "Not long left," he added when the silence became too much.

"Take care of yourself, too, Kai. Don't let them take your soul."

Too late. "Never. I'll see you in a couple of hours."

"Ich liebe dich," Sally said, bringing a smile to Malachi's face. His grandmother was already fluent in German when she switched to Spanish, soaking up the languages quicker than anyone he knew despite her reaching past eighty years of age. She had used the same "I love you" phrase in German the moment Malachi had burst out laughing, thinking she'd said she loved dick. He was grateful his family weren't prudes because they threw sexual jokes and innuendos like best friends would.

"I love you, too, Abuela."

"See you soon."

Malachi hung up and headed for the kitchen to make a coffee, delaying the inevitable for as long as possible. When the coffee steamed in his mug and he inhaled the aroma with a blissful smile, he drifted towards the desk in the corner of the room, its only saving grace being the view behind the house. Each step was like trudging through knee-height snow, but he gritted his teeth and sat at his computer, booting it up. While it did its thing, he put his notepad down and checked the recording on his phone. He had the entire visit recorded, but he relied on notes as well, just in case his phone failed.

By the time he was ready to start his article, he had bolstered himself against the words he had to write. He always wrote the hardest article first because then he could counteract his words, and the words of other reporters, in the easier one. Plus, he needed the pick-me-up after writing such soul-destroying things about the royal family.

Staring at the cursor blinking on the empty page, he held his fingers over the keys. Breathing deeply, he started typing, wincing and swallowing hard with every blade he sliced through the royal family. When he finished, he stared down at his arms, expecting blood to be dripping from his vein where he'd torn them apart. Shoring himself up again, he read through the article, checking for errors, and finally emailed it through to Tucker.

Then he raced to the bathroom and threw up. Same routine every time.

He flushed and splashed water over his face before pouring himself a glass of water from the kitchen. He sipped it, hoping the coolness of the liquid would settle his stomach, but only one thing could.

His counter-article.

The Malachi Sanders title was *Is The King Ill?* But the Kai Ruffers title was *Leading By Example*.

Writing the positive side of the event soothed his soul but made him feel no better about what he'd already done. The stress of his job didn't help his health, and insomnia was a friend he wished wasn't so faithful.

When he was done, he slumped back in his seat but smiled. He wouldn't release this version until after the other reporters had released their own. He'd need to check that he counteracted any of their remarks as well. Before he finished, he checked his emails, unsurprised to find one from someone who had been in his inbox many times over the past few weeks. They seemed to enjoy his Malachi articles, and often commended him on his choice of words and commiserated that the country was beholden to the royal family. Fans were everywhere, and he responded to some emails from them, but that one... Something was off about him, though he'd spoken to him several times as a source, he still emailed in after every article was published.

After checking the clock, he switched his computer off and headed for the door, and by the time he arrived at his grandmother's house, he'd relaxed somewhat. The underlying tension from his first article wouldn't disappear for hours, but he needed his family right then.

"Kai!" his mother said, dragging him into her arms when she reached him. He stumbled with one shoe on and the other half off.

"Hey, Mum. How are you?"

Emily pulled back. "I'm good." She cupped his cheek, tracing beneath his eyes with her finger. "You look tired again."

He tried for a smile. "I'm okay. I promise." He changed the subject. "Anyone else here yet?"

"We beat you here, loser!" Zara called from the region of the kitchen.

"Zara!" Their grandmother went off in a tirade of German, which none of them could understand fluently, but no one could mistake the telling-off tone of her voice.

"Yes, Grandma," Zara said as Malachi entered the kitchen. She probably had no idea what Sally had been saying, but they knew not to argue.

"Kai!" Sally enveloped him, and he clung to her, closing his eyes and breathing in his grandmother's scent. Whatever it was soothed him time and again. "You need to stop this, Kai. It's destroying you," she whispered.

"Not long left." He pulled back and smiled. "I visited the hospital today. They were talking about blood donors and how they always needed more people to donate. It's something to consider."

He settled at the dining table while his mother bustled around. She was someone who enjoyed taking care of her family and wouldn't let anyone help. Except when it came to setting the table and making drinks for everyone. Oh, and washing up afterwards. Those chores were down to the kids.

"Have you finished being mean to the royal family yet?" Ben, his brother, asked.

Malachi shook his head and pursed his lips. "Not yet. Soon, though."

"I don't know why you let him control you like you do. There are other jobs available."

It was an argument they regularly had. "There aren't as many journalist jobs as you think. Everything hinges on who you know. Reputation is everything in this job, and if I can just finish this contract out, I'll be home free."

"You hope," Ben countered.

Malachi didn't answer because it was something that scared the hell out of him. Yes, contractually, he didn't have to work for the Windsor Chronicle at the end of the following year, but what was stopping him from making his life hell and blackmailing him into working for him longer? Malachi would do everything in his power to keep his family safe, healthy and to keep food on the table, but Tucker was capable of a lot of things Malachi chose to ignore. After all, if he ignored them, they weren't happening. He didn't need any more burdens on his shoulders.

"Enough work talk," Sally said. "Ben, any luck in the romance department?"

Thankful for the distraction, he joined in with ribbing Ben about his lack of luck with girls. It would turn on him eventually, but he didn't mind. As long as they weren't focused on how he was destroying his soul, he could weather anything.

Sharp assessing eyes flitted through his head, followed by a turned-down mouth and creased forehead. Malachi shook the image away. He couldn't think about that bodyguard now because every time he did, his body fought between cold and hot. Cold because those eyes could spear anyone with hatred, and hot because the man was sex personified. It hadn't been that long ago that Malachi had stared at the screen with a dawning sense of horror as he watched the king's assassination attempt where too many bodyguards were killed or hurt, including Nick Tennant. One particular camera had caught Nick slamming to the ground and blood pouring from his wounds as his head hit the pavement and he stopped moving.

At the time, Malachi had thought he was dead, and he'd been barely able to breathe himself, but the news had reported him alive. Unlike some of his colleagues. He wished he'd been able to say something to them, but the only thing he could do was allow his alter-ego to send his sympathies to them.

One day, he might be able to face them without dreading the hatred that would no doubt be on their faces.

One day, he would be able to hold his head up high and say he didn't write that crap.

One day, he could make amends for what he'd done.

3

Nick

I s Prince Frederick the right heir for the job?

By Malachi Sanders

We've had this discussion before, but nothing shows as being incapable as messing up an official meeting with the heads of several countries in attendance. But leave it to Prince Frederick to do so.

Once again, the heir to the throne has shown how much he still has to learn before he can follow in his father's footsteps. Not that the king is doing a much better job, but at least, he's learnt some tact.

Nick growled at the article, ready to shake the reporter until his thoughts rattled around in his head and created some sense rather than the bumble of craziness he vomited onto the pages of his column.

"Stand down, Nick," Brett said.

"He's...infuriating!"

"He is, but he's not the only one. We have eyes on the ones we think have the potential to deteriorate and cause problems, including Malachi, but we don't have concerns with them yet."

Nick sighed. "It's not right."

"That's the freedom of speech for you. Regardless of whether it makes sense or is true, anyone has the right to say anything," Felix added.

"Isn't there any way of stopping him from attending this evening?"

Brett shook his head before Nick had even finished talking. "No. We're not going to single him out when everything has been confirmed. That's the perfect way to bring about chaos."

"We'll need to keep a closer eye on him, and those others, whenever they're near the king and princes."

Brett nodded. "That we will do. Okay, let's continue the topic around to tonight's dinner event," Brett said. "To confirm, we have King Andrew, Prince Consorts Kean and Kendal, Princes George, Timothy, Eddie, Christian, Oscar, Patrick and Kieren in attendance. There will also be CEOs of several companies, members of Parliament and other high-ranking officials, including some military higher-ups. On top of that are the reporters, including Nick's favourite. There will be ten of those in attendance."

"This is going to be a shit show," Landon muttered.

"Hopefully not," Brett deadpanned. "We will have all the exits guarded by people we trust, and the king will have his usual guards surrounding him, as will the princes. I'm working with the military personnel to confirm which of their guards they are bringing so we have a complete attendance list to go by. I will be working behind the scenes this time, while Locke guards Christian in my stead. We have extra security attending also; you will receive photo confirmation of these people before the evening begins."

The meeting continued, but the frustration built inside Nick. He was an easygoing guy most of the time, but when someone hurt the people close to him, that could change in an instant. It was hard to find the humour most people expected from him in times like those.

"Okay. Get to work, and we'll reconvene at five o'clock this afternoon," Brett said.

Nick took one last look at the headline and shook his head, leaving Sec HQ for his post at the king's office. He was due to swap with Colt and would work for a couple of hours before getting some rest before the event that night. It wasn't supposed to be a long evening, but it would be a stressful one. They always were. He was good at hiding it, though.

The journey to the event was a short one, with it only being at the Fairmont Hotel on the outskirts of Windsor. It had five-star reviews and cost upwards of seven hundred pounds a night. The event room was a logistical nightmare with far too many windows, exits and entrances for anyone's peace of mind. But they made it work. Brett and Felix had worked with the event coordinators to reduce the risk as much as possible, but that didn't mean it was completely gone. As with anything, there were areas they couldn't cover, no matter how much they tried.

Nick, Dominic, Viola and Landon climbed from the cars, studying their surroundings before Dominic gave the nod for the king to get out of the car. Kean and Kendal had arrived in a separate car a few minutes prior, and the princes around half an hour before. Staggering arrivals worked better than having everyone arrive at the same time. Far too many targets all at once when that happened. It was unavoidable sometimes, but they tried to stagger them whenever they could.

Entering the hotel, Nick barely saw the decorative embellishments of the place, concentrating as he was on whether there were any threats, but he'd already studied everything about the place he could. He'd memorised where every possible exit was, every hiding place, every nook and cranny of the place to ensure he could get the king out if something happened. He refused to allow the previous unnecessary deaths to happen again.

"London has entered the building," Dominic said into the radio.

"Roger that," Brett replied from his stakeout in the security room of the hotel. They had cameras at every possible angle, some they had placed specifically for this event to avoid any blind spots. "Oxford, Cardiff and York are mingling in the hall."

Having pseudonyms for the royal family only worked when people didn't know who they were talking about, and most of the world had figured it out by now, but they still used them for the major players. Habit, probably, more than anything else.

As Andrew entered the hall, the charity organisers stepped forward to shake his hand. They spoke for a few minutes before one organiser, Adele, gestured for them to move further into the event. That was the time it became more difficult to keep control of the situation. When people congregated around them to meet with the king, they became obstacles between them, but with years of practice, they worked as a team to ensure Andrew was safe.

As the guests settled into their seats for the dinner part of the evening, Nick relaxed a little, at ease against the wall between the king and the reporters, funnily enough.

"I'm sure you did this on purpose," Nick muttered into the radio as his gaze rolled over the man who sent the recently banked embers of frustration back into an inferno.

"I thought you might prefer having him in your sight. That way, you can keep an eye on him," Brett replied.

"Hmm," was all he said in response.

He couldn't keep his gaze from drifting to Malachi, checking he wasn't misbehaving, but he seemed to be enjoying the meal set before him, laughing and chatting with those seated at the table with him.

When the dinner finished, the organisers stood before their guests and spoke about the charity—one that benefitted children from all walks of life for whatever they needed, no matter their status or background—and had several guest speakers talk about their interactions with the charity. Even though Nick concentrated on the security side of things, the charity sounded good. The problem was that there were so many fantastic charities around and not enough money in his pocket to donate to them all.

Once the speeches ended, it was time for the second part of the mingling, another time to be on alert.

"Nick, keep to the perimeter," Brett said.

"Done."

He was happy to stay back because he could see the wider picture, and it also meant he could monitor the reporters. Everything seemed to be going well. At least until Malachi disappeared.

Nick scanned the ballroom over several minutes, giving the man enough time to return from a bathroom break if he'd been on one, but after twenty minutes, he still hadn't returned.

"Brett, any eyes on Malachi?"

"Looking now. Why?"

"He's been absent for twenty minutes now."

"Anyone else missing?"

Nick scanned the area again, already having checked but wanting to triple-check. "Not that I can see. Everyone else is present and accounted for."

"We have him on the cameras leaving the ballroom with a server." Brett paused. "They went into a room down the hall. I'll send someone to check."

"I'll go," Nick said. He froze as he waited for Brett to argue.

"Okay. Jade, pull back and take Nick's place."

"Understood," Jade said, and Nick watched her break away from Patrick and head towards him.

Jade nodded when they swapped, and Nick headed to the nearest exit.

"Which room, Brett?" he asked as he strode down the hallway.

"Next on your left."

Nick paused at the door, listening for any sounds inside but couldn't hear anything. "Do I announce or enter immediately, boss?"

"Enter," Brett confirmed.

Nick tried the doorknob, but it wouldn't open. "It's locked. I'm booting it down."

"Okay."

He stepped back and kicked at it, the door flying back on its hinges. He took in the scene in one glance, and fury flowed through him. Before he realised it, he had the server in his hands and held him to the floor, sitting on him when he struggled. He peered at Malachi, who was completely out of it with his clothes half off. He mumbled something incoherent, and Nick growled.

"Brett, get first aid in here, and the police. The fucking server drugged Malachi. He was trying to—" He broke off, unable to say the words. Memories of his sister flooded his head, and it took everything in him to wipe his mind clear so he could think. Malachi wasn't in any danger at that moment, so he let him be, but the server still bucked and cursed beneath him.

"You have no right to hold me!" the guy shouted.

Nick leaned down, his mouth right at the guy's ear. "I have every right," he growled. "And I'm going to make sure you pay for this. My reach is long, and I guarantee I can find something in your past to show you've done this before." The guy paled at Nick's guess, and Nick tightened his hold. "I will find every single person you have done this to and make sure you spend the rest of your life in jail. You feel me?"

The guy fell silent and stopped trying to dislodge him. Nick wished he would fight so he had an excuse to knock him out, and he almost decided to let him up so he'd have the excuse, but the cavalry arrived before he could lose his mind.

"We'll take him from here," two police officers said.

Nick let them take hold, but he grabbed the server's chin. "What's your name?" The server licked his lips but didn't reply. "Either tell me or you spend your hours with me instead of them."

The guy paled further and muttered, "James Richardson."

"Date of birth?" Nick asked.

"29 November 1989."

Nick shoved him away. "Do not let him out of your sight," he told the police officers. "This isn't the first time he's done this."

"Yes, sir."

They took him away, and Nick refocused on Malachi, ignoring the ache in his calf. He was fully dressed again, and the medic tended to him. Nick swallowed repeatedly, glad he'd been able to stop something so heinous from happening but wishing he'd not had to. Despite Malachi's need to drag the Sutcliffes through the mud, he wouldn't wish what had happened on anyone. He exhaled and rested his hands on his hips, watching what the medic was doing.

"Is he okay?" Brett asked—from beside him instead of in his ear.

The medic glanced at him. "His blood pressure is fine, and I can't see any signs of issues, but I think a trip to the hospital would be a good idea. If he was going to react to whatever he was given, he would've had it by now. It just needs to work its way through his system now."

Brett nodded and nudged Nick. "He's in excellent hands, Nick. I need you back in the main room."

Nick growled and turned away, stalking from the room and into the hallway. Brett caught up with him, tugging him to a stop.

"Nick, calm down."

He glared at his boss. "Calm down? After what almost happened? Jesus, Brett." He stalked off, Brett's parting words following him.

"The king needs you."

Nick swallowed hard and entered the ballroom. "Understood, Brett. Understood," he replied through his radio.

Pushing what happened to Malachi aside for the moment, which was more difficult than it should have been, he focused on the king and on making sure he survived the night. He wouldn't want his inattention to be the cause of more casualties, so every time Malachi's face floated into his head, he wiped it clear and recentred himself. It happened more than he wanted, and by the time they were in the car and on their way back to Windsor Castle, he could barely keep his eyes open.

"Nick, what happened tonight?" Andrew asked.

On that journey, he was sitting in the back with the king with Emmy, and Colt sat in the front. He inhaled. "A reporter was drugged, but he's at the hospital and being looked after now."

Andrew sat forward, piercing Nick with his gaze. "Tell me what happened from start to finish."

Nick replayed the events that led up to finding Malachi, and when he finished, Andrew fisted his hands.

"I want regular updates on the attacker and Malachi Sanders. In fact, as soon as Malachi is feeling better, I want a personal meeting with him at Windsor. I will get Randall to arrange that. It's the least I can do after what happened."

"Is that the best idea, Your Majesty? After all, he is the one writing nasty things about you in the media."

"Everyone has the right to say what they want, Nick. You know that. It's how we react to it that makes the difference. If it was someone else, I would've offered the same thing, so I refuse to not offer it to Malachi just because of what he writes."

Suitably chastised, Nick nodded. "Yes, Your Majesty."

"And anyway, think of it as a chance to change his stance on us."

Nick didn't think that was possible with how much hatred Malachi seemed to hold for them, but he allowed Andrew to think he could change his mind. And knowing the king as he did, Andrew might be the only person in the world who *could* change Malachi's mind.

Dominic and Colt took Andrew to his suite when they arrived back, and Nick headed for Sec HQ, bracing himself for a telling-off from Brett. He didn't get one, though.

"Are you okay?" Brett asked instead, pulling him aside.

Nick exhaled. "Yeah. Thanks for pulling me back."

Brett chuckled. "I would've happily let you go at him, but I needed you there. I'm happy to arrange a 'meeting' with the guy if you like?" He smirked.

Nick huffed and shook his head. "Better not. You might end up having to bail me out."

"It'd be worth the money." Brett sighed. "I checked up with the hospital. Malachi is sleeping it off. The doctors can't see any reason he would have an adverse reaction to the drug—which they found out was Rohypnol—but they're keeping him in until he's fully coherent and drug-free, to be sure."

Nick's chest eased with the news. "Thanks. As much as he drives me insane with what he writes, I'm glad he's okay." He exhaled. "Has Andrew told you his plan?"

"What plan?"

"He's inviting Malachi for a meeting once he's better."

Brett rubbed a hand over his face. "Wonderful." His tone implied it was anything but.

"He's hoping he can change his thoughts on the royal family."

"Doesn't surprise me that he'd try." Brett clapped him on the shoulder. "Go home. Get some rest. I'll see you in a couple of days."

As Nick headed out, images of things that had happened merged with things that could've happened, and when he arrived home, he dropped into bed without getting undressed. Curling onto his side, he closed his eyes against the torrent hitting him. His stomach cramped as he remembered his sister, Eliza, in the aftermath of her attempted rape. The same sense of helplessness he felt then was back with him. As much as he wanted to physically check on Malachi himself, he knew it wouldn't help. When Malachi realised what had almost happened to him, he possibly wouldn't want anyone he didn't know near him.

Nick would have to wait until Malachi accepted the king's offer. Because he would. Who couldn't resist the lure of something they wanted when it was handed to them on a plate?

4

Malachi

Waking up in the hospital was a scary thing. Especially when Malachi couldn't remember why he'd ended up there. He lay still in the bed as cool air drifted over him from the air conditioning and tried to recall anything after arriving at the event. He couldn't.

His mother and grandmother chatted between themselves after having checked on him and made sure he was feeling as good as could be expected. The doctor would be in to see him soon, and he wanted to ask a few questions. His mother, Emily, had explained that he'd been found in a room, delirious, and had asked him if he'd taken any drugs. Malachi had frowned at her and growled, "No!" She seemed placated, but his grandmother had narrowed her eyes on him. After that, he hadn't wanted to talk, and he'd closed his eyes, trying to recall anything, but other than the powerful scent of flowers, he couldn't remember anything. It was terrifying and made the headache much worse, so he stopped.

The doctor finally bustled in, and Malachi opened his eyes.

"Good morning, Mr Sanders. I'm glad to see you're awake. I'm Dr Andrews. Can you tell me how you're feeling?"

Malachi cleared his throat and tried to figure out the answer. "Um, I feel a little sick, and my head hurts. I can't remember why I'm here, to be honest." The doctor shared a look with Malachi's mother, and he bristled a little. "What happened to me?"

The doctor glanced at Malachi's mother again, and Emily scooted closer. "Sweetheart, someone drugged you and took you into a room." Her voice caught, and she blinked back tears, but Malachi shook his head.

"I... What?" His breathing increased as he stared at the three of them. "I was drugged? When? How? I don't remember!"

"It's okay, Mr Sanders. You're fine now, and your body is clearing itself from the effects. Nothing happened to you while you were drugged. You had a saviour that night, that's for sure." The doctor chuckled, as if the words should've reassured Malachi.

They didn't.

His gaze darted around the room as he tried to remember, his head driving spikes into his brain. "I don't..." He rubbed his head. "How?"

"We're not sure exactly," the doctor said, "but the police are here and would like to talk to you. Are you up for a visit?"

"I really don't think now is a good time," his grandmother said. "He needs to rest."

"I understand that more than anyone, Mrs Hopkins, but the sooner they get information from your grandson, the quicker they can investigate. I'll give you something for your head as well." He bustled around while Malachi tried to collect his scattered thoughts.

"I don't remember anything," Malachi protested.

"It won't take long, Mr Sanders," the doctor persisted.

Malachi sighed. "Okay." He didn't want to talk to them, but if it would get them off his back, he would.

Dr Andrews smiled and went to the door, speaking to someone outside before gesturing for them to enter. Malachi knew the Police Commissioner, but why was he was the one to be there?

"Mr Sanders, I'm Commissioner Thomas. I'm sorry for what you've been through, but we have a few questions for you, if that's okay?"

"It's Malachi. I'm not sure how much help I'll be because I don't remember much." Commissioner Thomas glanced at Malachi's mum and grandma, and Malachi shifted on the bed. "Mum, you and Grandma can take a break now," he said.

"No, it's okay. We can wait," Emily said.

Sally pushed herself to her feet. "Come on, Emily. Let's grab some tea from the restaurant and leave these people to talk."

Emily opened her mouth to argue, but a glare from her mother set it closed again. She stood and grabbed her handbag before leaning over Malachi. "I'll be right back, sweetie." She kissed his cheek, and he barely stopped himself from crying.

"Thanks, Mum." He waited until they and the doctor left before focusing back on the Commissioner. "Okay?"

"The event you were at last night was a large event with some royal family in attendance. Do you remember that?"

Malachi nodded. "It was a dinner event for a charity."

"That's right. What we need to figure out is if what happened to you was focused solely on you, or..." Thomas grimaced, "if you were the wrong target."

Malachi opened his mouth and then closed it again. Then he sighed, his head throbbing but beginning to ease. "Okay, ask your questions, but I'm not sure how much help I'll be."

"Thank you, Malachi." Thomas settled into a chair beside the bed. "What do you remember from last night?"

Malachi sighed again. "I remember arriving at the event and entering the hall. There were many people, which I expected. I remember sitting down to dinner." He winced and rubbed his head. "I don't remember anything after that."

"Do you remember what you had to eat and drink?" Thomas asked.

"I had a bottle of water when I first arrived, and then at dinner, I had…" He closed his eyes, trying to picture sitting at the table with the other guests. "I had the chicken dish and…a glass of wine."

"Do you remember if that wine was the one from the table or if a server brought you it?"

A wave of nausea flowed over him, and he breathed through it. "Sorry. Nausea is a bitch," he muttered.

"It's okay, Malachi. Take your time. Would you like some water?"

He nodded. "Yes, please." The Commissioner stood and poured some water from a jug into a small cup and handed it over. "Thanks." He sipped a little at a time, testing his stomach. When the nausea abated a little, he exhaled. "Um… oh, right, the wine. Um, the table only had red wine, which I don't like, so I asked the server for a glass of white."

Thomas's mouth tightened. "Do you remember who your server was?"

Malachi closed his eyes again, trying to follow the image. He only had a distorted memory, something blurry and unhelpful. "No, I can't remember. I can't recall his face."

"He? Why do you say he?"

Malachi blinked and thought hard. "I don't know, but I get the feeling they were a man. I don't know if that's true or not, though. I'm sorry." His stomach rolled again. "Can you tell me what happened?"

Thomas nodded. "I will tell you everything we know, but I'd like to get your statement first. I don't want anything I say to change what you remember. Does that make sense?"

Malachi nodded and then wished he hadn't. He breathed slowly again, sipping his water. "Of course."

"What was the last thing you remember?"

"That. Sitting at the table, asking for some wine. After that, everything is fuzzy and distorted or completely blank until I woke up in here."

"Okay, one more question and then I'll answer yours." Malachi nodded. "Can you recall anything else at all from last night? Scents, sounds, textures, tastes. Anything at all?"

"Flowers," he said, licking his lips. "I remember the overpowering scent of flowers. The kind of scent when you go into a florist."

"Anything else?"

Malachi closed his eyes again and rested his head back. "A flash of light. Just briefly. As if a light had flicked on and then went off a few seconds later. And a shout but sounding as if it was far away." He opened his eyes and met Thomas's gaze. "I couldn't hear what they said."

"Thank you, Malachi. That helps a lot." Thomas put his notebook away and clasped his hands in front of him. "I know you will have a lot of questions, and I will answer what I can. I'm prefacing this with something you need to know. Other than being drugged, nothing else happened to you last night. Okay? I need you to remember that."

Malachi swallowed hard and nodded. It didn't ease his mind completely, and his heart rate tripled at the words, but that was more because he was worried about what Thomas was about to tell him.

"From what we can ascertain, a server at the event drugged you, possibly with that glass of wine. When you started showing signs of being disorientated, the server offered to help you find somewhere to sit down. He took you into a room down the hall from the event, closing you both in." Thomas sighed. "This is where some of our information stops. We don't know what happened to you between the closing of that door and the time it opened twenty minutes later, but we do know you were not sexually assaulted. The king's bodyguard broke into the room and found you with your shirt unfastened, but the rest of your clothes were still on and unaffected. I know that might not be a comfort, knowing he had you that vulnerable. The guard pulled the server off you as soon as he entered the room." Thomas's mouth twitched as if he wanted to smile.

Malachi frowned. "What?"

"Nick left his mark on the man, I promise you."

Malachi's stomach swooped. "Nick?"

Thomas nodded. "Nick Tennant. The king's bodyguard. He was the one who went looking for you."

Malachi wasn't sure what to do with that information. He knew Nick didn't like him, so to have him being the one to save him was...unnerving, almost. It was better to focus on that part of the Commissioner's words than to think about what could've happened if Nick hadn't been there.

"Do you know—" He cleared his throat and started again. "Do you know why he did it?"

Thomas's mouth tightened. "No. Unfortunately, the guy isn't talking. We're still working on him. As we have video evidence of him taking you into that room, and we have Nick corroborating that he was straddling you when he entered the room, he will not get out of jail anytime soon."

"Straddling me," Malachi squeaked, his voice finally giving up.

Thomas's gaze softened. "I'm sorry. Yes, when Nick entered the room, the server was straddling you on the sofa."

Malachi closed his eyes against the tears threatening to spill over. He breathed through the fear rushing through him. The what-ifs. The maybes. He hated not being able to remember, but in the same breath, he was glad he couldn't.

"Do you have any other questions, Malachi?" Malachi shook his head. "In that case, I will leave you my number and you can call me anytime if you have questions or if you remember anything else. Okay?"

Malachi inhaled and lifted his head. "Thank you, Commissioner."

A knock sounded, making Malachi jump, and the second police officer, who had entered with the Commissioner, raised his eyebrows at Malachi. Malachi nodded, and he opened the door, revealing someone Malachi never expected—the king's personal assistant.

"Ah, Randall. I was wondering whether we would cross paths today," Thomas said, rising from the chair and holding out his hand to the other man. They shook hands, and Thomas turned to Malachi. "This is Randall—"

"Metcalfe. The king's personal assistant," Malachi interrupted.

"Good morning, Mr Sanders. I wondered if you could spare a minute to have a word, please?"

Malachi nodded, unsure how much more he could take.

Thomas pulled a card from his pocket and laid it on the bedside table. "There's my number, if you need anything at all. Please don't be afraid to call."

"Thank you, Commissioner."

"I'll leave you in Randall's capable hands."

Malachi shifted in the bed, ignoring his rolling stomach and slightly less throbbing head as he watched the Commissioner leave with the second police officer and Randall take his place.

"How are you feeling?" Randall asked, perching on the edge of the chair Thomas had occupied.

"As well as could be expected, I think." Malachi didn't mean anything by his words, but Randall still flinched.

"The king is sorry for what happened at one of our events. He is concerned for your health and your well-being, so if there is anything we can do, please let us know."

Malachi waved him away. "Honestly, unless you were the ones to set this up, it's not your fault."

"I promise we had nothing to do with this, but the king would like to offer something to apologise for what you're going through." Randall paused, and Malachi frowned. "King Andrew would like to offer you the chance for a behind-the-scenes, up close and personal look at Windsor Castle and what goes on there. As I said, he feels responsible—even though he wasn't—and would like to help in any way he can. He's also offering you whatever health, emotional and mental needs you have."

Malachi wasn't sure what to think of the offer. While Randall had said they felt bad about it, why would they be offering such a thing, especially knowing what he wrote about them? He said as much.

Randall shifted in his seat. "I will be perfectly honest with you. The king is against violence of any kind, but what happened—or could've happened—to you is something we all detest. Nobody should be put through what you have, and we want to help in any way. That being said, if giving you this opportunity to watch us behind the scenes helps to...adjust your view of us, we wouldn't be opposed." Randall's mouth twitched, and Malachi couldn't help his laugh. If only he could tell him what he really thought of them.

"I'm a reporter, Mr Metcalfe. I certainly won't turn down the opportunity for a close-up of the royal family, but please let me say that this is in no way anyone's fault but the person who did this." Malachi frowned, realising he didn't even know who the guy was. "Whoever he is."

Randall relaxed a fraction. "I agree, Mr Sanders. But the king still feels responsible, as he does for anyone who is covered by the monarchy. And one more thing. We do not wish for you to keep this quiet if you do not wish to. We are happy for you to write about what happened in any way you want to."

Malachi knew this and loved the king even more for his generosity, but he couldn't show it completely. After all, no one knew his alter ego. "Then, thank you. I accept His Majesty's offer."

Randall beamed at him and stood. "Thank you so much, Mr Sanders. I'll leave my card next to Commissioner Thomas's, and when you are feeling up to it, please get in contact to arrange the visit. I look forward to seeing you then."

The door opened, and his mother and grandmother entered. "Oh, who's this?" Sally said, a visible twinkle in her eyes. She knew exactly who it was.

Randall held out his hand to the older lady. "Randall Metcalfe, at your service, Mrs Hopkins. Mrs Sanders. It's lovely to meet you both. I won't take up any more of your time, though." He turned back to Malachi. "I echo the Commissioner's words, Mr Sanders. If you need anything, please don't hesitate to get in touch."

"Thank you, Mr Metcalfe."

When Randall left, Malachi exhaled long and loud. "Well, that was interesting," he muttered.

"What did he want?" Emily asked, bustling around to ensure Malachi's covers were where they needed to be, something she had always done whenever he was ill as a child.

"Well, Commissioner Thomas wanted to ask what I remembered and then told me what information they had about last night, and Mr Metcalfe wanted to offer me a behind-the-scenes tour of Windsor Castle whenever I was up to it."

Emily narrowed her eyes and pursed her lips. "They want you to keep quiet about what happened."

Malachi shook his head and wished he hadn't. He closed his eyes and rested his head back. "Not at all. They gave me permission to write about it all."

"Seriously?" Emily said, and Malachi met her gaze and nodded. "Huh."

Sally chuckled. "They're the good guys, remember, Emily? They have their bad eggs, but most of them are good." His grandmother loved the royal family as much as Malachi did.

Emily sighed and patted Malachi's arm. "Get some rest, sweetie. I'm sure the doctors and nurses will be bustling in again soon. You might as well get as much rest as you can."

He didn't even argue with her, almost instantly feeling himself drifting away. But what kept floating around in his head was the image of a certain bodyguard who was apparently even willing to save someone he hated. Who would've thought? He'd have to remember to thank him when he next saw him. If it hadn't been for him, who knows what could've happened to Malachi. He shivered at the thought, and then his mind slid into the depths of sleep.

But even in his sleep, he couldn't escape the dreams of a faceless man leaning over him, and it was only when he woke himself or the nurses woke him that he was free of the nightmares that would undoubtedly dog his sleeping moments for the foreseeable future. Not that he slept much, anyway.

After waking for what had to be the tenth time—blessedly to an empty room, after his mum and grandma had left to go home earlier—he decided to take the king up on his offer of help. Seeing a therapist might be the only way to get over what had happened—or could've happened.

5

Nick

Nick stared at Brett, mouth tightening. "Not a chance."

Brett raised his eyebrows. "I don't remember asking your opinion, Nick. I gave you an order."

Nick stood, threading his fingers through his hair as he paced between the chairs. He stopped and glared at Brett. "You're seriously giving me that order when you know how I feel about him? Seriously?" He gritted his teeth.

"You are the best person for the job." Brett crossed his arms over his chest.

"How do you work that out?" Nick snorted. "I'm more likely to strangle the guy."

"You're obsessed with him, Nick. You'll watch him like a hawk, and for good reason. You already know a lot about him. You will know if he does something unusual, or if he looks like he's not being truthful about something. You know him better than anyone. I can't think of anyone else who is as well versed in Malachi Sanders."

Nick tried not to feel embarrassed about his obviously not-so-secret obsession with the offensive reporter. He stared at his feet, his fingers gripping his hips, and he exhaled. "Fine."

"I'm not doing this to be an ass, Nick. You will see through any charming acts he puts on because *you know him.*"

He couldn't disagree, and he hated that fact. "When?"

"He's arriving on Friday."

Nick's jaw dropped. "Right before Kean's birthday?"

Brett shrugged. "The king thought it would be a good time to show him their human side, so to speak."

"That's one hell of an invitation," Nick muttered.

"You'll be sharing a suite with him just down from here. We don't want to give him any chance of sneaking around, and this was the best option. Friday will be more laid back, getting to know Windsor Castle, so you'll be giving him a tour and answering his questions, and then on Saturday, the king will have a meeting with him, and he will meet with some others if they agree. Sunday, he will have access to the grounds and house again, and then Monday, he'll be heading home with hopefully higher opinions of us than he has now."

Nick had taken all that information in, but he'd stuck on the first thing. "I'm sharing a suite with him!" He threw his hands wide. "Why not give me full access to killing the guy?"

Brett sighed, and Felix chuckled. "Nick, you'll be fine. It's four days, not the rest of your life."

"Unless I kill him and end up behind bars."

"Don't worry. We'll help you hide the body," Felix said.

Brett glared at Felix, who snorted in response. "No bodies will need hiding. No lives are forfeited. No deaths will happen. You'll be fine." He rounded his desk and settled in his chair. "Now get home."

Nick opened his mouth to complain again, but Brett turned his glare on him, so he swallowed it back. He grabbed his stuff and headed out of Sec HQ. Four days with Malachi! How the hell was he going to manage that? He was a fun-loving, easygoing guy mostly, but when someone messed with his people, he held a grudge. He muttered and grumbled the entire way home—or rather, his parents' home. They'd invited him and the rest of them for dinner, and Nick had a feeling they were going to announce their next cruise. Since they retired, they'd been going on cruises several times a year. Some closer by, like Gran Canaria, and some further afield, like the Caribbean. Nick was jealous in some ways. He'd love to try a cruise, but he hadn't got on one yet. Eventually, though. The pictures his parents took and the experiences they described sounded amazing. Maybe he'd take one after the debacle with Malachi.

He parked down the road from his parents' house and locked the car. He knocked but let himself in as they were allowed to. Nick didn't like the house being unlocked all the time, but his parents wouldn't listen to his opinions about it. People weren't as nice as they had been when his parents were younger, but he couldn't get through to them. He just had to hope that the security measures he had put in place for them held up if they needed to.

"Mum! Dad! I'm here!"

"We guessed that, sweetheart."

His mother, Rebecca, was in her early seventies and had a curly mop of grey hair framing her thin face. She didn't mind growing older and was vocally happy about enjoying every year she had. She kept up with yoga and pilates but had stopped running after a fall in a park with no one being there to help. Despite her usual resilience, it had scared her, so she'd kept her activities within a building or closer to home after that.

He kissed her cheek. "Hi, Mum."

Rebecca patted his cheek and smiled, her crooked front teeth peeking from behind her lips. "Hey, sweetheart. How was your day?" The reminder of what Brett had told him made him tense, and she noticed. "Bad, huh?"

"Not...bad as such," he hedged. "Just...annoying."

Rebecca frowned. "Annoying?"

He sighed. "I have an assignment I don't particularly want, but..." He shrugged. "It is what it is."

"Tell me about it before everyone else gets here." She headed for the kitchen, and Nick followed, poking his head quickly into the living room to wave at his dad before continuing to the hub of the house. "I'll make you a coffee."

"Can I have one, please, darling?" his dad shouted.

"Since when do I forget you?" his mum teased, rolling her eyes in Nick's direction.

Nick loved the visible signs of love his parents showed daily. They weren't stingy with their affection or their words, and it had shown Nick that it was okay to show those things, something he'd taken to heart with his friends and family. He showed his love for them every time he saw them. And when they asked for his help, he agreed without hesitation. Love was his language, and one day, he hoped he'd find someone to share his life with. One day.

"Sit down, sweetheart. What's this assignment? If you can tell me, that is."

His mother understood the necessity of his NDA and never pushed when he told her he couldn't talk about some aspects of his job. That assignment, however, he could explain. It wasn't public knowledge, but they also weren't hiding it, Brett had told him.

"A reporter is coming to stay at Windsor for a few days, and I have to stay with him all the time he's there. Even at night. I'm staying in a suite with him." He sighed and thanked her when she brought his coffee over.

His mother said nothing for a moment but then raised her eyebrows. "And this is a problem, why?"

Nick inhaled. "Because it's Malachi Sanders." Rebecca pinched her lips together, and Nick shook his head. "It's not funny."

"It's a little funny, sweetheart. Let me take this in for your dad." She disappeared, and Nick wrapped his hands around his mug, inhaling the roasted beans. His parents always bought the best coffee, some of which came from the different countries they'd visited.

Rebecca returned and settled beside him with her tea. "So, Malachi Sanders, eh? Does your boss know you're more likely to kill the man?"

Nick chuckled at how well his mother knew him. "I told him, but he said he had faith in me." He rubbed his lips, reluctantly smiling. "He said I knew Malachi better than anyone and I wouldn't take any shit he doled out."

"That's true."

"But I am likely to kill him before the time is through."

Rebecca sipped her tea and chuckled softly. "Think of it as a chance to find out *why* he's writing what he is. Something must've happened for him to be so antagonistic towards them."

Nick's stomach soured. "What if it's a ruse to get close to them?" He voiced his worst fear.

"Then you will be there to stop whatever he has planned." He focused on his coffee, his stomach churning, but his mother continued. "No one made a mistake that day, Nick. No one did. That man decided to do that, and no one did anything wrong. People still got hurt, but it wasn't anyone's fault but that man's. The king survived. Others didn't, but as much as I hate to think about it, that's the job you've signed up for. Bodyguards can do everything right and still bad things happen. If you continue to second-guess yourself, Nick, you won't be able to do your job."

Nick's throat closed up, and his chest ached, a physical pressure that made it hard to breathe. So many people had lost their lives, both that day and other days, and it was heartbreaking. He would happily give his life to save someone else's, but it sucked all the same. His mother had been there through his physiotherapy and helped him to get around while he was healing, and she knew how he felt because he spent many hours talking about it.

"Mum! Dad! I'm here!"

Nick cleared his throat and chuckled, grateful for the interruption, and his mother sighed and shouted back to Jonah, "We guessed that, sweetheart." The standard response to their children's standard greeting. A greeting he had no idea when it started.

His brother strode in, his suit still in pristine condition despite spending the day at work. Nick had never kept his suit that clean. Jonah worked in an office, using his financial genius to make investments for people. He was the image of their father with lighter hair and blue eyes, whereas Nick, Eliza and Rye took after their mother more with dark hair and eyes.

Rebecca rose and hugged Jonah before heading to the oven. "We have half an hour before the lasagne is ready, so go talk to your dad, both of you."

"I've just got comfortable!" Nick said, though he didn't mean a word of it.

"Then get uncomfortable," Rebecca replied, a twinkle in her eyes.

Nick groaned halfheartedly and grabbed his drink, following his brother into the living room.

"I wondered when someone was going to visit with me," his dad, Don, said, his tablet held tightly in his hand as his fingers worked the screen, undoubtedly setting more people working on the game he was obsessed with.

"You're busy working, Dad. I thought I'd give you some peace," Nick teased. He dropped onto a cushion on the sofa, Jonah settling at the other end.

"What's new?" Don asked, his eyes still on the screen.

Jonah crossed his legs. "Absolutely nothing."

Nick snorted. "How much money did you make people today?"

Jonah's cheeks flushed. "Enough." He loved his job, but he openly admitted he hated making certain people money. People he said didn't deserve it. He happily did it for others, including his family. "How many assholes did you beat up today?" Jonah returned the teasing.

"Not one, unfortunately." Nick sighed as if he was disappointed.

"Mum! Dad! I'm here!" Eliza's voice called through the house, and Rebecca sighed her usual greeting. His sister poked her head into the room.

"Where's Rye?" Nick asked.

Eliza shrugged. "He told me he was making his own way here tonight." She disappeared again.

Nick and Jonah shared a look. It wasn't often Rye arrived home by himself. Eliza and he lived close to each other, and she always picked him up along the way.

"Wonder what he's been doing," Jonah murmured.

"Leave him alone when he gets here," Don said. "You don't have to know everything about his life or anyone's lives."

"But it's so much fun teasing them," Jonah said. "You taught us that."

Don sighed and shook his head, glancing at them over the top of his glasses. "I taught you to be nice, too, and look where that got us."

Nick snorted, and Jonah pointed a finger at their dad. "See! You're just as bad."

Don's mouth twitched as he went back to his game, but he kept the conversation going. "How are you both?"

They spoke for a few minutes before Eliza joined them, and then the front door slammed again.

"Mum! Dad—"

"We know, sweetheart!" Rebecca shouted back, interrupting Rye's greeting.

Nick snorted. It was always the last child who got interrupted because his mother got fed up with the greeting by that point.

Rye didn't appear before their mother shouted them for dinner, but he was sitting at the dining table when they entered. Nick cupped his nape, squeezing gently, before sitting opposite him and next to Eliza. Jonah took the chair beside Rye, and their father and mother at either end.

"Thank you for dinner, Mum," Nick said before tucking into the cheesy, meaty, vegetable wonder that was his mum's lasagne tower. With four kids to feed, she made a lasagne big enough to feed six of them with meat and lots of vegetables, too. And because it tasted so damn good, not one of them had complained about the vegetables when they were younger, even though they hated them—the complete dish, all mixed together, was delicious.

The conversation, filled with innuendos, teasing and laughter, settled something inside Nick. It always did. Whenever he felt upset or uneasy, a trip to his parents' house or a visit with a sibling was all he needed to reset himself. He loved them all so damn much, and sometimes, it was overwhelming.

"Not long now until the wedding, is it?" Eliza asked. Her curly black hair settled around her shoulders, bouncing whenever she moved, a lot like her personality.

Nick shook his head. "A month to go. With four weddings in a year, they've got it down to a fine art now."

"I can imagine it's a huge undertaking," Rebecca said.

"It is, but Randall is amazing. He worked the first two himself, and then he brought other people in but gave them his task lists, his contacts and everything they needed. All they had to do was follow his instructions and timescale, and it was done. I hope he never leaves because I'm not sure what we'd do without him."

"How are the princes feeling?" Rebecca asked. Her concern was always palpable when she spoke about the royal family.

"They don't seem at all nervous, which is good. Both Patrick and Kieren are used to the limelight, and although Kieren was usually behind Patrick in the spotlight, he's doing okay with his additional responsibilities."

Nick gave them as much as he could without crossing the edges of his NDA. He clung to his contracts, even knowing his family wouldn't betray any confidences.

"What happened last week?" Eliza asked. "I read somewhere that something happened at the event."

Nick clenched his jaw, not wanting to bring back bad memories, so he simplified his answer. "Someone attempted to hurt a guest, but it was stopped."

"Who?"

Nick shook his head. "I can't say." How they'd kept Malachi's name out of the media, he didn't know, but Mav must've done his magic to keep his identity a secret, being a social media wizard as he was. He'd lost count of the times Prince Douglas's husband had stopped news from getting out. Nick was all for the freedom of information and all that, but sometimes, someone just needed to be protected, and that was that.

"Fair enough. Are they okay, though?" Eliza asked.

Nick nodded. "They are." He hadn't heard otherwise, so he assumed Malachi was doing okay since his release from the hospital.

The conversation turned to other subjects, and Nick studied his family as they spoke. Despite his and Rye's discussion a couple of weeks ago, the dark circles beneath Rye's eyes seemed to have lessened. He wasn't sure what had caused it, but he was happy all the same. He'd make sure to speak to him at some point. Eliza had steadfastly worked through her feelings and worries over the past ten years and had found a way to deal with what had happened to her. It had been a long journey for her, but he was so proud of what she'd accomplished. Jonah, on the other hand, had a spark in him that hadn't been there before. Nick had noticed it when they'd been talking in the living room but couldn't figure out where it had come from. If he had to guess, he would say Jonah had found someone he liked, but his brother wouldn't discuss anything until it was a done thing, almost. Not wedded bliss done, but when he was confident in the relationship. Far too many times over the years, Jonah had brought people home to meet everyone, and they'd turned out to be duds. None of them had been lucky in the romance department so far.

He could deal with that for himself, but he truly wanted his siblings to be happy. To find someone or several someones to share their lives with. It was what they all deserved.

By the time they'd cleaned up after dinner, it was getting late and still no accouncement, so Nick said goodnight and hugged each of them before heading home. He hoped he would see them soon, but after spending a weekend babysitting Malachi Sanders, he wasn't sure he wouldn't be serving life in jail by that time the following week.

Four days later, he still wasn't sure. As Malachi stood chatting to Andrew as the king welcomed him to his home, Nick's entire body trembled with the need to stop Malachi from being an asshole. He needed to spend the long weekend figuring out how to "persuade" the reporter to change his stance on the royal family, unable to contemplate having to read another disgusting report from the man.

"Nick, can you show Malachi around, please? And Malachi, please join us for dinner tonight."

Nick tensed. That hadn't been on the agenda. He pulled his phone from his pocket and messaged Brett, telling him what Andrew had just offered. Brett acknowledged the new information, and Nick took a breath before putting his phone away again.

It was going to be a shitshow.

6

Malachi

"Thank you, Your Majesty. I appreciate the offer, but I don't want to intrude." Malachi still couldn't believe they had invited him to stay at Windsor Castle. He'd visited the property before with the open house they did for the public, but that time, he would get to see what the public didn't. It was exciting and nerve-wracking all at once.

The king waved his hand. "You're not intruding at all. We'd love for you to join us." He turned to Nick. "Thank you, Nick. Take care of him. I'll be at the luncheon today, but if you need anything, please let Brett know."

Nick winced and nodded. "I will, Your Majesty."

Malachi could see the tension in the bodyguard's body, and he sent him a smile, hopefully conveying how non-threatening he was. Nick narrowed his eyes, so Malachi didn't think he was successful. He couldn't blame him. After all, they all knew what he wrote. Could he explain to them? Would they care? No, he couldn't let them know. It was his problem, not theirs.

When Malachi had told Tucker about this opportunity, his boss had rubbed his hands and grinned. He'd known what would be ordered of him before Tucker even opened his mouth but to hear the words still hurt his insides. Finding whatever bad stuff he could on the royal family wasn't what he wanted to do, but he wouldn't be able to get away with not providing something. If he claimed they were "clean," using the word Tucker had despite hating it, the potential for repercussions concerned him.

Regardless, he would still be able to get his experience out there with his Kai name, even if he had to cover what he said with words about hearsay and whatever else he could use to hide that he was both people.

The king bid goodbye and headed off with several guards, and Malachi turned to Nick. "Where is the dinner tonight? Do I need a certain outfit?"

"It's at The Langley in Slough. I would recommend a suit if you have one. If not, we can arrange for one." Nick's words were gritted out through a clenched jaw, but at least he gave the information.

"I have a suit, so it's fine. I brought several, just in case I needed them." He gestured to his suitcase, and Nick winced.

"If your suits are in there, our first stop is the suite because you'll need to get them out to stop them from creasing."

Nick strode off, leaving Malachi to fumble behind him and catch up. His cheeks flamed at the rebuke, but he ignored it. Nick made no attempt to hide his contempt for him, and it was something Malachi was going to have to deal with during the long weekend. But for a behind-the-scenes look at his favourite pastime, he could deal with it. He'd barely slept for the past few days, not only because his nightmares showed flashes of images that he wasn't sure were real or not—images from that night—but because he was so excited to be there.

"I received a basic outline of what was planned while I was here. Can you expand on any of it?" he asked as they hurried down the corridors, so similar to the ones the public could see in their part of the castle.

Nick sighed, his vast shoulders lifting and falling as if he was shaking off a heavy weight. "Today, I will give you a tour of Windsor Castle. You will see some rooms and areas the royal family use."

Malachi's stomach gave a whirl, and he barely stopped himself from squealing like a child when they'd been given something they'd been asking for. He couldn't believe his dream was coming true.

His mother or grandmother were the best people to ask about when his infatuation with the royal family started. He could only remember that he'd spent far too much time as a child watching and reading whatever he could find about them. Funnily enough, he'd wanted to be a bodyguard and had taken up shooting as a hobby. It wasn't that he was obsessed as such, although some people might think he was—and they would probably have a good argument with that—but they were an enigma, in some ways. The Sutcliffes, to him, were the most visible family that showed how much the dynamic could change depending on the people who were at the pinnacle. But it wasn't just that. It was also that, over the years, he'd been able to see how much they had changed. How opinions had changed. How behaviours had changed. And how much more inclusive they were—if he ignored the bad seeds. Everything the royal family did was in the public eye, except for what happened behind closed doors, but even then, sometimes snippets of their personal lives managed to sneak out through the loose lips of former—or even current—employees.

That irked Malachi a little because he believed in trust, and for a current employee to talk about their employer, especially to a reporter, was not something he agreed with. Unfortunately, due to his wonderful boss—sarcasm was amazing when he needed it—he had the fantastic opportunity to talk with one of those staff members and write an article about it. Every single word of it felt like he had etched it onto his skin with the dullest blade he could find. It hurt. Soul deep hurt. And he'd called off sick from work for almost two weeks because of it.

Whenever he discussed why he wrote what he did with his grandmother, she always asked him the same question. *Why do you do it?* But she didn't mean it in the basic sense. He did it because he needed to make money, and he couldn't find a job that would take him to write anything else. When she said why do you do it, though, she meant it in a different way. And every time, Malachi didn't have an answer for her. Not one she would accept.

"Am I able to put my clothes away before we go on the tour?" Malachi asked Nick, distracting himself from his circling thoughts.

"I'm taking you to the suite now, but the clothes will have to wait—except the suit." Nick sighed. "I don't know how much they told you about how this is going to work, but we're sharing a suite this weekend. Don't even think about trying to sneak out and tour the place by yourself. You will have a guard with you at all times. Most likely me. It's a twenty-four-hour thing, and we *will* be sleeping, we *will* be eating, and we *will* be resting in between the activities we have planned. Do not make us regret our offer."

Nick's words were harsh and said through gritted teeth, and despite Malachi understanding where it was coming from, it hurt.

"I understand completely. I have no plans to do anything that would fuck this up."

"I'm going to hold you to that," Nick said, staring over his shoulder as he continued down the corridor.

Malachi swallowed hard and averted his gaze, looking at the decoration on the private side of Windsor Castle. His suitcase barely made a noise on the highly polished floor, and in intermittent places, there stood tables with plants on top. He wasn't sure if they were real or fake, but they looked well cared for.

"Here we are," Nick said, pulling a key from his pocket.

He unlocked the large ornate door and held it open for Malachi to roll his suitcase through. Malachi might have been on the public side of the building before, but it amazed him to be physically in one of the rooms himself, rather than seeing it from the rope boundary that stopped anyone from stepping inside. His eyes were only good enough to a degree, and the photos didn't do the room justice. The ceiling was vast, with a circular design surrounding two light fittings. The room itself was a living area with three large sofas, a large coffee table, several armchairs with tables between them, and a large table to the side holding a kettle and everything they would need to make drinks.

"Wow," Malachi said. "I can't believe I get to stay here."

"This is your room," Nick said, brushing past and heading for the door furthest from the entry—for obvious reasons.

Malachi withheld his sigh and followed him into the bedroom that could easily hold his house.

"Bloody hell. If you don't see me for a few days, you might have to send a search party," Malachi joked, but all he received was a glare. "I thought you were the funniest of the guards. That's what I was always told."

"Humour has its place, and it isn't now."

Malachi bit his lip to stop him from saying anything. He couldn't argue because all they knew was that he was Malachi Sanders, the reporter wanting to watch the royal family fall. They didn't know Kai Ruffers, the reporter wanting to celebrate the Sutcliffes in everything they do.

"I want to say thank you for what you did." He didn't stop what he was doing.

"It's no problem."

Knowing Nick didn't want to talk about it any longer, he left his suitcase beside the bed after removing the suits. "Are we heading out straight away?"

Nick tilted his head. "Why? Do you have somewhere else you need to be?"

Malachi wasn't one for confrontation, and even after giving himself that pep talk, he still wanted to stand up to Nick. But he refrained. For how long was another question.

"Nope. Just asking."

Nick put his hands on his hips and stared at the floor for several seconds before clearing his throat. "It's supposed to rain soon. I'd planned for us to visit the gardens before the weather stopped us. Is that okay with you?"

Malachi nodded. "That sounds great, thanks." He'd already seen it from his public visits, but he would take whatever olive branch Nick was offering—even if it was with gritted teeth.

Following Nick down the corridor after hanging his suits, they walked out into the gardens, and despite what Malachi had thought, it was an amazing sight. Being able to look down on it from where they were gave a different viewpoint from actually walking in it. He stared into the distance, the grey storm clouds swirling above their heads making visibility less than a clear day, but it was still impressive.

"I'm waiting for permission from Prince Frederick for a tour of Frogmore Cottage. Whether he agrees is up to him," Nick said.

Malachi hadn't even known that was on the table. It was so rare to see that house. "Oh, absolutely. I don't want anyone uncomfortable at having me around."

"Well, that's impossible. You're a reporter, and one who rakes the royals through the coals. How could anyone be comfortable around you when they have no idea how you're going to take their interactions? When they're worried you'll misconstrue everything they say or do."

Malachi looked away, ashamed once more. He wasn't wrong, but having it thrown in his face like that was never easy. If only he could tell him... It wouldn't matter. Nick had his opinions, and nothing Malachi said would change his mind.

"Maybe I should just go," Malachi said, his fingers digging into the stone wall surrounding the gardens.

Nick sighed. "No. The king wants you here. I'll do everything that's asked of me, but I don't have to like it." He put his hands on his hips and stared at the ground for a long second before meeting Malachi's gaze. "I apologise. I will try to temper my words."

"Please don't." Malachi surprised himself with his words, but when he thought about them, it was true. He leaned back against the wall and crossed his arms over his chest, unable to meet Nick's penetrating eyes. He decided to tell some truth. "You might not believe me, but I don't want to write this. And your comments help remind me that while it's necessary, it's short term. So, please, feel free to tell me exactly how you feel." *Even if it cuts into my chest every single time.*

Nick didn't reply, and Malachi turned back to the view, letting the guard stew over his words. When raindrops hit the back of his hands and his face, Nick spoke again.

"We didn't have as much time as I thought, sorry."

Malachi waved him away, and they returned inside. "Where to now?" he asked instead.

"From here, we can visit the dining room and kitchens, the receiving room and Prince Consort Kendal's office. Is there anywhere in particular you were hoping to see? I can't guarantee it, but depending on what it is, I might be able to."

"No, thank you. This is wonderful." And it was. Just because they didn't like him didn't mean he couldn't get some pleasure out of living his dream.

"Okay, then."

Nick led the way back inside, and Malachi followed, desperate for every glimpse of the place he'd wanted to visit as a kid. It was similar to the public side—he assumed that was to keep in tradition with the family's ancestors—but there were small differences. Like the flowers on the hall tables. They were different varieties to those on the public side. Was that a conscious effort to have flowers the family liked, or was it nothing of the sort? Or was Malachi thinking too deeply when it was nothing of notice? Probably, but he wanted to know everything about them. He always had.

"Here is the Sutcliffes' family dining room. As you can see, it's not much different from a usual dining room, if you exclude the size." Nick's mouth twitched as if he was making a joke, and Malachi smiled.

"I bet even this isn't big enough when everyone comes for dinner," he said, studying the light fixtures hanging from the ceiling. They were chandeliers but much different from the ones he'd seen before.

"Not with how much the family is growing, no."

"Can I ask, is this where they always eat or just on special occasions?"

Nick cleared his throat. "They're like any other family, I think. They try to eat together as much as possible, but it's not always. Sometimes, they like some quiet time and have dinner in their suites." Nick glanced at him. "They're human, Malachi."

"I know, but it's sometimes hard to see that with what is in the media." He knew he'd said the wrong thing the minute he finished and wasn't at all surprised when Nick crossed his arms over his chest and huffed.

"You can't trust the media, though. They spread lies like wildfire. Even the most mundane word, action or behaviour gets misconstrued into something not even remotely like it was intended."

"That's true." It was all he could say. No one would believe he was doing the best he could with what options he had, so there wasn't any point in trying to change their minds.

After a brief, strained silence, Nick said, "You'll be joining them for dinner this evening. Not here, but at the opening of a new restaurant in Slough."

"Is a suit okay to wear? That's really all I brought."

Nick nodded. "It will be fine. If you need anything you don't have, we can arrange for it."

"No, please don't go to any trouble. If I don't have something at home I can collect, I just won't attend to make it easier on everyone."

Nick stepped closer. "But that won't make it easier. People know you're here, and if you don't attend certain things, it will look poorly on the royal family. Like they were keeping you from seeing everything. I won't allow you to make them look worse than you already do."

Malachi's breath left him, and he stared at Nick, seeing the protective air around him almost visibly shimmer. It wasn't possible, of course, but that was what it looked like. Nick's shoulders were broad enough to take over much of his vision, but he couldn't tear his eyes away from his face. All rigid lines and harsh features. Even his lips were strong and full. He'd probably be able to crack a bone with those lips. When he realised he'd been staring at Nick's lips for too long, he blinked and met his gaze again. Something sparked in those depths, and he wasn't sure if he wanted to know what it was. Recalling Nick's last words, Malachi nodded, accepting the truth in them.

"Okay then. Let's visit the private kitchen."

Malachi followed Nick like a lost puppy, trying hard to ignore the attraction he had just realised he had. It explained a lot about why he sought Nick out when he covered events and visits. But why did he have to have a crush on one of the most out of his league, no way in hell people on the planet? Nick wouldn't touch him with a stick if he was the last person on the planet, so what did it matter?

The kitchen was already bustling, and the scents of the food together created an unusual mix. He received a few smiles from the household staff and a few glares, but he'd needed to get used to that quickly in his job. Soon, though. Soon, he could tell everyone that he was Kai Ruffers. Soon.

"Do you have any questions, or are you ready to move on?" Nick asked.

"Moving on is good."

He did have some questions, but they were more for the staff, and he wasn't sure he was allowed to talk to them. He'd ask later and then request another visit if he was.

In the meantime, he had to get through a couple more hours of hostility before he could escape to his room to get ready.

7

Nick

Nick was being an asshole. He couldn't help it, though. Malachi just rubbed him up the wrong way. How the hell was he supposed to babysit him for the weekend without killing him? He steadied his breathing as they continued towards the receiving room. As far as Nick knew, no one was supposed to be there at that time but that didn't mean someone wasn't going to surprise him. Only time would tell. If he was a betting man, Prince George might make an appearance.

Knocking before entering any room had become standard procedure since the princes had found their partners. After walking in on personal moments too many times, he had made it mandatory, even if he knew there was no one in the room. And it was what he did when they reached the receiving room. No one answered, so he entered and held the door for Malachi, his inbuilt manners not able to defy him, no matter who the recipient was.

"Oh, wow. This room is huge. You said this was the receiving room, so you mean for meeting heads of state and such?" Malachi asked, meandering around the area.

Nick leaned his ass against a sofa and rested his hands on the back. "Yeah, sometimes. Initially, that was all it was used for, but since the family expanded, it's used more for family get-togethers than anything else now."

"I'm assuming that's mainly for birthdays and anniversaries and such."

Nick had been told what information he could and couldn't share with the reporter, but he baulked at that one because he wanted to keep it quiet. "It's—"

"We use it regularly. Nothing beats spending time with family in any capacity possible."

Nick stood, stepping closer to Prince Frederick and trying to hide his surprise and displeasure, especially when he didn't appear to have his guards. "Your Highness," he said, bowing his head.

"Oh!" Malachi's face flushed, and he bowed low. "Your Highness. Thank you for allowing me to visit your home."

Freddie smiled. "You're welcome. I have read many of your articles, Mr Sanders. Your writing skills are incredible."

Malachi lowered his eyes. "I...um, thank you, Your Highness. I wish..." He didn't finish his sentence, but Nick would've loved to see what excuse he came up with for writing such crap.

"You truly do have a talent. Your prose is eloquent and not at all flowery, which I've found in many reporters. Is the role you're in the one you envisioned for yourself?"

Nick bit his lip at Freddie's choice of words.

Malachi's cheeks reddened further. "Not in so many words, no. Unfortunately, not everyone gets to have their first choice of employers."

It was the second time Malachi had implied he wasn't doing the job by choice, but if that was the case, why wasn't he leaving?

"Such a truthful statement. As I was saying, this space is used primarily for our family now. It's big enough to house us all, and we don't have to worry about anyone finding out we weren't the prim and proper royals we *should* be."

Why hadn't Brett given Prince Freddie his job because his words, while fairly benign and truthful, were on the spot with making a point about Malachi's content? No matter how powerful his prose was, his words were hurtful all the same.

"Definitely, Your Highness. Not everyone needs to know your secrets."

"Never has a truer word been spoken," Freddie said with a smile.

Nick silently tagged on, "by you," but it wouldn't do any use adding it out loud.

"Are you attending the dinner later, Your Highness?" Malachi asked.

Freddie shook his head. "I have a prior engagement, but I'm sure my father will be a wonderful companion."

Malachi smiled. "I'm looking forward to talking with him some more."

"Well, I must be getting back to Damon. He'll be wondering where the popcorn is."

"Thank you for your time, Your Highness," Malachi said.

Nick moved closer to the prince and lowered his voice. "Your Highness, please consider bringing your guards the next time you want to talk to him. I am only one person and can only do so much."

Freddie's mouth curved. "He won't harm us physically, Nick. He's got too much to lose."

Nick frowned. "What do you mean?"

Freddie shook his head, glancing over Nick's shoulder to Malachi. "He won't hurt us, Nick. Maybe check your preconceived notions at the door and see him as a person rather than a reporter first."

With that not-so-subtle reprimand, Freddie left, and Nick saw Locke as the door opened. Whether she'd arrived with Freddie or after him, he wasn't sure, but either way, his tension lowered slightly, knowing he had some backup should he have needed it.

Three hours later, they were both dressed in suits and headed to the restaurant the king was opening. There would be a select few—King Andrew and Prince Consort Kean, food critics and celebrities—in attendance, so security was slightly easier, especially with Landon, Colt, Viola and Emmy joining him, and the several guards the celebrities brought.

After the official opening ceremony, short and sweet that it was, he followed them to their table and then stepped away, pausing when the king said his name.

"Your Majesty?"

"Please join us for dinner tonight, Nick."

Nick gaped, but he shook his head slightly. "Thank you for the offer, Your Majesty, but I have to decline. I am needed as part of the security team tonight."

Andrew sighed but nodded. "I won't get a different answer from you, will I?"

Nick smiled. "No, Your Majesty."

"One of these days..."

Nick cleared his throat instead of laughing at the king's veiled attempt to discourage the use of his title and call him Andrew and headed to his perch near the bathrooms. It was one of the few places Malachi would go if he was to leave the table, and he wanted to be close in case he got any stupid ideas. Malachi had flushed cheeks and laughed several times throughout dinner. Andrew and Kean joined in with the humour. At one point, Nick witnessed Kean's hand covering his mouth just as he'd taken a sip of his drink, his shoulders bouncing with laughter. What had been so funny? The partners were careful with their affection, not too much, but not too little, and Malachi had keen eyes, which seemed to take everything in despite the flowing alcohol he seemed to drink.

When Malachi rose, Nick tensed until he was away from the tables and heading his way. He was pale and a little unsteady on his legs, but his gaze never wavered.

"Maybe ease up on the alcohol," Nick murmured as Malachi pushed the bathroom door open.

Malachi nodded but said nothing, and Nick sighed. He wasn't the man's father, so he couldn't make him do anything he didn't want to do—mostly. If he wanted to drink himself into a coma, Nick had no choice but to let him.

A sound of metal against wood met his ears, and he strained for anything other than what his mind supplied of someone kicking the bin into the cupboard, but then a soft thud reached him, and he slammed through to the bathroom to find Malachi on his knees with an EpiPen in his thigh. His face was dotted with sweat, his lips tinged blue, and his eyes wild. Nick dropped to his knees beside him, cupping Malachi's jaw.

"What do you need?" Malachi shook his head with a jerk. "Did it all get in?" Malachi nodded and sank into Nick's hands, Nick barely catching him as he took all his weight. "What are you allergic to?" he asked as he tugged Malachi into his body.

Malachi yanked the needle from his leg, and Nick took it from him. Most EpiPens were not allergy-specific, but a little label had been stuck on this one with "peanuts" on it.

"Peanuts? You're allergic to peanuts?" Malachi nodded. "Was it in your food?" Malachi didn't answer, but he gave a slight lift of his shoulders. Nick sighed. "We're not having much luck with you and royal invitations, are we?" He tried for a joke, but he wasn't feeling so humorous. "Let me call for backup."

Malachi shook his head, the colour already seeping back into his face. "Won't...ruin...it."

"You have to go to hospital, Malachi."

"I will... Not yet."

Nick shook his head and spoke into his radio. "We have an issue. Malachi has had an allergic reaction. He's okay, but he needs to go to the hospital. Can someone bag up his food? Because I'm assuming he didn't purposefully choose something that had peanuts in it, so it needs to be investigated. Do the same for the king's and Prince Consort Kean's, just in case. We don't want any surprises."

"Do you want an ambulance?" Colt radioed back.

"No. I don't want to bring attention to this." He met Malachi's grateful gaze. "I'll take him out the back in a little while and call for a driver to take us there. Divert people from using this room for now."

"Understood."

Nick refocused on Malachi. "We'll wait here for a few minutes and then get you up and to the hospital, okay?" Malachi nodded, blinking lazily, probably so tired from the incident. "Where's your other pen in case I need it?" Malachi patted his pocket. "Okay, tell me when you're feeling up to moving."

It took a few minutes, but Malachi finally said, "I should be okay to get up now."

Nick helped him to his unsteady feet, keeping his arms around him to take his weight. "Does this happen often?"

"No, but it has happened. I know what to do. Hospital, as much as I hate it, is essential to make sure nothing else happens. I could do with a bucket in case I'm sick, though."

Nick grabbed the small waste basket, tipped the contents into the nearest sink and passed it to Malachi. The reporter snorted inelegantly but held onto it. Having been trained in first aid, he knew what had to be done in that situation, but he had never had it happen on his watch before. Going to the hospital had also not been on his agenda. His stomach, however, was cramping at the thought of something happening to Malachi; just like it had done at the event when he'd seen that guy straddling him. Whatever that was about was something for him to decipher another day.

They exited the bathroom, which was luckily in a hallway off the main restaurant area, and headed towards the back door, supporting Malachi as much as he could. He pushed the door open, hoping it didn't set off some sort of alarm, and helped Malachi to the black town car that waited for them. Once they sat in the back, the bin on Malachi's lap, Nick relaxed a bit.

"Thanks, Brandon. To the hospital, please," he said to their driver.

"Fast and rocky, or slow and steady?" Brandon asked as he manoeuvred from out of the alley behind the restaurant.

Nick glanced at Malachi's pale face and his grip on the bin. "Slow and steady for now. I'll let you know if we need to speed up."

"Understood."

Malachi closed his eyes and rested his head back, giving Nick time to study the man closely. What a conundrum he was. In repose, he had a pale complexion, made paler by that incident, with freckles speckled across his slightly flared nose. His lips were parted with every deep inhale he made, the thin upper lip trembling gently, and his tongue glancing across the thicker lower lip. His skin looked as smooth as it probably was having been freshly shaven before going out that night. His light brown hair was cut close to his head, similar to his own.

When Malachi's hand fell, Nick caught the bin before it went rolling away from them. Propping it on the other side of him, he slid his fingers around Malachi's wrist to check his pulse. It was fast, but he wasn't sure what Malachi's usual rate was, so he had nothing to compare it to.

Nick shook Malachi gently, wanting him to wake to check on him. When he didn't respond, Nick did it a little harder.

"Malachi? Open your eyes for me." No reply. "Brandon, speed up a little, please."

"Got it."

The car increased its speed, and Nick tapped Malachi's cheek. He was still breathing, which was one thing Nick was consoling himself with. Maybe he just crashed. Whatever had happened, they needed to see a doctor as soon as possible.

Nick's phone rang, but he didn't answer it, keeping his eyes on Malachi's breathing, and his fingers on his pulse. Malachi's eyelids were also fluttering as if he was dreaming. No way on this earth was something happening to the reporter on his watch. It would just be his luck that Malachi died and he ended up in the media as someone who killed him.

Nick shook his head and swallowed hard. He couldn't admit that he hated the idea of the man being ill. Well, he couldn't admit it aloud. Malachi had some sort of hold over him, and he hated it, especially with how awful he was to the Sutcliffes. It was as if Nick couldn't reconcile Malachi's reporter side with how else he saw him. The human side of him that seemed so different to the words he wrote.

Was that what Malachi meant when he'd implied he wasn't doing the job he wanted to do? Did he not want to be writing all that? If that was true, then why was he, and why didn't he stop?

They were all questions Nick couldn't answer, and neither could Malachi at that point.

"We're here," Brandon said, the car lurching to a stop hard enough that Nick had to stop Malachi from sliding off the seat.

"Malachi? Can you hear me?"

Malachi mumbled something Nick didn't understand but didn't open his eyes.

"Looks like I'm carrying you then," Nick muttered to himself.

He climbed out of the car, went around to Malachi's side and moved the bin, reaching in and slipping his hands beneath and around him as best as he could. He wasn't a light man, but he wasn't heavy either. His head lolled back as Nick lifted him out of the car, and Brandon helped by leading the way and getting a doctor as soon as they entered. Nick eased Malachi onto a gurney but couldn't find the energy to move away. When they started wheeling him down the corridor, he kept pace.

"Name?"

Nick blinked and then came to his senses. "Malachi Sanders. He had a reaction to peanuts and took his EpiPen around half an hour ago. He was coherent for all of it until around ten minutes ago, when he appeared to fall asleep. His pulse was fast, but I don't know if that's usual for him or not. He never stopped breathing at any point. He was mumbling when I got him out of the car but wouldn't open his eyes."

"Some people who use an EpiPen get really tired afterwards and fall into a deep sleep, almost coma-like, but it's not one," a doctor said. "He'll be fine and will wake up soon." The doctor focused on a nurse. "Fluids and get another adrenaline shot just in case he has a relapse."

"Will he?" Nick asked. "Have a relapse?" he added when the doctor frowned at him.

"It's hard to tell. Some patients do, some don't. It's best to have one on hand, just in case."

The doctor shone a light into Malachi's eyes, and he grumbled and turned his face, which settled Nick's concerns a little. If he was complaining, he couldn't be too bad. At least, he hoped.

Nick's phone kept ringing, but he ignored it. Until he had something more concrete to go on, he wasn't going to answer anyone's questions. He leaned against the wall, keeping out of the way of the doctors and nurses dealing with Malachi, but his gaze stayed on him. Every inhale the reporter took helped Nick to breathe easier.

They needed to figure out how he had been given peanuts. He knew he was allergic, so he wouldn't have chosen a meal that had it in. So, either the restaurant made a mistake and gave him the wrong option, or Malachi chose the wrong option, not realising it had peanuts in it, or something else sinister. Was this related to the event? Nick frowned. Why would it be? He tried to follow his train of thought, but there was a ruckus outside the room, and Andrew came barging in.

"Nick, update me as you haven't been answering your phone," Andrew said, and Nick immediately straightened from the wall.

"I apologise, Your Majesty. I was waiting for an update from the doctor before I answered to ensure I could give anyone an answer."

Andrew's stern expression eased, and he nodded. "Understandable. I was, however, concerned when Malachi left the dinner and never returned, and when Colt told me what happened, I wanted to make sure he was well cared for." Andrew's mouth curved. "At the hospital, not with you, Nick. I know you would take care of him."

Nick nodded, and his gaze found Malachi again. This time, his bright blue eyes gazed back at him, glazed though they were.

"You're big," Malachi whispered, ending in a loppy smile, and Nick's mouth twitched.

"There you are, Mr Sanders. I'm glad to finally meet you," the doctor said, gaining Malachi's attention. "Do you know where you are, Mr Sanders?"

Malachi's head swivelled around, his eyes widening slowly. "Hospital?"

The doctor nodded. "Yes, Mr Sanders. I'm Dr Livingstone. Can you remember what happened?"

Malachi stared at Nick again, and the loopiness in his eyes visibly eased. "Peanuts. I had a reaction."

"You did. You seem to be on the mend, and you're in good hands. You're hooked up to some fluids now, and we'll keep monitoring you for a few hours to make sure everything is on the up and up, but you should make a full recovery."

"Happened before," Malachi muttered, his eyelids blinking slower.

"You're an old hat at this, then." The doctor chuckled. "Get some rest, Mr Sanders. We'll keep you safe."

Nick would keep him safe. He had to.

8

Malachi

Malachi woke slowly, warmth surrounding him, but when he tried to push off the covers, something pulled at his hand.

"Hey, slow down. You'll pull the IV out," a voice said, and Malachi blinked several times to bring them into focus. Nick.

He cleared his throat, his throat a little sore, and opened his mouth to ask where he was before everything came rushing back. "Hospital."

"Yeah, you're in the hospital. Are you with me, Malachi?"

"Kai," he said absently, pushing himself to sitting. Nick propped the pillow behind him, and he rested back with a sigh. "I bloody hate it when that happens."

"What?"

"Allergies. They suck. I always crash after having a shot."

"That would've been nice to know. You crashed in the car, and we ended up breaking speed limits to get here." Though Nick's words were a rebuke, they were softened by his tone and expression.

"Sorry," Malachi's cheeks heated. "I should've said."

Nick shook his head. "It doesn't matter. You're on the mend, which is all we can hope for." He sighed. "Do you know where it came from? The peanuts?"

Malachi shook his head. "Usually I can taste them if I've eaten them by accident. They have a distinct taste that I've learnt to recognise. Preemptive, if you like. But I didn't taste a thing."

"We're having your meal analysed to see if something was in it that shouldn't have been, or if you were just given the wrong meal. We're speaking with the restaurant, too. This shouldn't have happened, especially on the opening night of a restaurant whose owner had others with high ratings. It's strange."

Malachi reached for the water jug, but Nick beat him to it, filling a plastic cup and handing it to him. "Thanks." He gratefully drained it, his throat thanking him.

"This seems to be a regular occurrence," Nick murmured. "Are you prone to ending up in hospital?" Nick's mouth twitched as if he didn't want to break into a smile. "Just so I know for future reference, you know."

Despite how tired he was, Malachi chuckled. "Funnily enough, no, it's not. The last time I ended up in hospital with my allergies was around...seven years ago."

"Well, at least we can cross off accident-prone on your list. That'll save me some work."

Malachi chuckled weakly and yawned. "This hospital malarky is pissing me off now. Do you know if they've let Mum or Grandma know?"

Nick's eyes widened. "I don't know. I never thought... Sorry, I should've thought about contacting them. Do you want me—"

"No! Really. I'm glad they haven't been told because they'd only get worried. I'll tell them once I'm up and about again. Although, maybe the grapevine will work, and they'll already know by the time I'm out of here." He huffed a laugh and closed his scratchy eyes. "Saves me a phone call."

"Get some rest, okay? I'll be right here."

Malachi wanted to stay awake, but his body was telling him, no way; therefore, it was several hours later when he woke in a dimmed room, which sent his heart racing.

"Are you okay, Malachi?"

Nick's voice had the instant tension easing away, and Malachi breathed through the panic of being alone. He wasn't scared of the dark or of being alone, but since that night, when he had no idea what had happened to him, he didn't like the unexpected.

"Yeah," he rasped. "I'm okay."

He rolled to his back, the tugging and rustle of the bed sheets making him realise someone had covered him. There was a slight chill in the air from the air conditioning, so he was grateful for the thought. Meeting Nick's gaze, he said, "What time is it?"

Nick rose, filled a cup with water and handed it to him before he answered. "It's about one in the morning," he murmured.

Malachi nearly choked on the water. "What? Shit, I'm so sorry. You don't have to stay. You must be exhausted. Go. I'm all right. They'll probably let me go home now, anyway."

Nick's mouth tightened, and even through the dim lighting, Malachi could see the action. "I don't think it was an accident, Malachi. Someone laced your food with ground peanuts. The pot your food came from had no traces of it. Only your plate."

It took a second for the words to sink in, and his stomach churned. "On purpose? Why?"

Nick shook his head. "I don't know. We need to figure it out. When you're feeling up to it and are back with us, we can go through some things to see if we can figure out who else you've pissed off."

Malachi closed his eyes. "Apart from the part of the British population who love the royal family, you mean?"

Nick grimaced. "Yeah. I never said it was going to be easy."

Rubbing his hands over his face, he sighed as the shittiness washed over him again. "We can go now. I'm sure I'm fine." He swung his legs over the bed, his head spinning for a second before righting itself again. "I'll sign that I can be discharged."

Nick held up his hands. "No, you'll only be going when they say you're well enough to go, so get those legs back up into bed."

Malachi ignored him and pressed the button for the nurses' station. Nick glared at him but settled back against the wall with his arms crossed. It took the nurse several minutes, but when she came, she was more than happy to send him on his way. Nick protested, but the nurse informed him that the doctor had signed off on his release after the last time he was seen. He needed to rest, and that was all, which Malachi knew already.

"I told you. This isn't my first rodeo," Malachi said, gingerly standing to make sure his legs took his weight. Nick stepped closer, his hand outstretched as if to catch him should he fall. *Maybe I should fake it and see if those muscles are as hard as they look.* He shook his head to clear the voice. When he walked the length of the room and back, getting stronger with each step, he grinned. "Told you."

"Well, then, cowboy, get yourself ready and we'll ride back to Windsor."

Malachi glanced at him. "Is that a good idea if someone has targeted me?"

"It's the best idea. There will be enough guards around to mitigate the chances of it happening again."

"But what if I bring it into Windsor?" His mind flicked to the emails he'd been receiving, kind of stalkerish, but he couldn't believe someone seemingly so happy with Malachi's words would want to hurt him. He wasn't positive, of course, but it seemed unlikely. He considered telling Nick about them but refrained.

"We'll know if they try to get in." Nick sighed. "With all the problems we've had over the past few years, our security is top-notch. It's highly unlikely for someone to get to you." He paused and narrowed his eyes. "Unless this is all a ruse you've concocted."

Malachi rolled his eyes. "Damn it. You caught me," he deadpanned. "Fuck, Nick. I don't want to hurt anyone."

Nick waved him away. "Let's not do this again. It's time to get back."

Malachi followed Nick out of the room once the nurse had confirmed he could leave, and they met someone at the entrance he vaguely remembered.

"I'm glad to see you're up and about again," the man said, nodding once.

"Thanks."

"This is Brandon. He drove us here."

Malachi gasped. "Have you been waiting here all night? I'm so sorry."

Brandon chuckled. "No, I went back to the restaurant to pick up His Majesty and the Prince Consort and took them back home. Nick messaged not long ago asking for a ride back. And here I am."

"I'm sorry it's so late," Malachi said.

Brandon waved him away. "Don't be. It's part of my job to be on call in case I'm needed."

"And are you needed often at three in the morning?" Malachi raised his eyebrows.

Nick cleared his throat and glared at him, making Malachi realise how his question might be construed. "Shit. Don't answer that. I'm not asking for secrets or whatever. It was a genuine random question I would've asked anyone who'd said that. Sorry." His stomach rolled, and this time it wasn't from the allergy. He hated that Nick thought the worst of him, but the only way to alleviate some of that was to tell him the truth, but what would that accomplish?

He climbed into the car and rested his head back against the seat, closing his eyes with a sigh. Not long left. Soon, he'd be free. He just had to keep reminding himself of that.

Nick nudged him awake when they reached the castle, and he rubbed his face and yawned before climbing back out of the car. Sleeping so much when he was used to insomnia was a mind-fuck.

"Thanks, Brandon," he said, waving at the driver before he pulled away. They headed inside, and he dragged his feet, his body too heavy for him suddenly. He was so tired, which was what always happened after an incident like that.

"Come on. Let me help," Nick said. He draped his arm around Malachi's waist and took some of his weight. Malachi automatically wrapped his arm around Nick's waist and gripped tightly.

God, he is as hard as he looks. And he smells divine. It took every ounce of willpower he had not to inhale deeply and keep that scent in his lungs for as long as possible. As in, passing out possible.

Nick leaned him against the wall while he unlocked the suite door and then helped him into the room. "Let's get you to bed, and then I'll lock everything up here."

Malachi stumbled with every step, but he managed to not fall flat on his face, but only because of Nick. When he sat on the bed, he let out an enormous sigh.

"Is this usual?" Nick asked. "Being so tired?"

Malachi nodded, barely able to keep his eyes open. "Always." He listed to the side, and Nick helped him to lie down.

"Do you want to undress?" Nick mumbled.

"Nah... tomorrow," he muttered.

Nick said something else, but Malachi faded away, only to be abruptly woken by his phone sometime later. His head was full of cotton wool and surrounded by a bubble, but he fumbled around in the area of the bedside table, only to find it empty. The obscene noise continued as he rolled to his other side and opened one eye to see if his phone was there. It was, and the brightness of the screen lit up the unfamiliar room. He looked around through squinted eyes, finally letting his brain catch up with the rest of him.

"Windsor," he muttered through his dry lips. His phone stopped but started again almost immediately. "All right. All right." He grabbed it and exhaled when he saw it was his mother. "Hello?"

"Malachi Edward Sanders! Where have you been? All I get is this notification that you've been taken to hospital with a peanut reaction, and I can't get hold of you, the royal family, your boss, no one! I've been out of my mind worrying about what happened to you! I finally received a lovely message from someone called Nick, and he told me that you were okay but sleeping it off. Well, it's ten o'clock the next morning, and I've still not heard from you!"

He waited a few seconds to see if she'd run out of air enough for him to talk, and when she didn't continue, he said, "I've been sleeping, Mum. You know how this gets. I'm sorry I didn't message you, but my brain was not working properly last night...or early this morning as it was."

"Did they figure out what happened with the peanut thing? How did you end up ordering something with peanuts in it?"

Not wanting to worry her, he said nothing about what Nick had told him earlier that day. "I think I might've been given the wrong plate. They're investigating it because, obviously, they don't want it to happen again."

"Damn right they don't. They're lucky we're not suing them. They were so careless. It could've killed you, Malachi! If you hadn't had your pen with you, it could've been a completely different story." She finished on a sob, and he let her calm down a little while he dragged himself up to lean against the headboard, realising he was still fully dressed.

"I know, Mum. Things could've been much worse, but the royal family will investigate and get to the bottom of it. I promise you."

She sniffed. "How are you feeling, sweetheart?"

He chuckled. "Oh, now you ask about me," he teased. "I'm doing okay. Very tired, but no other lingering side effects."

"Remember to keep hydrated today," she said, and although he knew extremely well what he had to do, he also knew it was her way of looking out for him, even though he didn't need it any longer.

"I will. I don't think we have a huge amount planned today, anyway, so I can take regular breaks." That wasn't strictly true, but he wasn't going to worry her any more than she already was.

"All right. Sorry to wake you."

Malachi chuckled. "It's okay. I needed to get up, anyway. Hydration, remember?"

Emily snorted inelegantly—something he got from her. "Ring me later?"

"Will do. Love you."

"Love you, too, sweetheart."

Malachi's hand fell to his lap when the call ended, and he closed his eyes, wanting to fall straight back to sleep, but he needed to get himself up. Before he could contemplate moving, though, a knock sounded.

"Come in."

Nick poked his head in the door. "I heard voices, so I assumed you were awake. How are you feeling?" He stepped in a little further but didn't enter fully.

Malachi, glad he was dressed, though fully aware he probably stunk to high heaven, swung his legs out of bed. He didn't try to stand up yet, not sure if his legs would fully support him, and he didn't want to seem weak in front of that man again.

"Tired, but that's to be expected. I'm sorry I slept so long. I know we had plans today. I'll get ready and we can get going for the day."

Nick waved him away. "It's fine. His Majesty has said we can have the meeting whenever you feel up to it."

"I'll be fine once I've had a shower."

"Okay, well, you do that, and I'll get some breakfast...um, brunch organised."

Malachi nodded, distracted by the uncertainty Nick showed. Where had it come from? He was usually ready to rip people apart at the drop of a hat, but that morning, he seemed almost...worried.

"Shout me if you need anything," Nick added, giving more credence to the worried description.

"I will, thanks."

Nick closed the door, and Malachi stared at it for a while longer before he tried to stand. His knees wobbled until they gained strength, and then he took a few tentative steps. Each step grew stronger until he felt a little more human. And after the shower, he was a new man. Well, he wasn't, but the sluggish feeling had ebbed away, and his stomach growled, which made him think he was getting back to normal. After dressing in tailored trousers and a shirt—but no tie or jacket—he went into the living area and froze.

On the coffee table were several plates of food, from scrambled eggs and toast to a full English breakfast to cereal.

"Wow, that's a spread."

If he wasn't mistaken, Nick's cheeks darkened, but his skin was tanned, so he couldn't be sure. "I wasn't sure what you liked, so I got a few things. Choose whatever you want."

Malachi settled into a chair on the opposite side to the guard. "Thanks. Can't go wrong with scrambled eggs." He picked up the plate and a fork and dug in. It was seasoned to perfection and reminded him so much of how his grandmother made them. "Delicious."

Nick's mouth curved at the corners into something resembling a smile, but it was more than Malachi remembered him sending his way before.

"I don't want to mess up the king's day, so I'm happy to rearrange our meeting if he has prior appointments, which I'm sure he does."

Nick swallowed the coffee he'd just drank and shook his head. "Actually, he doesn't. The only plans he had today were spending time with his family, and he's been doing that this morning and will do so after your meeting. It's all fine."

Malachi couldn't believe the change in Nick. Was that what a near-death experience did for him? Made him nicer to him? Maybe he should do it more often. After thinking that, he dropped his eyes and cursed himself. Why did it matter what Nick thought? He couldn't do anything about the articles he wrote as Malachi Sanders, and Nick didn't know about Kai Ruffers. He was stuck between a rock and a hard place, and he hated it.

Soon he'd be free.

"What happened to that guy from before? At the event?"

Nick smiled. "Too much evidence against him. He's in jail and not getting out any time soon."

Malachi liked the sound of that, but he changed the subject. "So, you contacted my mother?" he said as a distraction from his thoughts.

9

Nick

Nick felt his cheeks heat at the question. He straightened a little in his seat and inhaled. "If it was my mother, she'd be frantic. I thought it might help."

Malachi smiled at him, cheeks bulging with eggs and toast as he nodded. "It did," he mumbled. He chewed quickly, his hand covering his mouth while he did. "She was thankful she'd been told and said you were very kind, so thank you for reassuring her."

"You're welcome."

"I'm sure she'll lynch mob me when I see her next." Malachi chuckled. "Grandma won't, though. She knows I can look after myself." He paused. "Not that my mother doesn't, but she worries." He waved his hand, his fork circling the air. "What are the plans for today?"

"Well, it's Prince Consort Kean's birthday today, so apart from your meeting with the king, I thought we could speak with Randall, the king's assistant, and he can answer some of your questions. If you have any other requests for things to see and people to talk to, let me know, and I will see what I can do. Prince

Freddie has agreed to a brief tour of parts of Frogmore Cottage, and we can do that tomorrow."

Nick crossed his ankle over his knee, a little uncomfortable with how open the royal family was being, but rather too comfortable with Malachi's company recently. Was he concerned about the two hospital visits and whether it was a regular thing? A little. His gut was telling him something was wrong, but he couldn't figure out what. If things had been happening to him or one of the bodyguards, then he would've guessed it was that idiotic, stalkery weirdo that had been after Dominic and Owen, but it wasn't aimed at him. And there was nothing between him and Malachi to make whoever it was think they could get to him through the reporter.

No, whatever was going on—if anything was—was related to Malachi himself. Nick needed to figure out what it was and whether it was something of concern to the royal family. He would not put them in danger if he could help it.

"That's amazing!"

It took Nick a moment to follow the conversation again, and he must've taken too long to reply because Malachi looked down at his plate and put his fork down.

"I promise I won't do or write anything to cause problems. I really am just grateful to have this opportunity to see the castle and to meet everyone."

If Malachi had said those words before, Nick would've brushed them off as empty platitudes, but something niggled at him. Both Brett and Freddie had told him to look beneath the surface with Malachi, and Nick hadn't. But maybe he should.

Nick smiled across the space, and if Malachi's wide eyes were anything to go by, he'd not done it before. Fuck, he was an ass. "I know you won't." He tilted his head, continuing to meet Malachi's stare. "There's something you're not telling me, though, Malachi, and I *will* find out what it is. But...I know you won't hurt anyone."

Something akin to relief, maybe, and possibly a touch of fear passed across Malachi's expression, but the man gave a small chuckle and put his plate back on the table.

"I have no doubt that you already know all my secrets, Nick, but thank you for trying to make me think you don't." Malachi frowned down at his hands and then met his gaze again, squaring his shoulders. "I will tell you this, though. I have less than a year left on my contract with Windsor Chronicle, and I *will* be moving on to decidedly greener pastures afterwards."

Nick raised his eyebrows. "Well, that's one thing I didn't know. Any reason?"

Malachi rubbed his lips together for a minute. "I would like to go in a different direction to where they are."

Nick almost grinned at the vague answer, but instead, he nodded. "Fair enough." Deciding they had spoken enough about serious topics, he dropped his foot to the floor and clapped his hands on his thighs. "Are you ready to speak with the king?"

Malachi's smile grew. "Without a doubt."

Nick carried the empty dishes to the trolley and piled them up neatly. When Malachi joined him with their cups, the reporter chuckled.

"Siblings?" he asked.

Nick snorted. "How did you know?"

"I think many people know how to tidy up after themselves, but only those with siblings understand the pain of not piling things properly and having the entire pile of plates and cutlery come crashing down when there are more than a couple to deal with." Malachi bit his lip. "I have four."

Nick couldn't stop his grin that time. "Three. All younger pains in my butt. Wouldn't be without them, though."

"The joys and pitfalls of siblinghood."

Nick frowned. "Siblinghood? Is that even a word?"

"Don't care if it is or not. It should be."

"Says the writer."

Malachi held up his hands. "Hey, if fantasy writers can make up their own words for items, so can I."

Nick chuckled and checked everything was in place before tilting his head towards the door. "Ready?"

"Yes—no! Let me grab my notebook. I don't know if this is on the record or not—either is fine. I just want to be prepared." Malachi rushed around, gathering things into a small satchel-style bag, and then stopped in front of him. "Ready."

Nick placed his hands on Malachi's shoulders, immediately realising it was the first time he'd touched him outside of needing to help him, and tried to ignore the need to drag him into his body. "Malachi? Breathe. He's just a man."

"Yeah, a man who runs a country! Do you know how much work that must be? Of course, you do. You see him work every day. He never takes a day off, I'm told. And I could believe it, too, with how much he's done for us all. He's—"

"Breathe, Malachi," Nick said again more forcefully, moving his hand to cup his neck, and this time, Malachi stuttered to a stop and took a shaky inhale. "And again."

He could feel the reporter's pulse fluttering beneath his palm and the heat of his skin seeping into him. A wave of protectiveness washed over him, and he wanted to pull Malachi into his body and shield him from everything. It was that thought that made him step back. Surely, he couldn't change his tune that quickly. He never had before.

"Okay. Let's go."

He held the door open, locking it behind them, mainly to keep Malachi's items safe from nosey staff members. No one was above wanting to know more about those people coming into their orbit, and he'd hate for something to come out about Malachi that had nothing to do with reporting.

He almost stumbled his steps. What the hell was he thinking? This man beside him had been saying hateful things about the royal family for the past two years or more. Why was he defending him? He deserved every ounce of hatred and mistrust anyone wanted to throw at him.

But something inside Nick told him to stop thinking that way. To listen to what Malachi was and wasn't saying. To do some deeper research he should've done in the beginning rather than relying on the surface stuff he could find easily. Was that what Brett and Freddie had been getting at? That there was something he'd missed? If there was, he'd have to wait to find out because he wasn't leaving the king alone with the reporter unless he had no choice in the matter.

"Afternoon, Colt," he said, receiving a nod in return from the bodyguard stationed outside the offices. They each took a turn either in the hallway or outside the office door, especially after what happened to Randall a while ago. Having secret entrances was not always the best idea.

They entered the offices. "Hey, Randall." He smiled at the man who rushed around the table to hug him—something he'd not long started doing since he began a relationship with Dominic.

"Nick! Malachi! Are you well after last night?"

Nick let Malachi take the lead on the conversation, knowing Randall could be a force of nature when he wanted or needed to be, especially when someone was hurt. He nodded at Landon, who was on duty outside Andrew's office that day.

"I'm good, thanks. Plenty of sleep and a lovely breakfast was just what I needed."

Nick ignored the surge of pleasure that flowed through him when Malachi glanced at him when he said, "breakfast." He wasn't at all happy that Malachi enjoyed what he'd ordered him. Truly he wasn't.

"King Andrew is ready when you are," Randall ended the conversation politely, and Malachi smiled.

"I won't take up much of his time. I promise."

Randall waved him away. "You'll take as much of his time as he'll let you. But yes, maybe less is more today. He'll want to get back to Kean."

"We can reschedule," Malachi said.

Randall shook his head, smiling. "He won't hear of it. I tried already. To be honest, it'll be good for him. It'll give Kean and Kendal some time together."

Nick did not want those images in his head, so he headed for the office door. "Do you want to announce us, Randall?"

"Yes, of course."

He knocked and popped his head through the door, mumbling something Nick couldn't decipher, and then he came back out and nodded. "Go on in."

Malachi hesitated and looked at Nick, so he smiled and nodded. "He won't bite."

"I know. I just..." Malachi shook his head and sent a small smile back. "Never mind."

He knocked as he pushed on the door, and Nick followed, thanking Randall before he closed them inside.

"Mr Sanders! How are you feeling today?"

King Andrew rose from his chair and headed towards them, hand outstretched. Malachi took it and shook.

"I'm all good, thank you. Nothing more than a reaction. It's inevitable at some point."

"Still. Are you well? There are no adverse side effects from what happened?"

Malachi shook his head. "Everything is fine. I've been through it before, and it's why I have my pen. I just get really tired afterwards."

"I can imagine it takes a toll on your body. Would you like something to drink or eat?"

"I'm good, thanks. We've just had breakfast." Malachi glanced at him again, a small smile curving his lips.

"Nick?" Andrew asked.

"You know me. I would never say no to coffee, but I can get it, Your Majesty. Would you like anything?"

"Tea, please." Andrew returned his attention to Malachi and gestured to the uncomfortable sofas he purposefully had in his office. He said they made people leave quicker than they would if they were comfortable, so Nick couldn't begrudge him.

He made two drinks while eavesdropping on the pleasantries most people started a conversation with. Nick carried a mug of tea over to the king and settled at his usual post against the wall, sipping the hot nectar of the gods. He wasn't sure how any of the bodyguards survived without coffee, but somehow they must.

"Nick, come and sit down," Andrew said.

"I'm okay, Your Majesty. Thank you." Those sofas were not to be trifled with.

"I insist. Come join us."

Nick inwardly sighed, knowing his butt was going to ache after that meeting, but he dutifully sat next to Malachi and crossed his ankle over his knee.

"So, Malachi," Andrew started. "What questions do you have for me?"

Malachi looked startled and fumbled with his notebook. "I, um..." He paused, inhaled and glanced at the king. "I have so many questions, but what I'd really like to hear about is your family. Whoever you're willing to talk about, if anyone. And it's completely fine if you don't want to. It's just..." He stared down at his notebook again. "Family is important to me, and I know it is to you, too. I have never seen such a...wonderful dynamic as yours. It's fascinating."

Nick gaped at him. Okay, he hadn't expected him to ask about family, but from his words, there were no snide remarks, no comments bordering on nasty. He wanted to talk family, which could be a minefield in itself when it came to what had happened a couple of years ago, but was fairly benign compared to other topics.

Andrew smiled, broad and loving. "I am always happy to talk about my family, Malachi. I can honestly say that it has taken me far too long to realise that my sons and my nieces and nephews are grown-ups. That they can deal with their own problems on their own without me needing to help them." His expression was pained, and Nick could guess his mind had gone to his late wife, and his next words confirmed it. "Before Louisa died, she was the one to set us straight. To show us the way. Now she's gone, I find I'm asking myself, 'What would Louisa do?'" He smiled again. "Even Kean and Kendal ask me the same thing whenever I ask their opinion on something."

"In our family, we go to Grandma. She's the soul of the family," Malachi said. "Always helping us to see our own paths by working us in circles until we figure it out on our own."

"She sounds like a wise woman. Just like Louisa was."

They chatted a bit more, Malachi seemingly keeping to benign topics, almost as if he didn't want to push his luck. They covered a variety of information in those minutes, though. In Nick's opinion—and he wasn't a writer—Andrew gave Malachi something to talk about for each of the princes, but what he would do with that information, only time would tell.

"I don't want to keep you any longer because I know it's Kean's birthday, and you want to spend the day with him, but thank you so much for talking to me."

"I've enjoyed talking with you, Malachi. If we have time before you head out, we'll get together again and talk some more. I'd love to hear more about your family, too."

Colour stained Malachi's cheeks. "Thank you, Your Majesty. I'd like that."

They rose, and Nick withheld the wince he wanted to give, along with a lengthy groan at the ache blossoming in his ass cheeks and tailbone. Andrew clapped him on the shoulder.

"You're a good sport, Nick. Now go rest your butt on some comfortable chairs."

Nick snorted. "Thank you, Your Majesty. I just might do that."

When they headed back down the corridor towards their suite, Nick said, "Why didn't you ask any other questions?"

Malachi sighed. "Because I'm not the monster I appear in writing. I'm truly not. And..." His cheeks darkened again. "I really am fascinated by the royal family. They're the epitome of everything, and they do it willingly, without fail, without complaint and without thanks. Many people would fail under those circumstances, but the Sutcliffes have bloomed. They are what the world should be."

Nick stared at him as they entered the suite, but he said nothing.

"I'm going for a quick nap if that's okay. I have time, right?"

Nick nodded. "As much as you need. Do you need me to get anything?"

Malachi shook his head. "No, I'm good, thanks. Wake me if I need to be somewhere."

"Will do."

He watched Malachi enter his room and close the door. The moment he did, Nick grabbed his laptop from his room and settled onto the comfier chairs in the living area. Booting up the computer, he set to re-reading the information he'd gathered on the reporter. An hour later, he still couldn't figure him out. What was he missing? He grabbed his phone.

"Felix, what have I missed?"

"Took you long enough," Felix replied, clicking away on his computer if the noise was any indication. "There. You should have the file you hadn't been able to find or were too lazy to look for."

"Hey!"

Felix chuckled in his ear. "You only saw what you wanted to see, Nick. You know what happens when you only dig so far."

"You're eaten by the wild bears," he muttered.

"Ain't that the truth? Happy reading."

He ended the call and pulled up the file Felix had emailed him. By the time he was done, Nick was stunned. He had no idea how anyone would guess that Malachi Sanders and Kai Ruffers were the same person. Why, if Malachi loved the royal family so much, was he writing such garbage about them? It made little sense to him. But then he remembered something Malachi had said about having less than a year left. Had the newspaper hooked him into a contract and made it impossible for him to disobey? Nick wouldn't put it past them because he saw it all the time. How had he kept Kai Ruffers a secret, though? And why was that knowledge sending sparks of heat through Nick?

Fuck. He knew why, but he didn't want to admit it. How could he admit that the reason he was so obsessed with the guy and whatever he wrote about the royal family was because he had a crush on him?

Nick dropped his head against the back of the sofa and groaned slightly. When Malachi spoke from behind him, he jumped, having not heard him at all during his pity party.

"How long have you known?"

Nick lifted his head, glanced at his laptop to see what exactly was on-screen, and met Malachi's gaze. "I knew you were a conundrum from the beginning, but I didn't know about Kai until just now. Why do you do it?"

Malachi rubbed his hands over his face and through his hair, giving Nick the chance to study his fresh-out-of-bed look. He exhaled and dropped into the seat beside him.

"If I leave now, I'll lose certain benefits I can't afford to lose."

10

Malachi

Some of the tension Malachi had been holding released, and he slumped into the chair. He was relieved that Nick knew. Keeping secrets was hard work, and he hated it, especially when Kai was more Malachi than Malachi Sanders was, which could be extremely confusing some days.

"What benefits? Surely you can get them elsewhere?"

Malachi's stomach twisted. "Four years ago, Mum got breast cancer. She went through all the chemotherapy and everything else they told her to do, and she beat it. Because I had additional health care benefits with the job, it made it easier, and she was able to get additional care."

Nick shifted to face him. "If she beat it, why are you still there? I'm not being mean, Malachi. I just want to understand."

That was the answer he never wanted to give his grandmother, but for Nick... He closed his eyes. "I'm scared she'll relapse and I won't have the benefits she needs to recover again. I can't lose her." It was his worst fear.

The sofa dipped, but Malachi refused to open his eyes in case tears fell, but the moment arms came around him and he was tucked against Nick's chest, they broke free anyway.

"Jesus, Malachi. You've been keeping this bottled up inside?"

He didn't answer. He couldn't. His throat had closed up, and he was at the very edge of his control. The arms surrounding him tightened, and Nick's heartbeat pounded against his cheek, soothing him. No one had ever held him like that before. Like he was precious. Like he had someone who cared—excluding his family. But then he brushed that thought aside. Nick didn't like him like that. He was just being kind. It was that thought that had him pulling away, but Nick seemed reluctant to let him go.

When they separated, Nick took his hand. "You don't have to carry this all on yourself, Mala...Kai."

Nick's eyes bore into him, and Malachi finally relented and wished the bodyguard would kiss him. He'd been attracted to Nick from the moment he'd started working for the royal family years ago, and he'd enjoyed reading about the comments people had overheard him making—funny anecdotes or jokes to break the seriousness of any situation. Few companies or businesses would let a guard do that, but the Sutcliffes appeared to appreciate the levity.

When his mind stopped wandering and refocused on Nick, he found them closer than they had been. All Malachi could see was Nick. The sharpness of his jawline, his full lips and the depth of those eyes. He wanted to rub his cheek against his stubble to see if it was rough or soft.

"Kai...?" Nick whispered.

Malachi didn't want to believe what he saw in Nick's eyes. Want. But the man raised his hand, cupped his jaw and brushed his thumb across Malachi's cheek. His heart raced, his breath choppy and unbelieving. Did Nick want him as much as he wanted Nick?

"Do you want this, Kai?" Nick asked, his breath fanning across Malachi's lips.

Malachi's eyelids fluttered as his deep voice rumbled through his body. "Yes," he breathed, his eyes closing fully.

The first brush of lips against lips was tentative, but Nick rubbed their skin together again and again before tugging at Malachi's bottom lip with his own. Malachi groaned and opened to him without prompting. Nick's hand slipped to the back of his head and pulled him closer—if that was possible—fusing their mouths.

As if a match had been lit, Nick held his head in both hands, as carefully as if he was made of glass, and devoured him. His tongue slipped inside, sliding against his own, duelling for the supremacy that Malachi happily rescinded to him. He wanted to feel Nick all around him, taking his scent into his lungs so he was deep inside him, too.

One of Nick's hands left his head and wrapped around his waist, tugging him closer until he had no choice but to straddle Nick's lap. No denying what they both felt when their groins met in the middle. Malachi threaded his fingers through the strands of Nick's hair, his other hand gripping his shoulder for balance. All the while, their lips sipped, took and gave, leaving him breathless and lightheaded.

He couldn't help the need to move against him, reaching for more, even though he knew it was too fast. Nick's hand slid down his back to his ass, squeezing his cheek, even as he gentled the kiss. Malachi didn't want to stop. He tightened his hold on Nick's neck, pressing their mouths harder and needing to get as close as possible.

Nick, however, had other plans and tore their mouths apart with a groan. "Fuck, Kai." He didn't stop Malachi from rubbing against him, though. "Shit. We need to stop. There's... We're...

Fuck." He dropped his head back while Malachi nipped and sucked at the skin of his neck.

Feeling mischievous, Malachi dragged his teeth down the column of his neck and latched onto his collarbone. Nick grabbed his hair and tugged, pulling him free.

"Bad boy, Kai," he grated, just as breathless as Malachi was. "We need to talk properly before this goes any further."

Malachi tried not to pout. "About what?"

"Everything." He sighed, gentling his hold on his hair and brushing his hand down his cheek. "I don't want you to think that I only wanted you after I found out you were Kai. I suppose it's kind of true, but I always wanted you. Right from when you first became a pain in our asses. I just tried to deny it when I thought you were a mean person."

Malachi smiled and cupped Nick's jaw, loving that he could touch him however he wanted. "It's okay. I would've done the same. I suppose it's inevitable that people will find out. I hadn't wanted anyone to while I was still working at the Chronicle, but if you found it, then maybe it's already happened."

Nick shook his head. "Felix sent me this. There's not much Felix can't find, but the average person wouldn't figure it out. I don't think you have to worry for now."

Malachi couldn't resist. He rested his head in the crook of Nick's neck and closed his eyes when Nick wrapped his arms around him. "I can't seem to find the energy to care if anyone knew at the minute. I'm so tired of it all, but I can't give it up yet. Soon, though." Something niggled at him, something he should remember, but he couldn't figure out what, so he pushed it aside to think of at a different time. Instead, he luxuriated in being able to touch and hold Nick. Someone he had thought unattainable—to him, anyway.

"What do you want from this, Kai?"

Malachi loved being called Kai, but it was such a fuss to teach people to use a different name when he'd been using Malachi for so long. Maybe it would catch on, eventually. He lifted his head.

"I've been attracted to you for a long time, but I never, ever believed you would feel the same. It's kind of like a dream that I don't want to wake up from."

Nick pulled him down and kissed him again. Unfortunately, it lasted all of a second, but he was grateful for every one he received.

"I'm not one for going fast in a relationship—not that this is a relationship...unless you want it to be." A fumbling Nick was a cute Nick. "What I mean is that I want to take my time with you, Kai. I want to get to know the real you, not the one I thought you were."

"Does that mean you want to wait for sex?" Malachi blurted out, his cheeks heating the second the words left his mouth.

Nick laughed, long and loud, and Malachi stared at him, grateful to have received one of the famous Nick Tennant laughs. He hadn't thought he would ever be the cause of one of those. Locking away the sound for a time when he believed Nick would tire of him, he grazed his lip with his teeth.

"I'm happy to have sex whenever. There's no timetable. But we don't need to rush anything. If you're not ready, that's fine."

"I'm so ready," Malachi breathed. And it was true. He had a physical need to feel Nick's hands on his body. Everywhere. Truthfully, he couldn't remember a time when he had felt such a visceral need for someone. Even with his one-nighters and casual relationships, he never felt as important as that did. He wasn't sure why it was Nick, but he also didn't care. Now that Nick knew his secret, he wasn't going to push him away when he could grab him with both hands. No one else knew everything about him, and there was always something missing. It was nice to relax about keeping things to himself.

"Then let's see how the evening goes, yeah?"

Malachi nodded. "What's the plan tonight? I can't remember what you told me."

"Dinner with the royal family, of course."

Malachi stared at him, his mind flickering offline. "What?"

Grinning, Nick said, "Now before, I would've hated giving you this opportunity, but now I love leaving you speechless. I might have to think of other ways to do it." He tugged Malachi towards him and kissed him, sending more blood away from his brain and making it even more difficult for him to comprehend.

He pulled back. "Dinner with the royal family?"

Nick nodded and pulled him into another kiss. Malachi lost himself before he lifted his head again. "But it's Prince Consort Kean's birthday!" Nick nodded again and threaded his fingers into Malachi's hair, but before he got distracted again, Malachi slapped his hand over Nick's mouth. "I shouldn't be there for that! It's private!"

Nick raised his eyebrows but said nothing until Malachi realised he still had his hand over his mouth. Nick licked his lips once he was free. "They would love for you to join them, and as you're such a huge fan, it'll be perfect for you."

"But what will I wear!" Malachi tried to rise, but Nick gripped him.

"Kai, shush. Breathe. You don't need to worry about this. Everyone is glad for you to be there."

"But they hate me!"

Nick smiled and brushed his thumb over Malachi's cheek. "I think more than one knows who you are. I was one of the last ones to figure it out. Too blinded by my frustration." He winked. "And attraction."

Malachi swallowed. "Are you sure it's okay?"

"Absolutely." Nick slid his arms around him again. "Now, can we kiss some more before we have to get ready?"

He didn't answer. Instead, he slammed their lips together, closing his eyes as the taste of him hit his taste buds. Their tongues tangled, and Malachi lost himself in him again, still unable to believe the difference from that afternoon to right then. He'd dreamt of it but had never believed it would happen. Malachi with a royal bodyguard. He chuckled into Nick's mouth, and Nick cupped his face.

"Most of the time, I would be upset that someone laughed while kissing me, but your little giggle intrigued me. What are you thinking about, Kai?"

He sighed. "Fairy tales."

"I'm assuming that makes sense to you." Nick pressed a kiss to the corner of his lips. "Let's get ready. Is it too soon for a shared shower?"

Malachi thought he might've squeaked at the idea, but Nick's expression didn't change, so he might've been quieter than he seemed. "Not for me."

Nick's mouth twitched. "You might need to get off me."

Malachi's eyes widened. "I...can do that."

Nick stared at him, eyebrows slowly rising the longer they looked at each other. "Well, are you going to?"

Malachi glanced down between them, seeing the bulge in Nick's trousers. He reached for the button, pausing when Nick's hands covered his. "What are you doing?"

"You asked me to get you off."

Nick pursed his lips, but a smile broke through. "Thank you, but what I actually said was that you might need to get *off* me. As in, climb off my lap so we can shower." He squeezed his hands. "I'm not saying no, just not yet."

Malachi closed his eyes in mortification, heat invading his cheeks until he was sure he was sunburnt. He climbed off Nick's lap as quickly as his legs would allow him, stumbling into the coffee table.

"Sorry."

Nick rose and slipped his arms around Malachi's waist. "Don't be. You're the first person I would ask to get me off, but when I get my hands on you—properly—I want to take my time." He tucked his finger under Malachi's chin, lifting his head to meet his gaze. "Don't ever be embarrassed with me. Although I'm enjoying finding out all your *squeaky* charms."

Malachi closed his eyes and dislodged Nick's finger, tucking his face against Nick's chest while groaning. "Kill me now."

"Nope. No time. We have to shower."

Nick grabbed his hand and dragged him to the en suite bathroom—Nick's en suite bathroom.

"I need my clothes!" Malachi spluttered as they entered.

"You can get them afterwards."

Nick turned on the large shower and began stripping. Malachi swallowed his tongue as bare skin came into view. Skin with amazingly detailed black swirls and designs. The man had muscles for miles and seeing it on display was more than his heart could stand. He wanted to see his hands on him, to see the difference in skin tone and temperature, and whether he was as smooth as he looked.

"Like what you see?"

Malachi blinked and refocused. Seeing the lightness in his eyes had him smiling. "Without a doubt in the world."

"Then let me see what you have. We have little time."

His hands shook as he stripped off his shirt and trousers, pausing when he was down to his briefs, a lot self-conscious. But when Nick stepped closer and slid his hands from his shoulders slowly down his arms and tangled their fingers, he found the courage. Because Nick wasn't pushing. He wasn't making him do anything, and it gave him the confidence that Nick did actually want him—even though Nick's cock was also talking. It might not have been the longest, but it was thick, and as the head peeked from the foreskin, red and ready, Malachi's confidence soared.

Keeping his fingers tangled with Nick's, he hooked his thumbs in his briefs—not as easy as he thought it would be, but he managed—and let them fall to the floor before kicking them away.

It took him a few seconds to comprehend that he was naked in a bathroom with a famous bodyguard, just about to shower with him.

"Ready?" Nick asked.

Malachi met his unwavering gaze and nodded. "Didn't think I'd be doing this today, but yes. I'm ready."

Nick tugged him into the shower cubicle, which was a tight fit with Nick being so broad and muscular, but they managed. Malachi felt small and cared for in his shadow, and he didn't care about what that might have said about him. Nick manoeuvred him into the spray, and Malachi closed his eyes, letting Nick wet his hair and body. When Nick moved him again, he didn't fight it, and though it was colder outside of the water, he didn't complain. Nick's scent washed over him, and Malachi opened his eyes, watching as Nick squeezed some shampoo into his hand. He rubbed it into Malachi's hair with slow but sure fingers, and Malachi groaned. He hadn't realised how sensual something like that could be.

"Let's wash it out," Nick murmured. He banded an arm around Malachi's waist, giving him the first feel of their bodies against each other, and he couldn't help rubbing his hips when Nick's cock pressed against him. "You keep doing that and this shower is going to turn into something else."

Malachi smiled as he tilted his head back to wash the shampoo free. When that was done, Nick glided soapy hands all over his body, washing away his sins. He opened heavy eyelids to meet Nick's gaze, and as the lust in his eyes hit him, he surged onto his toes and gripped the back of his neck, pulling his mouth down to meet his.

Malachi gasped as his back met the cold tiled wall, but Nick used that as his chance to slip his tongue inside. Malachi sucked on it, his fingers threading into Nick's hair and holding him in place while their bodies slipped and slid against each other. He didn't want it to end, but he also knew they didn't have time, so he pulled back with a gasp and smacked his head back against the wall, groaning.

"Fuck," he muttered. He dropped his hands, pressing them against the cool wall. "Wash. Quickly. I'm not sure how much willpower I have with you like this."

"You're not the only one."

Malachi watched as Nick flew through his routine, throwing suds all over, but he was mesmerised by the need to lick every inch of his body.

"Don't look at me like that, or we'll miss dinner completely," Nick growled.

Malachi swallowed and slipped from the shower before Nick could grab him. Someone needed the sense in that relationship, and it would rarely be him. It was difficult when he had someone like Nick in his life. Who wouldn't want to spend a stupid amount of time around someone intelligent, gorgeous, funny and talented?

Wet arms came around his waist, and a wet, fully erect cock pressed against his spine. "You're not the only one who can't believe this person wants to spend time with him," Nick mumbled in his ear. "You are exquisite, and I'm sorry for thinking badly of you."

Malachi spun in his arms. "You don't need to be. I just wish I'd explained sooner."

Nick swooped down and feasted on Malachi's lips. When his knees threatened to buckle in an embarrassingly short time, he tore his mouth free.

"The king."

Nick groaned and buried his face in his neck. "Tell me again why we agreed to this?"

Malachi laughed, lighthearted and happy.

11

Nick

It was hard to keep his hands to himself on their walk to the dining room the Sutcliffes usually used for dinner. Originally, Nick had been pissed beyond measure to hear that they intended to let Malachi into their space, but since their chat earlier—and subsequent kisses and fondling—he didn't mind at all. Did that make him two-faced? Maybe. Regardless, a smile crossed his face when Malachi gasped at the room they entered. He'd seen it the day before, but he was so happy to be there.

They were, perhaps, a few minutes later than planned, and the entire royal family was waiting for them.

"I apologise for being late, Your Majesty," he said to the king.

"You don't need to apologise, Nick. Things happen, and we've not been waiting long." Andrew smiled at them. "Malachi, would you like to join us here?" He waved at the seat between Kendal and Douglas—the seat usually reserved for Douglas himself. "That way, you should be able to see and speak to all of us more easily."

"I don't want to get in the way, Your Majesty. I'm happy sitting at the end."

"Nonsense. One day of moving around won't harm anyone. Please, sit."

Malachi glanced at Nick, and he sent him a smile and a nod before taking his post against the wall. As Malachi took his seat, Nick met Freddie's gaze, and a barely concealed smirk. Nick rolled his eyes and shook his head, even as his cheeks heated.

"Did you get the chance to visit the kitchen this afternoon, Malachi? The staff make a wonderful afternoon tea," Kendal said.

Malachi cleared his throat. "We—I got a little distracted, so I didn't get the opportunity."

"Have you not eaten since you woke?" Andrew asked, frowning.

Nick's stomach grumbled at the reminder of his lack of food. He'd been too busy reading Malachi's file to think about eating, and then afterwards... Well, who wanted to think about food?

"I had a nap, but it's okay."

Andrew pierced Nick with his gaze. "Have you eaten?"

"I'm fine, Your Majesty."

Andrew sighed. "Sit your ass down, Nick."

Nick straightened at the king's almost curse, even as a chuckle wound through the room. "Honestly, Your—"

"Sit. Down."

"Yes, Your Majesty." Nick settled into the chair on the other side of Eddie, unwilling to disobey a direct order, and met Malachi's gaze. Malachi dipped his head but not before Nick saw his smile. "And happy birthday, Your Highness," he said to Kean.

Kean grinned. "Thank you, Nick."

"And a happy birthday from me, too," Malachi added. "I hope you've had a wonderful day."

"I have, thank you. Far too many gifts from everyone, and I feel decidedly spoilt, but it was fantastic. Is fantastic." He shared a smile with Andrew and Kendal, who squeezed his hand across the table.

Nick would've liked to be able to do the same to Malachi, but they hadn't covered the subject of whether Malachi wanted their relationship to be known, especially if he was keeping Malachi Sanders and Kai Ruffers separate. If he started a relationship with someone so close to the crown, would it affect his job?

A plate was put in front of him, and his stomach growled at the scents tantalising him. If he wasn't mistaken, it was chicken cacciatore, one of his mother's favourite recipes.

"Dig in, everyone," Andrew said.

The chicken melted in his mouth, and the tomatoes, peppers and mushrooms gave it a hearty flavour. It rivalled his mother's, but he would always choose hers over anyone else's, even if he had a gun to his head.

The surrounding conversation had the same feel as the dinners he had at his parents' when everyone was there. The muted individual ones as well as a larger one that everyone dipped in and out of. It was hard for him to describe it to someone who didn't know what he meant, but he could see it happening there. It was wonderful to see all of them include Malachi in it—though he'd expected no less. Malachi still seemed a little wide-eyed and starstruck, but at least he got his words out.

"If you look at him like that much longer, there will be no chance of denying your feelings for him," Eddie murmured.

Nick glanced at him and then away, focusing on his plate. "I don't know what you mean, Your Highness."

Eddie chuckled. "You won't get away with it. George has already figured it out if the glances he keeps sending you are any indication. Freddie seems to know, which means Damon knows. Andrew keeps checking on you with a small smile on his face. You're not as sneaky as you usually are, Nick."

Butterflies filled his stomach, but he couldn't deny Eddie's observations. "It's early days, Your Highness. We have yet to figure anything out other than we would like the chance to explore what it could be. I don't have more of an answer for you."

Eddie faced him. "You don't need to have an answer for me. You don't need to have an answer for anyone. The only ones who matter are you and Malachi. I'm sorry if my words came across as out of order. I was merely warning you in case you hadn't wanted to expose your thoughts."

Nick wiped his mouth with his napkin. "Not at all, Your Highness. You weren't out of order. Thank you for telling me. As I said, it's early days, and I've yet to confirm with him what his preference is for telling people."

"I have to admit, I'm a little surprised, though. I thought you hated him."

Nick wasn't sure how much Malachi wanted to tell anyone, so he hedged his words. "I didn't like that my attraction was to someone who could write what he did. But he's not what he writes. Those are just words. He's..." Nick glanced at Malachi, finding the man looking back at him. "Different."

"I'm glad to hear it. I wish you both the best." Eddie smirked. "You might want to bring him to the club," he whispered. "That would blow his mind."

Nick choked on the drink he'd just sipped at. He banged against his chest to clear it, waving away any help. "I don't think that's a good idea at the moment, Your Highness."

Eddie chuckled. "Maybe not. But if things go the way they seem to be headed, you might want to make time in your schedule to take him there. You might be surprised what he's into."

Nick studied Eddie. "Do you know something I don't?"

Eddie's mouth twitched. "Not at all. It's just what I can see from his body language. I've become adept at reading people."

When Eddie didn't continue, Nick sighed. "I'll consider it, okay?"

"Good for you." Eddie sipped his wine. "At least it should be."

Nick didn't try to get any more information from him because he knew a closed book when he saw one. If Malachi had any interest in BDSM or kink, it would need to be kept as far from Club Royal as possible until he finished his contract with the Windsor Chronicle.

"Nick," Freddie called. "I was just discussing a possible change in plans for tomorrow. A visit to Frogmore is still on the cards, but then we're heading to RAF Northolt to speak with some people there. Would it be okay for you and Malachi to join us?"

Nick took a breath. Changing plans was not ideal, but it was something that always happened. He'd been to Northolt several times and could see no reason to deny the visit.

"I'll double-check with Brett, but I don't see it being a problem."

Malachi's bright grin made his decision worthwhile, and he sent an answering one back. When Malachi turned back to Freddie, Nick met George's gaze, the prince grinning at him, much like Malachi had. Nick sighed and refocused on his food. He would never hear the end of this. He needed to warn Malachi as soon as possible that the princes had ulterior motives. What those motives were, though, was anyone's idea.

When the dinner ended, Malachi was full of chatter and smiles, making it hard to keep Nick's smile in check. As they headed to the door, following Princes Douglas and Mav, Andrew called to him.

Nick glanced at Malachi, who said, "I'll wait outside."

Nick shook his head, but Douglas said, "We'll stay with him until you're finished."

They didn't wait, but instead, headed for the door, closing it behind them and leaving Nick with Andrew, Kean and Kendal.

Nick strode over to them, hoping they'd get to the point so he could be with Malachi again. God, he had it bad already.

"How are you managing with Malachi?" A slight curve to the corners of his mouth accompanied Andrew's words.

Nick didn't sigh like he wanted to. "We're getting along fine now some misunderstandings have been cleared up."

Andrew's smile came out in full force with those words. "Glad to hear it. I have to say, it's not like you to take an instant dislike to someone. You've been wandering around the castle like you had a permanent rain cloud over your head."

Nick did sigh at that. "I know, Your Majesty. I didn't like what he wrote, and that stopped me from seeing the real him."

"Which is?"

Did the king know Malachi's alter ego? Did Nick have it in him to tell them about it? He exhaled, knowing he was going to break Malachi's confidence, but hoping Malachi didn't hate him for it. After all, Nick's priority was the crown.

"He only writes what he does because he's locked into a contract he can't get out of. However, he contradicts that writing by writing as another name, Kai Ruffers."

Kean gasped. "Seriously? I've read Kai Ruffer's work, and he has a huge affinity for all things royal." He glanced at Andrew. "Why didn't you tell me?"

Andrew smiled. "Because then we would've had two starstruck people at the table."

That answered the question of if Andrew knew. But of course he did. He knew everything.

"Also, I didn't know about this contract. I assumed he was there because he wanted to be." Andrew stared at him.

"I don't know everything about it, but from what I can gather, Malachi was locked into a contract right from the beginning. He has less than a year left, and he has no plans to renew the contract again."

"Do you think Mav might be able to help him?" Kendal asked. "With his reputation, I mean? It's got to be hard doing the work he hates under his real name. What's he going to do afterwards? Change his name to Kai Ruffers?" Kendal tilted their head, frowning. It cleared quickly, replaced with a grin and a chuckle. "Clever. Sanders and Ruffers. One sands things down, one roughs things up."

Clever indeed. Nick hadn't caught on to that, but it was something he needed to ask Malachi about.

"Is there anything else, Your Majesty?"

Andrew waved him away. "Go. Just remember the plans for tomorrow. And make sure you eat next time," he chided.

"Yes, Your Majesty. Your Highnesses."

He turned on his tail and strode for the door, opening it rather more forcefully than he meant to and closing it a lot quieter. Douglas and Mav stood a short distance down the corridor, but Malachi was nowhere to be seen. Nick's heart raced.

"Where is he?"

Mav pointed to the bathroom door, one door down from where they stood, and Nick settled.

"So, you and Malachi, huh?" Douglas said, grinning.

"Shut up. Your Highness," Nick said, staring at the door Malachi should appear from.

"I'm only messing with you," Douglas said, clasping his shoulder. "I'm glad you've found someone. I was starting to worry you'd be single forever."

"You weren't the only one, Your Highness."

After a little more chatter, Nick's stomach churned. Where was Malachi? He started down the corridor slowly, his mind telling him he was fine, but also remembering what had happened in the restaurant bathroom. What if Malachi couldn't shout for help? His brain—wonderfully creative as it was—sent more images of things that could've happened as he drew closer.

"What's wrong, Nick?" Douglas asked.

"It's been too long," Nick muttered. His gaze darted around, trying to figure out why his instincts were screaming at him. "Prince Douglas, Prince Mav, please retreat further down the corridor and call Brett."

"We can help—"

"No, sir. Please. I won't be good to anyone if I have to divide my concentration between you and whatever my instincts are trying to tell me."

He waited for them to move back to where they had been standing while Mav was on the phone. Then he concentrated on the door, leaning closer to see if he could hear anything, but the doors were thick and almost soundproof. Not wanting to advertise he was entering before he did in case something was amiss, he gripped the handle and pulled his gun from his holster. Inhaling, he twisted the knob and entered quickly.

Immediately, his gaze took in Malachi lying on the floor, blood dripping from his head, and as much as he wanted to go to him, he needed to clear the room first. He checked every toilet cubicle and every inch where someone could hide, but there was no one.

Nick reholstered his gun and crouched beside Malachi. He didn't move him. "Malachi? Can you hear me?" No response. "What is it with you and bathrooms?" he muttered. He checked him over, but other than a lump to his head beneath the cut that steadily dripped blood, he was fine. Had he slipped and fallen? Nick glanced around the room, checking the sinks and handles for any signs of blood. Nothing. What had happened?

"Is he okay?" Dominic asked, and Nick cursed, having not heard him enter.

"He's out for the count, but he has a steady pulse and is breathing."

"What happened?"

Nick shook his head. "No idea. We were waiting outside for him, but when he was in here for a while, I came to investigate because my instincts were blaring."

"Can't see any signs of him hitting his head on something," Dominic said, agreeing with Nick's quiet investigation. "The blood from his head looks like it started while lying down." He frowned.

"What do you mean?"

Dominic rubbed his chin. "If someone had fallen to the floor, there would be more of a splatter pattern as the blood exited his wound with the impact. But there are no drips in an arc around him at all. It's almost like he was either lying down when he started bleeding or..."

"He was positioned that way. Fuck."

Dominic was on his phone before Nick finished his words. "Lock down Windsor. Now!" he barked.

"No one was in here when I came in, and we were outside the whole time."

Dominic sighed and stood. He walked over to the corner of the room. The wall had a cut-out bit where Nick assumed the pipes were hidden, but Dominic pulled on the corner and the wall swung out, revealing a gap.

"It's a secret passageway," Dominic growled. "I'm sick and tired of these being used to hurt people. First thing tomorrow, I'm going to request every single damned one of these be permanently closed. They're nothing but trouble." Nick could understand his anger with what happened to Randall.

"Where does this one lead?" Nick asked as he checked Malachi's pulse again.

"If I'm not mistaken—and I might be because I don't know every inch of these tunnels, though I will—this one leads to the kitchen, but it also has maybe two doors off it, but I can't think where they go right now." He dialled again. "Felix, get the map of the tunnels up for me." He paused. "Yeah. This bathroom to where?" He listened and grimaced. "Thanks." He hung up. "The kitchen, as I said, but also the receiving room and outside."

Nick stared at Malachi's pale face. "So whoever they are has either gone or is in hiding. Household staff member, do you think?"

Dominic shook his head. "It could be anyone."

Nick exhaled roughly. "I don't like this, Dom. This is the third incident to involve Malachi. Are they aiming their wrath at *Malachi* or the royal family, and Malachi is merely convenient?"

"I don't know. But until we know further, I think we need to keep Malachi close by."

Nick cursed. "Jesus, Dominic. We were! We were right outside! How much closer do we need to be to stop this from happening? He deserves so much more than this shit," he finished in a mutter.

After retrieving another gauze pad and replacing it on Malachi's cut, he stroked his hand through Malachi's hair with his free hand. He hated that he didn't know what was going on. It reminded him of when the terror had reigned through the castle when the king's sister and brother had chosen to wreak havoc. That hadn't ended well.

His thoughts derailed when Malachi started moving and moaning. "It's okay, Kai. It's okay. Take it easy."

"Nick?" he muttered, barely able to keep his eyes open, which was unsurprising given the undoubted headache he would have.

"I'm here." He cradled Malachi's cheek. "I'm not going anywhere."

"Tah...ruh...mmm," Malachi murmured, his eyes closing again.

Nick panicked a second when he slumped once again, but a quick check of his pulse had him relaxing.

"What did he say?" Dominic asked.

"I'm not sure. Tah. Ruh. Mmm." Nick frowned. "Tarum? I can't think of anyone with that name."

"I'll get Felix on it. He'll put it through the computers to see what comes up."

The ambulance crew arrived and though it killed him, Nick stepped aside.

They needed to figure out what the hell was going on.

12

Dominic

What the hell was going on and why was Malachi bearing the brunt of it all? Seeing the pain in Nick's expression brought back all that uneasiness Dominic had felt when he and Randall were being targeted. It wasn't pleasant. Not even the second-hand version of it he was dealing with then.

He clapped Nick on the back. "We'll get the search started. Felix is already checking the security cameras, and Brett has sent people to check the tunnels from the other entrances."

Nick stared after Malachi and glanced back at Dominic. "I'm going with him."

"Of course you are. Go." He pushed a little to get him moving. "I'll keep you posted."

Nick disappeared from the bathroom, and Dominic put his hands on his hips and studied the area. There was no other option than for whoever it was to have come through the tunnels. They could've been lying in wait for Malachi, but Nick said no one had exited the room. That left the tunnels as their only exit point.

He moved over to the tunnel again, peering into the darkness. They needed to close the tunnels immediately; they'd been used too much against them in recent years and he refused to let it happen any longer.

Brett entered the bathroom. "How is Malachi?"

"Unconscious. He has a gash to his head, but he was conscious for a few seconds and said something like 'Tarum' to Nick, then blacked out again. Nick's gone with him." Dominic sighed. "We're closing these tunnels, Brett. I don't care what laws you have to break to get it done, but it needs doing."

Brett nodded. "It will be. It's something I planned to do anyway, but this has stepped it up the list faster. They'll be closed up as soon as I can arrange it."

Dominic left the tunnel access open and wandered around the room again, checking for anything out of the ordinary. He wasn't a detective by any means, and one would be there soon to check the room, but he couldn't see anything. It was too clean.

"What are you thinking?" Brett said from the doorway, having not ventured any further inside.

"It's too clean. Malachi was laid down instead of falling. Why?"

"What makes you say that?"

Dominic pointed at the blood on the tiled floor. "There's no splatter pattern from him impacting the floor that you would expect if someone had fallen. That only leaves him being carefully put in that position. Is there a reason behind that? Does the attacker know him and not truly want to hurt him? Or is that just to fuck with our heads?"

"You mean like it is doing?" Brett rubbed his forehead. "This entire thing is fucking with our heads. We need to find a connection between these events and if it's solely focused on Malachi or if they're using Malachi to get to the royal family." He sighed. "I fucking hate the unknown."

"Don't we all?"

Footsteps sounded, and Owen popped his head out of the tunnel. "All clear. Absolutely nothing apart from cobwebs and creepy crawlies. I did notice what looked like disturbed dust along the way, but I can't decide if that's just my imagination making it real."

"We'll get Brady's guy to check it over," Brett said. "He should be here any minute."

"We need to find this fucker; otherwise, Nick's going to lose his head," Dominic said with meaning. "If anything happens to Malachi..." He didn't need to finish the sentence.

"We'll find them," Brett promised, and though he couldn't make a promise like that, it made Dominic feel better.

13

Malachi

Once again, Malachi woke to the sterilised scent and decoration of a hospital room. That one was no less effluent than the previous one, but the pounding in his head was a recent addition. He tried to lift his head and groaned when pain shot through him. Reaching up to his forehead, he felt a bandage, and there was no denying the lump beneath it.

"What the hell?" he tried to say, but his voice wouldn't work properly.

It must've been enough, though, because seconds later, Nick was beside him. The low-level lighting could still pick up how pale he was.

"Hey," he said, grasping his hand gently. "How are you feeling?"

Malachi checked in with himself while Nick helped him to drink some water. "My head has a gymnast on a trampoline, and my right side aches a bit. What happened?"

"We're not certain. What do you remember?"

Malachi blinked, trying to remember what happened, his stomach churning with nausea. "I remember using the toilet and washing my hands. Then I felt a migraine blast through me. I must've lost consciousness."

Nick grimaced. "I don't think it was a migraine. Someone hit you with something and knocked you out. They used the secret tunnels to get in."

"Secret tunnels?" He frowned as he tried to figure out what Nick was telling him, but then his brain caught on, and he smiled. "They're real?"

Nick huffed a laugh, his shoulders lowering as he shook his head. "You and your reporter head. Yes, they are, but not for much longer. We've had far too many issues with them, so we'll be closing them up indefinitely."

"That's a shame. I bet they're handy." He felt his eyes growing heavy again.

"Truthfully, they're rarely used."

Malachi floated away. "I'm sure...we can think up...a story."

The next time he woke, he was more alert, though he was extremely glad the lighting remained low. He eased his head until Nick's prone form came into view. Slouched in an uncomfortable position in a chair not made for sleeping, Malachi guaranteed he'd be hurting when he woke up. Malachi took check of himself. His head still hurt, but it wasn't as bad as before. His side ached a bit more, but he assumed that had something to do with a bruise coming out. He touched the side of his head, gingerly pressing at the lump, causing him to hiss.

Nick woke immediately. "Are you okay?" he said, rising without a hint of an ache.

"How can you sleep like that and not hurt?"

Nick chuckled. "Many years of practice. It's almost like being in the Army. Catching snatches of sleep when you can and being alert the second you need to. But you're avoiding my question. How are you?"

Malachi sighed. "Aching, but I'm okay. Someone really attacked me in Windsor Castle?"

Nick exhaled and settled carefully onto the edge of the bed. "Yes. It's not the first time something like this has happened." He paused, his mouth twisting. "Off the record, those secret doorways were how someone got around the castle to hurt the royal family during those years of unrest. We kept that quiet."

Malachi blinked, his head spinning for a second. "Wow. I knew there had been whispers of secret tunnels, but nothing had ever been confirmed. I could understand it was to safeguard the family."

Nick nodded. "We have to have some secrets." He grinned.

Malachi chuckled and winced as a sharp pain shot through his head. "Okay, laughing is a no-no." He rested his head back again, breathing deeply.

"Sorry."

He gently rolled his head to the side to meet Nick's gaze. "You have nothing to be sorry for."

In an uncharacteristic show of uncertainty, Nick dropped his gaze to the floor. Malachi wished he could comfort him as much as receive comfort in return.

"Nick?" Nick didn't look at him. "Nick, look at me." It took a few seconds, but he did. "It's not your fault, okay? You weren't to know this would happen."

"I should've been keeping an eye on you instead of talking with the king."

Malachi sighed. "Nick...you couldn't have known."

"I should've!"

"Come on. Are you a mind reader now? No one could've predicted that."

Nick raked his fingers through his hair and stalked to the other side of the room before returning. "After what happened before, it should've been something that was on our radar. Even though those tunnels are not used, we still knew they were there and that some were open. We should've thought about the possibility of something happening. Not necessarily to you, but to someone."

Malachi nodded. "Maybe. But it's done now. We can't change what happened, only how we go forward. Do we know who it was?"

Nick shook his head. "Those tunnels don't have cameras, and we don't have any other cameras showing anything out of the ordinary. Either they managed to get out of Windsor completely, or they are someone who works there, and we wouldn't think anything of them being around." He winced.

"What's wrong?"

Nick settled into the seat he'd been asleep in and blew out a breath. "We need to figure out if these events are focused on you or whether you're just convenient and it's aimed at the royal family."

Malachi frowned, but his stomach churned faster, causing him to close his eyes and breathe through his nose for a moment. When he blinked open again, he said, "Why would it be focused on me?"

"I don't know. Maybe someone doesn't like your work? Have you had any hate mail or anything recently?"

Malachi chuckled and wished he hadn't. One Nick turned into two for a short time, and his head spun, but it eased fairly quickly. A wave of lethargy washed over him.

"Sorry," he muttered. "I'm assuming I have a concussion? I've had one before and it seems to be similar to this."

"Yeah. Concussions suck."

Wanting to chuckle, Malachi held his breath to stop it and then shook his finger at Nick. "Stop trying to make me laugh."

"Sorry."

Malachi muttered, "I think I need to donate blood with how often I've been here lately." He sighed. "I receive hundreds of hate emails every day. I no longer read them. Any one of them could take it further and I wouldn't have a clue. Other than that, there's no one…"

He frowned, winced and tried to follow his train of thought. His brain didn't want to lock on properly. Replaying his previous words, he grasped the tip.

"What's wrong?" Nick asked, settling beside him again.

"There was something… Oh, yeah. Tarrant Milton. He's a fan, and he sometimes sounds a little fanatical. But not in a hateful kind of way."

"Have you ever met him?"

"Once. We attended the same charity event. I wasn't entirely sure how he even came to be there, because he wasn't a reporter or anything like that. He introduced himself, and other than seeming a little flustered at meeting me, he was harmless." He didn't need to explain that there was something in the man's eyes that didn't sit right with him. That was just his personal opinions getting in the way. "I occasionally use him as a source."

"That reminds me. Do you know anyone called Tarum?"

Malachi reached for the cup of water, and Nick took over, holding it for him to sip from. He used the time to think through his acquaintances. When he'd had his fill, he said, "Not that I can think of. Why?"

"In that bathroom, you woke briefly and said, 'Tarum.' At least that's what it sounded like to me and Brett."

"It doesn't ring a bell."

A knock sounded, and Nick went to the door, opening it a crack before pulling it wider. "Should you really be here, Your Highness?"

"I'm sure you and my guards are more than enough to keep me safe, Nick," Prince Freddie said. "Plus, Damon is here, and you already have other guards outside. I think I'm okay to stop by and see how our guest is faring for a short time."

He focused on Malachi, who fought not to squirm and make himself feel worse. As it was, there were two of the prince when he looked at him.

"How are you feeling, Malachi?"

"A little foolish that things like this are happening to me. I'm sorry for making things difficult."

Freddie waved him away. "Don't even bother yourself with thoughts like that. We've had our fair share of problems, so we know what it's like to be the focus of someone's ire."

"You do think it's someone after me, then?"

"We went through everything with Brett and Felix, and from what we can gather—which isn't much mind—they have to be part of our household staff or they know someone who is, and they helped get them away. We've been through everyone present when we locked down Windsor, and no one brought up any red flags. All we can assume, right now, is that they somehow got out of Windsor undetected." Freddie frowned. "It's something we will be rectifying immediately. But don't worry yourself with that. Just get better. And as soon as you're released, you're welcome to come back—if you want to. Although we completely understand if you don't ever want to darken our halls again." Freddie's smile grew, and Malachi returned it.

"I would love to come back. But maybe I should visit my family first."

Freddie nodded. "I understand completely. Feel free to extend the invitation to your family as well, if it would make them feel better about you being there. Anyway, I better take my leave before I give Nick here a heart attack."

Malachi glanced at Nick, and sure enough, the vein in his temple pulsed wildly. He grinned, barely hiding another wince.

"If I was to have a heart attack so easily, I would've had a hundred by now, Your Highness," Nick said.

Freddie chuckled. "Get well soon...Kai."

Malachi's smile widened. He sure did love being called Kai instead, but he had to admit, he liked it best when Nick said it. The prince left, and Nick turned to him.

"Right. You need to rest. I'll even tuck you in."

"I'm already tucked in," he said as Nick tucked the covers tighter around his body. "Well, thank you, kind sir."

Nick settled back into the uncomfortable chair, and Malachi closed his eyes. Finally, his head stopped spinning.

"Nick?" he whispered.

"Yeah?"

"Will you read me a bedtime story?"

There was a slight pause, and Malachi didn't think he would, but then he cleared his throat. "Once upon a time, there was an evil reporter called...Guy..."

Malachi's mouth curved, and he drifted to the sounds of Nick's voice as he wove a tale of intrigue and madness. And when Malachi finally headed towards sleep, he knew he was safe.

"I understand if you don't want me there, but someone has to go with you," Nick stated, and by the look of his body language, there would be no changing his stance.

Malachi sighed and rubbed his forehead, bypassing the lump, as he resigned himself to having a guard while visiting his family.

"I'm happy for you to come, but I doubt you want to meet my mum and grandma so soon." He rose from the bed carefully. Most of the dizziness and double vision had disappeared over the last twenty-four hours, and only the blinding headaches remained, varying in strength, depending on the situation. But the doctors had cleared him for release, and he was going no matter what.

Nick readjusted his position against the wall, crossing one ankle over the other and staring down at them. "Whatever will make you more comfortable."

Enough was enough. "Nick, you need to make this decision, not me. I'm going home, regardless, and I would love you to meet everyone, but we've barely started our relationship. Few people introduce their bodyguard and boyfriend at the same time."

Nick's mouth quirked. "Could be a good story."

"Nick..."

Nick pushed off the wall and dropped his hands to his sides. "If you are sure you're happy introducing me, I am happy to come with you."

Malachi studied him, and Nick stared right back, unwavering, solid. "Okay. Welcome to 'meet the family' day."

As his discharge papers had already been completed, he followed Nick to the lifts and down the long corridors towards the exit. Murals decorated the walls in vibrant colours, letting patients and visitors take a journey through various landscapes. That one was a rainforest, and the work was so vivid, it felt like he was there.

"This was done by a thirteen-year-old, you know?" he murmured.

"She's definitely going into a bright future with this talent," Nick said.

Malachi mulled over that as they drove towards his grandmother's house. What he wouldn't give for a do-over, as long as it didn't affect the outcome. He wouldn't change a thing if it meant his mother didn't get the treatment she needed. But it would've been nice to choose a different path. One he didn't have to continually blacken his soul to keep. It was only because the Sutcliffes were the kindest people on the planet that he could finally write his evil words with less pain. They understood. Maybe not everything, but they knew he wouldn't be doing it without a reason, and by not asking him to give that reason, they had accepted it.

Shame other people weren't of the same opinions.

When they parked in front of the house, Malachi took a breath. He had never before introduced someone to his family, and his knees were a little shaky. He brushed off some imaginary dust from his trousers.

"Do you want me to tell them you're just my bodyguard?" he asked.

Fingers brushed against his cheek, turning his head towards Nick. "Not unless that's what you would prefer."

The sincerity shone in his eyes, so Malachi shook his head. "I've never done this before," he whispered.

"What?"

"Introduced a boyfriend."

Nick smiled. "We already have an audience," he gripped Malachi's chin to stop him from looking, "so why not break the news now to get it over with?"

Malachi swallowed hard, but then smiled and leaned forward, joining their lips in a chaste kiss. He'd been wanting to do it since he'd woken up but hadn't had the courage to just reach for it. Despite Nick's behaviour to the contrary, he had wondered if the man wouldn't want to continue anything because of what they'd surmised about the incidents.

"What do I tell them?"

Nick sighed. "The truth." Malachi's eyes widened, and Nick chuckled. "I won't have you keeping secrets when you don't need to."

Leaning forward, Malachi kissed him again as a thank you. He hated the idea of keeping things from them, but he would if he needed to. By giving him no restraints, he could weave a story as close to the truth as he wanted but leave out some details to protect the royal family.

"Let's go," Nick said and climbed out of the car before Malachi could stop him.

Nick rounded the car and opened Malachi's door, holding out his hand to help him out, which he was extremely glad for because he was still a little wobbly—from the incident and that talk. Nick let go of him, but Malachi threaded their fingers together, both to keep himself from running to hide and to help calm his nerves.

"Malachi! What happened?" his mother said, reaching for him and cradling his cheeks. Her eyes flitted over his bandage, and she turned his head this way and that to check for more. It was something she had always done whenever he'd been injured.

"I'm okay. I have a concussion, but I'm okay."

"You have a lump the size of Ireland on your head! Of course, you're not okay!"

"Mum, please, don't shout."

Emily's nostrils flared, showing that she was keeping herself from crying. "Sorry, sweetheart." She glanced at Nick, and Malachi identified his cue.

"Mum, this is Nick. Nick, my mum, Emily. Nick is...my boyfriend." He peered at Nick, who smiled and held out his hand.

"Mrs Sanders, it's lovely to finally meet you. Malachi speaks of you all the time."

At first, Emily didn't respond, but then she smiled and took his hand. "I don't need to ask what you do. I've seen you on the TV."

Nick nodded. "Yes, ma'am. I'm sure you have."

Emily studied them both. "Before we go inside to Grandma... Is this," she pointed at Malachi's head, "related to the crown or simply Malachi being clumsy?"

He could see Nick's approval, and why it mattered to Malachi that Nick see how intelligent and worldly his mother was, he didn't know.

"In short, we're not certain what the incidents were about, but we are investigating. I'm sorry to say we don't have any answers right now."

Emily raised her eyebrows at Malachi, and he winced. "Incidents? Plural?"

Nick snapped his gaze to him, eyes wide, and Malachi couldn't help but laugh. But then he was wracked with a throbbing head and a wave of nausea. By the time it eased enough for him to think, he sat in his grandma's living room. Nick handed him a cup of water and helped steady his hands to drink it.

"I really shouldn't laugh at the minute. It really hurts," he complained.

"I don't see how this is a laughing matter, anyway," his mother said.

"It wasn't the incident I was laughing at. It was Nick's expression when he thought he'd dropped me in it." Even now, the reminder made him smile, but he refrained from laughing. Nick scowled at him. "It's okay. They know everything...I think." Even he was getting a little rattled by what seemed to be happening. They needed to figure out what was going on quickly because he couldn't keep looking over his shoulder every day.

14

Nick

Nick couldn't believe he'd put his foot in his mouth within the first few minutes of meeting Malachi's mother. He was so stupid. And then, when Malachi almost fainted in pain, he felt worse. It didn't make any difference that Malachi reassured him he was going to tell them, he'd still messed up.

"Sorry," he said.

Malachi waved him away.

"I think a cup of tea is in order. Nick?"

He hated tea. "Yes, thank you."

Malachi smacked his arm. "You don't drink tea, you idiot. He'll have coffee, please, Mum."

Nick's face bloomed, and he glanced at Emily and ducked his head. "Coffee, please, ma'am. If it's not too much trouble."

He didn't look up until he heard her leave, and then he met Malachi's humour-filled gaze.

"She won't bite, you know."

"She's your mother. She should."

"Oh, she *could*. But she won't." Malachi grinned, making Nick feel a little better, though he didn't know why. Was it because he knew someone else had Malachi's back? He'd have to somehow let his family know that Malachi now had him, his family and the royal family behind him, too.

When Emily returned with their drinks, he settled properly next to his reporter and braced himself for the third degree.

He didn't get it.

"Malachi Sanders, what the heck have you been getting yourself into now?" a voice called from the doorway.

An older version of Malachi's mother entered, leaning heavily on a cane but in no way, shape or form did it diminish her personality. Malachi went to rise, and Nick jumped up to help him. He smiled at him before facing his grandmother.

"Hello, Grandma." He leaned down and kissed her cheek. "As usual, I'm a clumsy so-and-so."

Before Nick could wonder why they were keeping things quiet from her, Malachi's grandmother said, "You can't lie worth shit, boy."

Malachi laughed again, and Nick caught him as he stumbled. They needed to stop making him laugh. He helped him back onto the sofa and settled beside him. Sally settled into an armchair next to Malachi and patted his knee. While they waited for Malachi's pain to ease, Sally pierced him with her gaze.

"So, Nicholas Tennant. What are your plans for Malachi?"

Malachi groaned. "Seriously, Grandma?"

Sally didn't break their staring match, and the need to move intensified, but he had never shied away from anything, and he wasn't going to start now.

"I've always been attracted to him, and he's giving us the opportunity to see if this could go somewhere."

Sally narrowed her eyes and pursed her lips, continuing to stare at him. But then she cracked a grin, and Nick's heart resumed beating when it made her look ten years younger. He doubted he was out of the woods yet, by the expression on Emily's face, but at least one person didn't seem to hate him on sight.

"You are so mean, Grandma," Malachi said, though he still had his eyes closed. "Nick, stop worrying. No one is going to eat you alive. I promise." He rolled his head towards him and smiled, cracking his eyelids open. "I won't let them."

Nick smiled back. "Do you want some more paracetamol? You've been laughing a lot since we got here."

"It's because you're all hilarious," he deadpanned. "No, I think I'm okay, as long as I don't move too much." He rolled his head back towards his family. "I doubt anyone else is joining us, are they?"

Emily sighed, her expression softening but saddening. "No. I told them you were coming over, but they're busy." She smiled tightly. "So, Kai, what happened?"

Malachi went through the story, and Nick finished off the bits where Malachi was unconscious, surprised to find that Malachi couched nothing; he told them *everything*. He did have a moment of worry when it came to talking about the Sutcliffes, but they seemed to understand that he couldn't tell them certain things, and when he said so, they didn't pry. Maybe it was because he was there, but he didn't think so. It seemed to be a familiar experience for them.

"Thank you for being there, Nick," Emily said. "I don't know what might've happened if you hadn't been."

Nick didn't want the thanks because he hadn't done enough. Malachi should've never been hurt in the first place. Giving a tight smile, he nodded, but that was all he could do.

"Let's get some dinner inside you, and then we can get you into bed," Sally said. "You'll need constant supervision for the next few days, at least."

"No, I'm going home, Gran—"

"Not a chance," Sally stated. "You don't have anyone else to look after you, and it's easier for us to do it here. Nick has to work. He can't be at your beck and call when he's protecting the king, now, can he?"

She wasn't wrong, but if Malachi wanted him to, he'd take some time off to care for him. What the hell was happening to him? Within one day, his entire outlook on his life had changed. Well, his outlook on Malachi had changed. He could see them having a future, which was why he was so happy to go ahead with whatever was building between them. It didn't stop him wondering if they were going too fast.

Malachi didn't look at him, but he heard the sigh. "You're right. Okay, but I need to collect some things from home."

"You can give me a list, and I'll fetch them," Emily said before Nick could offer, but then, Malachi probably wouldn't want him in his space alone anyway.

"Thanks, Mum."

She smiled and clapped her hands on her thighs. "The food should be ready. It's been cooking all day."

"Are you sure I'm not imposing?" he asked.

"Not at all. Come on, you can help set the table," Emily said, and Nick's stomach churned. Here was where the third degree came in.

"Of course." Nick stood.

"Be kind, Mum," Malachi warned.

Following her into the kitchen, he braced himself. She didn't start talking until after she'd shown him where the cutlery was.

"I don't have any problems with you dating my son, Nick, if that's what's worrying you. It's Malachi's choice who he dates. I will accept anyone he chooses. If anything, you might be good for him." She shook her head. "He spends far too much energy on that paper, and I wish he wouldn't, but I can't persuade him otherwise."

Knowing what Nick did about Malachi's reasons, he could answer that, but he didn't. Despite Malachi seemingly sharing a lot of things with his family, that was one thing he didn't. He could tell that from their earlier conversation.

"He's got a level head from what I've seen and heard. He knows what he's doing."

She glanced at him, and Nick got the impression she knew exactly why he was still working the shit job. Nick said nothing else.

Emily snorted as she put plates on the side, something he'd noticed Malachi did, too. "He's been obsessed with the royal family ever since he saw them on TV when he was...what, five years old. Maybe even earlier. I don't know what he found so fascinating with them, but every time he saw them..." She smiled, pulling the lid from the slow cooker. "I thought he'd grow out of it. Instead, he grew *into* it." Shaking her head, she divided the dinner onto the four plates, and Nick watched, just like he did whenever his parents were cooking. "Do you cook?"

Nick blinked. "Um, I do, well, I don't...um..." He took a breath. "I know how to cook, yes, and I enjoy cooking, but I have little time to do it."

"That's a shame. Maybe you can make time?"

He smiled because it was such a mum statement. "Are Mums given a handbook?" he asked.

A crease appeared between her eyebrows. "A handbook?"

"My mum has said something similar. She was worried my job would stop me from finding someone. Obviously, it hasn't, but I get the underlying question beneath it." He inhaled and laid it out. "Now Malachi is in my life, I want to try to balance things better. I can't make promises for the near future because certain things are set in stone months in advance, but I can start to make the changes. I don't want to leave Malachi alone more than I have to." He held up his hands. "Not that I'll be a stalker, either. I don't mean it that way."

Emily chuckled and faced him, wiping her hands on a cloth. "As for your original question, no. Parents are not given a handbook. Not really. We muddle our way through bringing children up the same way we would've muddled through our lives if we didn't have kids. No one has a clue what they're doing, Nick. And if they say they do, they're lying."

"That makes me feel so much better."

"What does?" Malachi asked, wandering slowly into the kitchen with Sally at his back. "I came to see if she'd killed you."

Nick grinned and pulled him closer, pressing his lips to Malachi's uninjured temple. "Sorry, I'm still here."

Malachi's smile lit a fire in Nick's stomach, and he wanted nothing more than to kiss it off his face, but he remembered where they were.

"I might've had something to say about it if she'd scared you off."

"Not a chance."

"Right, settle in, everyone," Emily said, and they all took seats.

The dining table was well worn and seated eight people, which he assumed was needed with how many siblings Malachi had. Thinking that, Nick counted how many there would be if they were all together—fourteen if he didn't include his cousins who regularly came to visit.

He expected a lot more questions during dinner, but the conversation remained easy and non-confrontational. It was a lot like his own family—and he felt the sme peace during the meal that he felt at his parents' house. He offered to clean away, but Emily waved him away. He settled onto the sofa beside Malachi, but when he gave an immediate yawn, Nick decided he'd bothered them enough for one night. He sent a message to Brett, asking for someone to guard the house while he was gone.

"I'm going to head off. Are you sure there is nothing I can do to help before I leave?" he asked Malachi.

Malachi squeezed his hand. "No, I'm good. I've got stuff here I can use until Mum goes to my house tomorrow."

"I'd be happy to do that if it helps, but I'm sure you won't want me in your space alone."

Smiling, Malachi said, "I have no problem with you being in my space alone, but you've done enough already. Get some rest."

No chance of that. He was going straight to Windsor to figure out what the hell was going on. "I will. You make sure you do, too. Though I know you're in good hands." He smiled at Sally, and then at Emily when she entered the room. "Thank you so much for having me and for dinner. It was delicious."

"You're welcome." Emily sat and crossed her legs.

"There is going to be a guard outside the house overnight and potentially for a few days until we figure out what's going on. They will go wherever Malachi goes. You don't need to worry about them, though." He slid to the front of the sofa and faced Malachi. "I'll check in tomorrow, okay?"

Malachi nodded slowly. "I look forward to it."

Nick licked his lips but glanced at Malachi's family. Then he decided, to hell with it. He leaned forward and softly brushed his lips over Malachi's.

"Goodnight, Kai."

"Goodnight."

He bid goodbye to Sally and Emily, noticing the small smiles they both wore and hoping it meant they were okay with him. Only time would tell. But no one would be happy unless they figured out what—or rather, who—was plaguing Malachi.

The drive to the castle was quick, and he headed straight for Sec HQ. Even though it was getting late, guards were still milling around, finishing shifts, starting shifts, working on whatever tasks they had, and as expected, Brett sat at the front, immersed in whatever paperwork had a frown on his face.

"Bad news?" he asked when he approached.

Brett glanced up briefly. "It's not bad as such, but it's not great either. What are you doing here?"

"I've just left Malachi, as you know, but I wanted to start gathering information. Has anything new turned up?"

Brett glared at him. "Do you think you wouldn't know if something had?"

Nick held up his hands and backed up a step. "Sorry. I'll leave you to do your thing." He turned away, Brett sighing heavily behind him.

"No, sorry. Fuck it all." Brett sighed again and leaned back in his chair, the ever-present squeak a comforting sound amongst the stresses they were dealing with. "We've found nothing about who it could've been. Everything seems to check out. Felix is still working his magic, so he might find something, but so far, everything is horse shit, worthy of the stables at Sandringham."

Nick rested his ass against a table and crossed his arms. "I still don't know how he could've escaped so cleanly. There are far too many cameras covering every possible area."

"And that's why I'm so pissed off." He sighed, and Nick started worrying about his lungs. Surely sighing so much wasn't good for someone. "We're missing something. What did you find out about his family?"

Nick had been a little peeved—to put it politely—when Brett insisted he check out Malachi's family while he was there. The last thing he wanted to do was spy on his boyfriend's family on his first visit, but he didn't do much. "I didn't do any snooping." He held up his hand. "No chance," he said, stopping Brett's words. "His mother and grandmother are on the up and up. I didn't get to meet any siblings."

"Father?"

"Deadbeat. That much I do know. It's something I knew about him when I first started looking into him…" He trailed off, realising just how much he'd given away with those words, but Brett just smirked.

"That's not news, Nick. You were obsessed. *Are* obsessed."

Nick grinned. "With good reason."

Brett huffed and shook his head. "I'm happy for you. I really am." He glanced across the room and then down at the desk. "I suppose I need—"

"You fucking asshole!" Felix shouted, pushing away from the computer and running his hands through his hair. "Fucking shithead. When I get my fucking hands on you, I'm going to—" He stopped when he faced them and inhaled. "Sorry."

"News?" Brett asked.

"Yeah, he wiped the cameras. But not so that it'd stand out. What he's managed to do is splice them. So he basically cut a few minutes, but it was in such small amounts, I didn't notice."

"Which cameras?"

"Prince of Wales' Tower to Queen's to York. He must've walked damn fast because there are barely seconds missing from some cameras."

Brett stood. "He had to have help. There's no way he could've escaped and deleted all those cameras in the time it took us to start looking for someone."

Felix nodded. "No doubt. He's good, but he's not a magician."

"What did Malachi say about any hate mail?" Brett asked, turning to Nick.

"He gets it daily and ignores it. He did mention one guy, Tarrant Milton. Said he was not a hater, as such, but loved the work he did. Which is a bonus in Malachi's favour, but not in ours."

"If the guy loves Malachi's work, then he doesn't like the royal family. It could be him," Felix stated.

"Correct," Brett said.

"But I thought we were assuming this was about Malachi, not the Sutcliffes," Nick said.

"I suddenly remembered what they said about assuming." Brett sighed. "It makes an ass of you and me."

Nick exhaled and leaned back against the table again. "I feel exhausted all of a sudden."

"Welcome to my world," Brett muttered. "Go home, Nick. Start fresh tomorrow after your shift if you have the energy."

"I'm good now. I'll get started—"

"Go home. That's an order. You've been on duty for hours, even if it's not felt like it. Get some rest."

"No, I'm—"

"Go. Home."

Nick exhaled, knowing he wouldn't get a different answer. And it wasn't like he couldn't do some work from home. "I'll see you tomorrow."

"And if Felix tells me you logged onto the system, I'll stop you from organising anyone else's party for a year."

Nick gasped and spun around. "That's mean!"

Brett smirked at him. "That shows how serious I am."

Shaking his head, Nick headed for the door. "Evil leader," he muttered.

As he left, he caught Felix's gaze, and the man winked at him. He hoped that meant he'd keep quiet about whatever Nick got up to at home. Because he was going to research his ass off. If this was focused on Malachi, Nick needed to figure it out. He wouldn't stop until whoever was involved was behind bars or dead—he didn't care which. All he wanted was Malachi safe. And Nick would do whatever it took to make that happen.

And if it meant he was protecting the crown at the same time, then well done to him.

It was going to be a very long night.

15

Malachi

I t took over two weeks for Malachi's concussion to stop affecting him, and during that time, he'd received dozens of emails from Tucker, bemoaning the fact he couldn't work. He probably could've, but his mother made him promise to fully recover this time, and he listened to her. After all, he'd been living with them for the first few days.

The day he woke where he had no aftereffects was a win for him. Not only because his head didn't spin or hurt, but because it meant he could start persuading Nick to touch him again. The odd chaste kiss and handholding was nice, but he wanted—no, *needed*—more. He needed to feel Nick surrounding him. Above him. Inside him. His dreams were out of control, and every part of his body ached—and not because of the incident, either.

That day was his doctor's appointment, and he was hoping for an all-clear so he could begin his seduction. It might take him a few days to break down Nick's barriers, but he'd do it. Being able to get dressed without an ache anywhere was a godsent miracle. And to be dressed within ten minutes was another. He had no qualms about using his newfound confidence in their relationship to sway Nick to his side of things.

Nick had been a constant bright light in his life while he'd been suffering the aftereffects of the head injury. Daily visits, sometimes early morning, sometimes late at night, but every time, he would sit with him and talk to him about what he'd done and give titbits of information about the royal family's activities. The behind-the-scenes version. He loved it. When he had time, Nick cooked for him, too. But other than cuddles on the sofa or kisses in the kitchen, Nick had hardly touched him.

When the doctor told him he had the all-clear, he almost wept with joy. It had been a long road of thinking he was all right, and then having another headache or dizzy spell take him down. But now he was better—on the understanding that he still needed to be careful, and if he experienced any effects, he needed to go back—and he could plan his attack.

There was one unpleasant thing that came from getting better…

"Good morning," he said when he entered the office of the Windsor Chronicle. He received maybe two replies, but they had never been the sociable kind, at least not with him. He knocked on Tucker's door and entered when called.

"Fucking finally," his boss said when he saw him. "Stupid of you to knock yourself out while on assignment. You've wasted weeks now."

Tucker was a lean man, the muscles he'd grown in the Army having diminished once he finished working out regularly. His attitude, however, had only grown larger.

For once, Malachi didn't cower in his presence, though he was careful with his words, reminding himself of the lie the security team had concocted about what happened to him. "I have the opportunity to go back, which I will be doing today. You'll still have the inside scoop."

"If they haven't brought in someone else to do your job, that is." Malachi said nothing. "Get your ass back to work. I expect an article ready to go this afternoon."

If nothing else, Malachi knew what Tucker was like and had predicted this, so he already had an article he'd been writing during the past two weeks. One that made him physically ill to write, but he had known it was necessary. Nick, however, had told him to quit. He'd said he could look after any future hospital costs, or even the royal family could, but Malachi didn't want to depend on others. He was an independent, self-sufficient man, who had the ability to provide his family with private hospital care they wouldn't otherwise get by just staying in the job he hated.

He was a little concerned about what he would do once his contract was up. Then, he definitely wouldn't be able to cover the hospital costs should he need to, but he'd cross that bridge when he came to it.

"You'll have it."

Tucker said nothing further, and Malachi retreated. He rarely stayed in the office to do anything, and he didn't then either. He went straight for home, packed a bag and headed to Windsor like Nick had told him to. The guards let him in but asked him to wait in his car until he had an escort arrive to take him into the castle. He didn't mind. He loved looking at the area no public was allowed in, except in extremely specific conditions. Studying his surroundings meant he noticed when someone walked towards him. He recognised Felix immediately and climbed out of the car.

"Good afternoon, Malachi. Or do you prefer Kai?" Felix tilted his head as if studying his reactions.

Malachi smiled. "Either is fine, though I don't promote the Kai version."

"I'll stick with Kai, then. How are you feeling?" he asked as they headed inside.

"A lot better, thanks. Had the all-clear from the doc today."

Felix smiled. "That's great news."

They spoke some more, and it wasn't long before Malachi noticed they weren't heading towards the suite. "Where are we going?"

"Sec HQ."

"Why's that?"

"We have a few things we want to go through with you before you resume your visit. Is that okay?"

He wasn't truly asking, but it was fine—understandable, even—and he said so. "As long as I'm not heading for the gallows, I'm good."

Felix grinned, making him look much younger than Malachi initially thought he was. "You're good then. We don't execute people for their opinions anymore."

"Good to know. It's not my opinion, though. Just so we're clear. They're just words meant to make the royal family look bad, which I know is not a great job, but hopefully, my other articles counteract most of the damage I cause."

Felix paused by a door and faced him. "You don't have to explain yourself to us. We understand. So do the Sutcliffes."

Malachi briefly wondered if Nick had told them about the real reason he did what he did, but he didn't think the man would break a confidence like that unless he had to.

They entered the room he had never been allowed in before. Nick had probably been concerned he'd use it against them, and his mouth twitched at the thought. He'd have to ask him later.

"Nick is currently guarding the king, so you'll have a different guard for now. Me." Felix grinned.

Malachi chuckled. "Good to know. I'd hate to have to break in a new one already," he joked, and chuckles resounded around the room.

Felix snapped his fingers. "Nick will never live that down."

He wondered if he'd said the wrong thing, but the humour in Felix's gaze was contagious, and he couldn't find it in himself to worry. He doubted Nick would be upset, maybe just embarrassed.

"Brett would like to talk to you about what we've found out so far."

He nodded. "Okay, great. Not sure if I'll be much help, but I'd love to know what the heck's going on."

"You're not the only one," Brett said, heading their way. "We'd love to know, too."

Malachi's stomach churned at being so useless. He had seen nothing, and if he had, he didn't remember it.

"What can I do to help?"

"Tell us about Tarrant Milton, to begin with."

They settled into seats, and Malachi gave them everything he knew about the guy, which wasn't much. He'd hardly researched him because he hadn't thought it was necessary. He had been all talk.

"Well, we've found out he's attending the event at the end of the month. If you're in agreement, we'd like you to contact him."

"Why?"

Brett leaned back, crossing his hands over his stomach. "He's fairly benign in his messages, but there is a chance he could escalate and become a problem, if he hasn't already. We'd like to stop that from happening, so we want you to approach him, or let him approach you, and then Nick can get an opinion of him."

"So, I'll just debrief Nick when I'm done?"

Felix chuckled. "Nick will be right beside you as your date."

Malachi's jaw dropped. "He what?" He shook his head. "I don't want to push him to do that. He might not be ready."

Brett chuckled this time. "He's met your family. I think he's all in."

"How did you...?" Malachi grimaced. "The guard."

Brett smiled. "Not much we can keep from one another unless we try really hard. And besides, Nick's been obsessed with you for a long time. It wasn't a case of if he would fall, but when."

Brett moved on to other questions, but Malachi's head stuttered over his words. He'd implied Nick was in love with him. How did Malachi feel about him? Can people fall in love that quickly? He wasn't sure. All he knew was that he enjoyed being with the man, and he yearned for him whenever he wasn't with him. Was that love?

Eventually, they finished with the questioning, and Malachi slumped in his chair. "That was harder than my Spanish GCSE exam."

Felix snorted. "Brett's inquisitions usually are." He stood. "Come on. I'll take you to your man."

"He's not..." He paused at the expressions on both men's faces and swallowed. "Okay, thank you," he finished, nearly tripping over his bag as he stood. He was tired.

"Would you prefer I take you to the suite? I can tell Nick where you are?"

"Is that okay? I don't want to mess with your plans, but I'm so tired." Lethargy dragged at him.

"Of course it's okay. I'll get you settled and then find Nick. I'm sure he'll be there soon enough."

Felix led the way, and Malachi dragged his feet. He was a lot more tired than usual, but the doctor had said he would tire more easily while he was getting back to where he had been. When they entered the suite he had used before, he thanked Felix.

"There will be someone outside your door all the time. Not because we don't trust you. We want to make sure you're safe. Let them know if you need anything or anyone."

Malachi smiled. "Thanks. I think I'll just take a nap and recharge until Nick gets here."

"Sounds like a good plan. I'll see you later, I'm sure."

Felix's words sounded like a prophecy, but he chose not to think like that. When Felix disappeared, he only took the time to take off his shoes and trousers but left everything else on.

He couldn't remember falling asleep, but he knew how he woke. Cocooned, warm and surrounded by a scent that was already becoming familiar. Nick. Smiling, he nestled closer, and Nick's arms tightened around him.

"How are you feeling?"

"Much better. All the questions fried my brain." He chuckled and squirmed around until he faced him. "How was your day?"

"We're all alive, so I count that as a win." Nick's mouth curved on one side. "Are you still feeling okay? No lingering pain or dizziness?"

Malachi's heart thumped painfully at the concern in his voice. Nick always took care of those around him, and now it was time for Malachi to look after him. He pushed Nick to his back and straddled him, leaning down and rubbing their noses together with a smile.

"I'm fine. Just a little lingering tiredness, but nothing to worry about." He brushed their lips together, enjoying the way Nick opened for him without hesitation. Tongues tangling, the kiss deepened, Malachi loving how Nick let him take charge. He'd never had that before, having always chosen the wrong person to sleep with. It was hard for him to explain what else he desired from sex, so most of the time he let it lay dormant, ignoring the need like he ignored everything else he couldn't change. Maybe, in time, he could bare his soul, and Nick wouldn't throw him to the curb.

But right then, he had other plans to fulfil. Pulling away from Nick's tantalising mouth, he peppered kisses down his neck, unfastening the buttons of his shirt so his mouth could taste his skin. He dragged the ends of his shirt from his trousers and pushed the edges aside, bearing Nick's chest and stomach.

Meeting his gaze, he skimmed his fingers across the slightly bronzed skin, enjoying the warmth of it, and ran a pad of one finger across each nipple.

Nick hissed, his indrawn breath long and loud in the otherwise silent room. Malachi wanted to hear more of it, so he flicked a blunt nail over the tip, and Nick rewarded him with another sound. Unable to hold himself back, he lowered to his forearms and sucked a nub into his mouth. He didn't go easy. At his constant ministration, the nipple beaded, and when he was satisfied, he took it between his teeth, peered up at Nick and bit down gently.

The widening of his eyes and the gaping of his mouth was another reward, and Malachi wondered if his needs might meet with Nick's after all, but then he pushed it aside again. Just because there were rumours of the Sutcliffes owning or attending Club Royal didn't mean it was true. And he wasn't about to ask.

Laving the nub to soothe it, he then moved to the other, giving it the same treatment. Nick's fingers clenched around a fistful of covers, and Malachi smiled, breaking his hold. He reached up and kissed Nick again, spearing his tongue inside, needing to taste him again. Grinding down on him, an answering hardness met his, and he repeated the action, dragging a moan from Nick's throat and swallowing it down his own.

Nick tore his mouth away. "Fuck," he breathed as Malachi attacked his neck again.

Malachi's finger got busy fumbling with Nick's trousers, and within seconds, he dragged them down his legs, baring him to Malachi's gaze once more. Seeing him in the shower was nothing compared to having him laid out for him, and he licked his lips, eyes on his prize. But before he delved in, he undressed Nick completely, and then himself, shucking the T-shirt, boxers and socks he'd kept on from before he fell asleep.

When he met Nick's gaze, he spread Nick's legs and rubbed his hands up his thighs to where he wanted them. Then he paused. He studied Nick's quickening breath, his tight jaw, his flaring nostrils, and waited. He would never take something that wasn't his to give, and neither would Nick, so he waited for Nick to confirm he was okay with what they were doing. Within seconds, Nick relaxed and nodded, and Malachi beamed at him. Taking it slowly, he wrapped his hand around Nick's cock, the heat seeping into his palm, and stroked. Nick hissed.

Gone was the boy whose ideals had been dashed at his first job. Gone was the reporter who wanted a story to ensure his family stayed safe. Gone was the man who was scared to take control. In their place was a man who knew what he wanted.

And he wanted Nick at his mercy.

Leaning down, he licked the head, humming at the explosion of his taste. He did it again, needing more. And when that wasn't enough, he sucked the head into his mouth.

"Fuck, fuck," Nick murmured.

Malachi closed his eyes, concentrating on his taste and ensuring he made this the best he could. He needed to give this to Nick, a small piece of himself, and though it wasn't a tit-for-tat relationship, he wanted to show him how much he meant to him. How far he had fallen in such a short time. Though had it really been short? They'd both admitted to feeling the attraction from almost the beginning. Could they have had feelings involved for a lot longer than when Nick first found out about Kai?

He pushed the thought aside for thinking about later and concentrated on sucking. Malachi sank down as far as he could, loosening his throat to get further, and Nick thrust up.

"Jesus, Kai."

If he could've smiled, he would have. Instead, he went to work, bobbing and swallowing, sending Nick as close to the edge as he could without going over. And when Nick's words turned to babbles, he pulled back.

"Holy..." Nick panted, pupils dilated and eyes unfocused.

Malachi braced himself on his hands by Nick's chest and kissed him. He waited for him to come back to earth, their cocks nudging each other as Malachi circled his hips, keeping the arousal simmering. When Nick focused on him, he smiled and whispered against his lips, "Can I fuck you, Nick?"

Nick's gaze roamed across Malachi's face, and he didn't move, allowing him to make whatever decision was best for him. They hadn't talked about who was a top or bottom, and while Malachi was vers, he preferred to top. It didn't mean he wouldn't bottom if Nick needed him to, but he loved to be the one making someone lose control. It wasn't even that he needed the control, not totally, but being the cause of someone letting go enough to fly was a high he never tired of.

As Nick stared at him, he hid nothing of what he was feeling. He let Nick see it all because what was the point of a relationship if they were going to hide who they were? Nick reached up and cupped his cheeks, brushing his thumbs over his skin and pulling him down for a kiss. When they parted, Nick smiled.

"Make love to me, Kai."

16

Nick

Nick swallowed hard when he said the words. There was a distinct difference between fucking and making love, and he hoped he hadn't messed up. He hoped they were on the same page.

Malachi's smile lit up the room, and Nick's heart pounded. "Gladly."

Malachi joined their lips, sliding his arms beneath Nick's back and holding him tightly. Nick draped his arms around Malachi's neck and took everything he gave. He was more a bottom than a top, but he'd happily do either. From Malachi's demeanour when they first decided to try when Nick had found out about Kai Ruffers, he'd assumed he was a bottom, and Nick had been happy to top him, but that person was nowhere to be seen, and Nick loved it. For some people, it was difficult letting someone have that sense of control over them, but for Nick, he loved seeing what someone would do to him. Expecting the unexpected was something he enjoyed. Like what Malachi had done with his nipples. He'd known they were sensitive but had never expected that spark of pain to flood his veins with pleasure.

Malachi's hips ground into him, and he wrapped his legs around him, keeping him close. His calf twinged, but not enough to stop. His head spun as they kissed, air becoming an afterthought rather than a necessity...until it was. He pulled away, panting, and gripped Malachi's hair, going back for more even though he needed more oxygen. As their lips sipped and nipped, Malachi's hands roamed, and every touch was like a wave of electricity flowing through him. He needed...

"More," he gasped, and Malachi's lips and tongue led a path down his neck. Pulling away, Malachi peered down at him, eyes glazed, lips ruby red and swollen. He'd never looked more beautiful, but Nick panicked when he left the bed. "Kai...?" He rose to his hands, bereft of his warmth, but Malachi smiled at him as he stopped at his suitcase.

He unzipped it, rummaged through and pulled several items from it. Then he held them up, and Nick laughed, dropping back to the bed and covering his eyes with his hands.

"Shit. I thought you were leaving."

The words left his mouth before he thought how vulnerable it would make him sound. But it was Malachi, and he didn't care. He would be as vulnerable and truthful as he could.

He opened his eyes again when Malachi crawled from the bottom of the bed until he knelt in the same position he'd left. He dropped condoms and lube onto the bed, and Nick chuckled.

"I thought we might need these at some point, so I brought some with me," Malachi said, resuming his previous mouthwatering path across his skin. "I need to make sure you're ready." He hovered over Nick's mouth. "I refuse to hurt you."

Nick lifted his head, joining their lips. "I trust you."

Malachi took his mouth again, and Nick lost himself in the sensations bombarding him. It wasn't until Malachi's fingers rubbed over his pucker that his attention zeroed in on the area. He inhaled through his nose and pressed his head back into the pillow when Malachi slipped a finger past his rim, the lube making it easier. Nick was expecting a little pain because it had been a while since he'd last bottomed, but he was there for it. He wanted it. Wanted him.

"Nick, look at me."

Nick met Malachi's gaze, his eyelids fluttering in the battle to keep them from falling into the ecstasy. Especially when Malachi slipped another finger into him.

"Watch me," Malachi ordered.

Nick did, and the sensations of what he was feeling and watching became a loop of overwhelming need. Malachi nipped, pulled and tugged at his nipples, sending arrows of fire towards his groin and wrapping around Malachi's fingers in his ass.

"Fuck, Kai. More, please."

He was sure Malachi dragged it out as long as he could because, by the time Malachi pulled his fingers free, it felt like several hours had passed.

"Ready for me?" Malachi asked as he rolled a condom down his length.

Nick pouted at not having the chance to taste him but nodded. "Yes."

"Ask me again," Malachi said, and Nick frowned. Ask him what? Then he smiled and slid his hands up Malachi's stomach to his face, caressing his cheeks.

"Make love to me, Kai," he whispered.

"With pleasure." Malachi grinned.

Malachi kissed him at the same time he pushed against his hole, and Nick couldn't help closing his teeth around Malachi's lip. They both groaned as Malachi broke through the muscles and slid inside. Having done such a good job of stretching him, there was barely any burn, and Nick was able to concentrate on how it felt to have Malachi's cock in his ass. Fabulous was what it felt like.

"Fuck, please." He groaned, spreading his legs further and gripping Malachi's ass cheeks, trying to get him inside quicker.

"Patience...is a virtue...you don't seem...to have sometimes," Malachi panted.

With a final thrust, he bottomed out, and Nick wrapped his legs around his waist and his arms around his neck, wanting the connection. He buried his face in Malachi's neck, inhaling his scent while Malachi held still, probably waiting for Nick's go-ahead. Nick kissed up his neck to his mouth and murmured, "Go."

Malachi kissed him again and withdrew before sliding deep again. That electricity expanded, encompassing his entire body until he was nothing but a live wire with every movement and touch flickering with fire.

"Oh, fuck," he breathed. "More. More, more, more."

Malachi chuckled on an exhale. "Impatient fucker."

But he listened and increased his speed and strength, lifting to brace himself on his hands. Nick gripped his shoulders, holding on as Malachi reamed him. His cock bobbed between them, leaking precome in a long string of need that pooled on his stomach. He wrapped one hand around his shaft, hissing at its sensitivity.

"That's it. Stroke it for me," Malachi growled. "Show me how much you want it."

"*You.* How much I want you."

Malachi's eyes darkened further, and he pounded into him. Arousal turned into fire, which evolved into a ball of power set to burn him to a crisp, but still, Malachi took him higher until his breath left his lungs and his entire being clenched and jerked and came apart beneath the man he loved. His eyelids fell shut, his ears ringing loudly enough to block any other noise than the rushing of his blood, and his lungs ached for oxygen.

Finally, he slumped to the bed, his legs and arms falling to the mattress with a thump. His chest heaved, and he pulled his eyes open with effort, meeting Malachi's pained gaze. Nick frowned and opened his mouth, but Malachi beat him to it.

"Hold tight," was all the warning Nick got, and his lover began another series of thrusts, sending sparks through Nick once more, but he couldn't come again. Instead, he focused on helping Malachi to fall over the edge, and when he finally did, Nick was glad he'd come earlier because it gave him the chance to experience the sounds, sights, feel, scents and taste of him as he orgasmed—a sight he was unlikely to forget anytime soon.

When Malachi pulled free, Nick winced but pulled him closer, needing that connection before they cleaned up.

"Was that okay?" Malachi asked, a rasp to his voice, advertising the strain he'd put on it.

"More than. I hope you have more of that in you." Nick snorted. "For another day, I mean."

"You feeling your age, Mr Tennant?" Malachi teased, running his fingers up Nick's stomach and chest.

Nick laughed, catching his wandering hand and tangling their fingers. "Definitely. Though I'm sure I can go again soon if you need to be reminded of how good it was."

Malachi leaned over him and dropped a kiss on his lips. "I'll remember how good it was every day," he whispered.

They shared a grin, but then Nick broke the ensuing silence with common sense. "Come on. We need to clean up."

Once they had, they snuggled back into bed, Nick as the big spoon, and turned off the light.

"I'm glad you're back," Nick murmured against Malachi's neck.

"Me, too."

"I promise I'll keep you safe."

Malachi tightened the hold he had on Nick's arm. "I have no doubt."

The warmth that spread through him at the words was nothing short of love. There was no denying it. He didn't even want to. He never would. Loving Malachi was the easiest thing he'd ever done. He just hoped he could keep the promise he'd just made. Because it seemed like someone was out to get him, and they needed to figure out who it was, and quickly.

The rest of Malachi's visit was uneventful. Which was good and bad. Good because it meant Malachi wasn't in danger, but bad because it meant they were not much closer to an answer than they had been.

Malachi had thanked Andrew repeatedly for the opportunity, and though they knew some bad articles would come from the experience, they also understood the good would outweigh those dreaded words.

Nick had gone back to his usual duties, sleeping at home instead of at the castle, and it was strange. He still saw Malachi, but they had a few weeks of busy schedules ahead of them, including another royal wedding and Dominic's birthday party, and it meant their one and only night of passion had to keep them going for the next two weeks. It was only on the night of the charity event Brett had asked Malachi and him to attend that he saw his boyfriend in person for more than a passing few minutes or a shared night of exhaustion where they'd both fallen asleep immediately. It hadn't been the best start to their relationship, but they'd learnt how to communicate through the phone, that was for sure.

Nick had joked about phone sex, but Malachi had pulled a face, so he'd not brought it up again. Maybe they could talk about it face to face before he tried because he wasn't sure he could go so long without needing to share something with him again. Nick was desperate to touch him, hold him, taste him.

Which was why, when he knocked on Malachi's door to pick him up for the event, he almost swallowed his tongue at the sight of the freshly pressed tuxedo caressing his lover's body.

"Holy…" He blew out a breath and swallowed hard. "Yeah, we need to get this evening over with quickly."

Malachi flushed, and Nick watched it reach his ears. "You don't look so bad yourself."

Nick shook his head. "Your chariot awaits, Mr Sanders."

Malachi's smile lit up the small hallway, and Nick's stomach swirled. How he wished they didn't need to attend that night. He held out his elbow, and Malachi took it, locking the door behind him before letting Nick lead him to the black town car waiting to speed them to the event in the centre of London.

Despite there being around an hour of a journey to the event, Nick promised to be on his best behaviour. Well, he promised himself. No point in making the task harder than it needed to be by announcing it to anyone. Then, if he caved and sought out Malachi's lips or cheek…or body, he only disappointed himself.

"Is Tarrant definitely going to be there?" Malachi asked, his voice strained.

"He has an invitation and he RSVP'd, so we're assuming that means he's coming." Nick wouldn't object to the man cancelling his plans, even though he knew they needed to scope him out. He hated the idea of Malachi being so close to a potential suspect. Luckily, he was allowed to wear his gun, which was safely tucked into his holster beneath his jacket.

"I've been searching through the hate mail I get, but other than words showing their displeasure, there wasn't anyone who appeared to be wanting to take those words and turn them into actions."

"Thank you for looking. That must've been hard for you."

Malachi scrunched his face. "It certainly didn't make me like what I do any more."

Nick squeezed his hand. "Not long to go." And if Nick had his way, he'd be out of the job quicker than the contract end date. It was something Felix was working on. "How is your mum and grandma doing?"

Malachi smiled. "They're complaining because they haven't seen you." He waved a hand. "I've explained, but, you know. Family being family."

"It's on my agenda to come back, I promise. I think I'm off next weekend. Maybe we can arrange to have dinner? I could treat them to a nice dinner out?"

"I'm sure they would love that, but you don't have to. They'd be just as happy spending time with you at home."

"I know, but why not treat them like the princesses they are?"

Malachi chuckled. "I'll check to make sure they're free. Thank you."

"Invite the rest of your family, too. If you want, I could invite mine as well. Everyone could meet?" Nick had no clue what Malachi's answer would be, but he relaxed a lot when he received a smile.

"I'd love to meet your family, and I know Mum would, too."

"Great. Check with them, and I'll arrange it."

They talked about some of the things they'd done during the time they'd been apart, even though they'd spoken on the phone nearly every day. There was something different about doing it face to face, watching the play of emotions wash over Malachi's face. But far too soon, they arrived, and Nick exhaled.

"Show time."

Malachi gave a small smile. "At least we're together."

Nick's heart soared. "Nowhere else I'd rather be."

They climbed from the car and entered the building, giving their names to the guards on the door before being let through. The opulence was slightly overdone, but then, that was the point. Rich people were happy to bleed money when they were surrounded by wealth. Something about the environment lent an air of superiority to them. It changed nothing, though. There were still people who needed the money these people gave, and if holding fancy, expensive events was the way to get that money—and more—from their pockets, then so be it.

He kept his hand on Malachi's, which he'd slipped around his arm again as they'd entered, and smiled at people as he passed. They weren't there to schmooze, a good thing in his book. All they needed to do was talk to Tarrant Milton and get a feel for him. Was he the one messing with Malachi? Only time would tell.

Prince Christian waved to them, and Nick steered Malachi in his direction. Nick shook the royal's hand when they were close enough.

"How are you feeling, Malachi?" Christian asked.

"In myself, as if nothing happened. About being here, nervous." He gave a small chuckle, eyes darting around.

"I can understand that. Just remember, there are enough of us here if there's a problem, okay? Just shout and we'll be there." Christian tilted his head behind him, and Nick followed his direction to where Brett and Felix stood not too far away.

Felix smiled, and Brett nodded once, tapping four fingers against his arm to let Nick know there were four other of their guards around the room. Despite knowing his own abilities, he was grateful for the support. They didn't usually take six guards to cover two royals.

"If nothing else, the dinner should be lovely," Oscar said, his hand clasped in Christian's.

Malachi laughed a little easier this time. "Not sure I'll be able to eat, but that's good to know."

Nick cleared his throat. "We'll wander around and see if we can make contact."

Christian nodded. "Don't forget to use that money." He smirked, and Nick groaned.

King Andrew had insisted on providing Nick with a not-too-insignificant amount of money to donate to the cause that night. Nick had argued that Christian was there to do that, but Andrew had insisted that Nick also do something similar. He had no idea what he was doing, but he wanted to get rid of it as soon as possible.

They wandered around the room, picking up a glass of juice, and made conversation between themselves.

"What did he mean about the money?" Malachi asked.

Nick rolled his eyes. "They wanted to make sure I was seen as someone rather than a...lackey for want of a better word. The king thought it would be a good way to bring Tarrant to us, thinking he'd get the inside scoop of what we put our money towards. I hate spending other people's money," he mumbled, his stomach churning at potentially making the wrong choice.

The event was holding a gallery as well as a dinner, and anyone could buy the art. But as Nick had said, he hated spending other people's money when he hadn't been given clear instructions on what to buy.

"Let's check out the art, then," Malachi said.

Nick sighed. "Okay."

The artwork was held in a side room, and as they studied the paintings, Nick paused in front of one particular landscape. Instinctively, he knew this would've been one the late Queen Louisa would've chosen as she loved landscapes, but was it the right choice for the money? The more he studied it, the more he liked it, but he wasn't sure if the reminder was a good option.

"You know they'd love it," Malachi whispered in his ear. "They love the reminders of her."

Nick closed his eyes and sighed, loving that Malachi already knew where his thoughts had gone without him having to try to explain. After another breath, he filled out the form, enclosed it in an envelope and handed it to the person in charge of the art. When they exited, Nick didn't feel like he could breathe any easier—and he wouldn't until he knew if the Sutcliffes liked the painting or not.

They wandered around the outskirts of the room, and Malachi tensed. Nick followed his gaze and stopped, tightening his grip on Malachi's hand.

"You've nothing to worry about," he murmured. "I've got you."

As he watched Tarrant Milton move through the guests towards them, he took stock of him. And, in all honesty, there wasn't much to say. He was short, slender and had shocking blue hair. But the tuxedo he wore was far too big for him.

"Malachi, nice to see you again. Mr Tennant, nice to meet you finally." Tarrant's gaze locked on Malachi. "You've gone up in the world. Surprising, to say the least."

Nick didn't care for his tone and tensed, but Malachi shocked him with a laugh.

"Yeah, surprised me, too."

17

Malachi

Tarrant's thinly veiled words unlocked Malachi's uneasiness. They had talked before briefly, but there was something about him that made his stomach churn. He had to remember, though, that they were there to investigate him. He wasn't sure Tarrant would tell him anything because Malachi would seem to be in with the royal family now, even with the opposing words he wrote in the media.

"When love calls, you have to heed it," Malachi said, glancing fondly at Nick. Nick smiled back, though it was strained. "How are things with you?"

Tarrant nodded. "Good, thanks. I loved your latest article. In my heart, I'm hoping what you're writing is still true, but I still wonder if your opinion has changed."

Tightening his hold on Nick's hand, Malachi said the words he hated, knowing he needed to keep the ruse up. "Not at all. Just because Nick works for them doesn't mean they're any less unnecessary. A strain on the economy is still their major role."

The words tasted of flour, and he sipped his lukewarm orange juice.

Tarrant's face lit up. "Exactly! Same with all of this." He waved his hand around. "Why spend thousands of pounds to hold an event like this when that money could be given directly to the cause?"

Malachi knew why, but he just nodded in response. "The artwork is incredible. Have you seen it?"

Tarrant smiled, his shoulders losing the tension they'd found during their conversation. "They are incredible. Oh! I almost forgot. This is for you." He held out an envelope towards Nick, who frowned.

"What's this?" he asked before taking it. He slid his finger beneath the flap and pulled out a piece of folded white paper. Unfolding it, he looked at it, and Malachi saw anger overtake him. Nick dropped the paper and grabbed Tarrant's tuxedo jacket.

"What the hell is this?"

Tarrant struggled, hands covering Nick's on his jacket. "I was asked to give it to you! I don't know!"

They were drawing attention, and Malachi picked up the discarded paper and envelope.

#3

He frowned. What did it mean? Two guards came through the crowds that had formed, standing around them but letting Nick do what was needed.

"By whom?"

"A guy at the door. He said he had to get it to you, but the guards wouldn't let him in."

Nick shook him. "Why, then, did you think it was a good idea to offer to bring it in?"

Tarrant's eyes widened. "He said it was important!"

Nick cursed and dragged Tarrant with him, the two guards leading the way. Malachi followed, unsure of what was happening. What was the relevance of the number three? There was nothing he could put his finger on, but it was potentially a closely guarded secret. Whatever it was, wasn't good. He followed them into a smaller room, and Nick shoved Tarrant to the sofa, grabbing his gun from the holster but holding it down by his side.

"Who was it?" Nick asked.

Tarrant spread his hands. "I don't know! I'd never seen him before."

"Describe him."

Tarrant rubbed his hands over his face, his eyes glazing. "Um, taller than me, brown hair, wore a suit, unkempt beard. Um..." His face flushed. "Bright green eyes. Never seen that colour before. It's what drew me to him."

Nick huffed. "What did he say to you, exactly?"

"Just that the envelope needed to get to you in time."

"In time for what?" Nick stepped closer.

Tarrant shrugged. "I don't know. I didn't have time to ask because the guard shoved him away from the door."

Nick shook his head and peered at one of the guards who'd come with them. "They secure?"

"Already on their way home," one said.

Nick grabbed his phone, dialled and put it to his ear, walking away from them towards the window. "Yeah... Number three... Uh-huh... Do you think it's linked?... Okay. We're on our way back... Yeah." He glanced over his shoulder at Tarrant. "He'll spend the night talking with Brady. We need to figure this shit out and fast." He ended the call and faced them. "Owen, Sam, can you please escort Tarrant to Brady? He'll be expecting him by the time you get there."

The two guards moved, gesturing for Tarrant to stand, and though the guy sent Malachi a questioning glance, Malachi wasn't interrupting whatever it was. They must have their reasons for it. After they left, Nick exhaled.

"Sorry about that," he said, and Malachi shook his head.

"Why are you sorry? There's obviously a reason for it. You don't just go grabbing people for no reason." He would've liked to know the reason, but he wasn't going to push.

Nick put his gun away and held out his hand for the paper, staring at it for a long moment before putting it back in the envelope and tucking it inside his jacket.

"We have to get back."

Malachi nodded, his chest aching when no explanation was given. He understood. Nick couldn't tell him everything; he wasn't allowed. It still hurt, though.

They climbed into the town car and fell into silence. Nick was lost in his thoughts, and Malachi was trying to figure out the relevance of the number three. Three victims? Three chances? Three... He shook his head. He had no idea. Wishing he could help, he took a chance and covered Nick's hand with his own.

"Are you okay?"

Nick's gaze focused on him slowly, and he blinked as if coming out of a trance. He turned his hand over and squeezed. "Yeah. It's... There's..." He sighed. "Can we talk about it when we get back?"

"Of course."

He listened to Nick make several phone calls, though nothing that was said gave any indication of the topic. Malachi hoped it wasn't anything to do with him, and they were going to interrogate him when they got back. He'd answer any of their questions, of course, but he had no idea what was going on.

When they finally pulled up to Windsor Castle, Malachi trembled from worrying so much. It eased slightly when Nick took his hand when they climbed out of the car and led them down the corridors to what Malachi now knew was Sec HQ. Nick knocked and waited for someone to open it, and then they were inside.

"Where is it?" Brett asked. Nick let go of Malachi and pulled the envelope from his pocket. Brett pulled on some gloves and opened it, his eyes scanning the page and envelope. "Nothing else?"

"No. Just that and a brief description of who gave it to Tarrant."

"Did it ring any bells?"

Nick shook his head. "No idea who it was from that."

"Felix is getting us some photos to look at. Maybe we can get a facial recognition hit once we know which one he is." Brett glanced at Malachi and then back at Nick. "Fill him in."

Nick raised his eyebrows. "Are you sure?"

Brett stared at Malachi again. "The words you put in your articles are for self-preservation, right? You're not hiding anything from us, are you? Because if you are and we find out, your punishment will be far worse than what you could dream of."

Malachi's stomach revolted at the idea that he would do anything to truly hurt the royal family—though words can be hurtful, he supposed—so he shook his head. "I don't want anything to happen to them. I promise. It's purely self-preservation."

Brett nodded. "Fill him in, Nick. You never know, he might have an idea of what the fuck is going on around here. Owen, help him out."

Over the next hour, tucked into a corner of Sec HQ, Nick and Owen provided him with the information about the events that had been happening but kept out of the media as much as possible. Randall's kidnapping and Dominic being shot. Evan and Owen being blackmailed and blown up. And each of them being left with a number. It had confused the hell out of him until he realised they were all in relationships. Dominic and Randall. Owen and Evan. Nick and…Malachi. One guard, one partner.

"You're thinking the things that happened to me were because of you," he surmised, staring at Nick.

Nick nodded and peered at his hands. "I can't think of another reason. Not now we have this?" He pointed to the number three. "It fits." He swallowed hard and finally met Malachi's gaze. "I'm sorry for dragging you into this."

"If you are."

Nick frowned. "What do you mean?"

"The first thing happened before we were together. Are you certain they're related?"

He was glad Nick didn't instantly dismiss his thoughts and actually sat there and worked through it. "I can't be certain, but it's a good guess. Although we weren't together, we were attracted to each other, and if others could see it—which I'm sure they could from their comments—then it fits. I'm not ruling out that it could be two separate things, but as you've not found anything relating to anyone potentially going after you, I'm still erring on the 'me' cause."

Malachi could see where he was coming from. He didn't have any idea who could want to hurt him, but it didn't mean he had to like making Nick feel like it was his fault.

"Why are they targeting bodyguards?" he asked.

Owen shrugged. "So far, we have found nothing that points to anyone in particular. It seems to be that whoever is doing it is using pawns to do their dirty work. People who've got beefs with us outside of the top person's agenda. If we didn't have these numbers linking things, I don't know if we would've even figured out they were." He sighed and rubbed his face.

Malachi worked the information around in his head. Something niggled at him. "Could it be a former bodyguard with a grudge?" he said, trying to work through it. "A spurned lover from someone? Anyone have a past they haven't mentioned or refused to talk about?"

Owen scoffed. "Most of us have something in our past we don't want to talk about, but no. I can't think of anything right now. Brett would be the best person to ask that to, but I can't guarantee he'll answer. He's good at what he does, and keeping secrets is his best skill. After all, the king needs to trust someone with all their information."

"Someone knows about these tunnels, and as a reporter who researched them and thought it was all bogus, it needs to be someone *in the know*. Someone who was given the information. I doubt they could have just stumbled across the entrances. So, either someone is giving information out to others, or it's someone who already knows the information. Like a former bodyguard or staff household member."

Nick frowned. "I don't know who would fit that bill. We need to get access to former employees. I'm sure Brett has already done it, but we could cross-reference things."

Malachi loved puzzles like that, but he was less sure of himself when so much hung in the balance. "Who else could it be? Has anyone got information from Tarrant yet?"

"The Police Commissioner is interviewing him, but from what I've been told, he doesn't have much to say. He'd never seen the person before and had no contact with anyone prior who had asked him for information or to do anything for them. It almost seems like it was the wrong place and time kind of thing, but I don't trust it. Maybe Tarrant didn't know it was going to happen, but I have a feeling he was targeted."

"Why?"

"You. If this is going the same way as Dominic's and Owen's stories did, they used people around them to lure them in. This would be a way to lure you into the asshole's game, ensuring I take part, too."

Malachi shook his head. "I can't believe all this was happening, and I had no clue."

Nick grinned. "We can keep secrets if we need to." His expression changed but then brightened again.

"What was that?" Malachi studied him.

"What?"

"Something went through your mind right then. What was it?"

Nick licked his lips. "Nothing." Malachi raised his eyebrows, and Nick sighed. "Fine. Nothing I can tell you." He shook his head. "I'm sorry, but even I can't tell you everything. Not yet."

"I don't expect you to, Nick. I understand the need to keep things quiet, but you seemed... I don't know. Confused? If I can help in any way, I'd love to. But not at the cost of you telling me stuff you can't. I won't let you risk your job like that."

"I'm glad to hear it," Brett said from over Malachi's shoulder, making him jump. "Anything?"

"Not yet, though have we looked at former bodyguards?" Nick asked.

A wave of pain washed across Brett's face, but he hid it quickly. "We've looked at the most obvious ones. The ones who left on not-so-good terms. Maybe we should dig deeper."

"Or look into the pasts of the ones who are already here. Do they have someone who holds a grudge against them and is using the other guards to get to them? A way of making that one pay for a perceived slight." Brett stared at him, unblinking, and then he turned and walked away. "Did I say something wrong?" he asked Nick.

Nick watched Brett, shaking his head, but Owen answered. "Sometimes, he'll think of something and go off on a tangent. You might have given him an idea. His brain tends to focus on the new thing and forget where he was in a conversation. Especially when it comes to something like this. Something so important." Owen stood and headed after him.

Malachi could understand. If someone was trying to hurt his family, he would be distracted, too. He bet it was tenfold for Brett, both his guards and the royal family were important to him. They needed to find this son of a bitch and stop him.

"What can we do?"

Nick shook his head. "I honestly don't know. If this is related to me instead of you, we need to go through people I've upset, had arguments with or whatever. That'll be fun."

"If it's one thing I'm good at, it's research. What do you want me to do?"

"Get Felix to get you on a computer," Brett interrupted. "See what you can find out." He met Malachi's gaze. "As much as I want to trust you, Malachi, I can't afford to right now. So, your computer will be monitored."

"I understand, and that's no problem for me. I have plenty of tricks up my sleeve. You might even learn something." It seemed strange teasing the head of security to the royal family, but when Brett's mouth twitched, it was enough of a reward for him to know it was okay.

"Get to work."

"Yes, boss," Nick answered for them.

Malachi was exhausted, but he pushed it away, grabbed a cup of tea—to the turned-up noses of several coffee drinkers—and settled next to Felix. After the man had logged him on, he set to work. He wasn't entirely sure what he was looking for, but he took a name from the list Felix had given him and started work. Once he got into research mode, it was easy to forget bodyguards surrounded him—people who had thought the worst of him until someone had decided to research *him*.

And as he delved deeper into the names, he found out information he never thought he'd know about anyone. How many people were into BDSM that were friends with the royal family? Could there be any truth to the rumours of Club Royal?

Malachi had so many questions. Questions that not only pricked his reporter's brain but also pricked his personal one. If there was some truth to the rumours, could he finally be truthful about what he wanted from a relationship? After all, what man truly wanted a partner who wanted to be whipped before that partner then took control of the sexual acts that came afterwards? He couldn't even explain it properly. Anytime he tried, his partners looked at him like he was an alien.

He hadn't even gone as far as to attend a BDSM club to ask questions. Who could he trust with that knowledge? Who wouldn't recognise him and use it as some way of blackmailing him into doing something for them? And so, he'd shoved those needs down as far as he could and enjoyed a "normal" relationship.

But if there was any truth to the rumours, maybe he could ask for help to figure himself out. He glanced around the room. Despite not knowing most of them to talk to—though he knew all their names—he trusted them all. He'd seen how they worked together and interacted with each other and the royal family, and they were amazing people. Could he risk being laughed at again by asking for help?

Staring back at his screen, he exhaled. Maybe not yet.

"You're one of us now, Malachi. Start believing it," Felix muttered from beside him. "Whatever you need help with, we'll help. You just need to ask."

Malachi held his breath, letting that information seep into his brain. "Thanks."

Maybe. One day.

18

Nick

The last two days had been far too long, and he needed to get Malachi into bed, and not for any other reason than to sleep. As for when they woke—that was a whole other idea.

"Come on. Time to sleep."

"But—"

"Nope. No excuses. Up. Now."

He slid his arms under Malachi's armpits and pulled, dragging him to his feet.

"I need—"

"Sleep. You're right. You do. Come on."

Malachi slumped and rubbed both hands over his face. "Okay."

"Get some rest. I'm sure we'll see you later or tomorrow," Felix said.

Nick wrapped an arm around Malachi's shoulders and led him from the room, waving at Brett before they left. "You're going to have a cracking headache after looking at the screen for so long," he said. Malachi hummed, and Nick smiled. A tired Malachi was a cute Malachi.

They entered the suite, and Nick didn't even bother trying to shower because they were both exhausted. He stripped Malachi down to his boxers and tucked him in bed, even forgoing a teeth brush; one night wouldn't kill them. Malachi snuggled into the pillows, already on his way to sleep, and Nick undressed and joined him. Pulling him back against his chest, Nick sighed and pressed his lips to his nape.

"Sweet dreams, darling," he muttered, already sinking.

He was rudely awakened by his phone blasting through the quiet. Scrambling to reach the bedside table, he answered without looking. "What the hell?"

"Nick, we need you," Dominic said.

Nick sat upright, rubbing his eyes to clear the sleep. "What?"

"Get over to our place now. We need your help."

"Okay. I'm coming."

Dominic ended the call, and Nick scrambled from the bed, hopping over to his discarded clothes and dragging them on.

"What's wrong?" Malachi asked, yawning.

"No idea. Dominic needs help. I've got to go."

Malachi swung his legs over the bed. "I'll come, too."

They dressed quickly, Nick grabbing his gun, and within minutes, they were on their way. Luckily, Dominic didn't live too far from Windsor Castle, and with it being the middle of the night, they were there faster than usual. He parked haphazardly in their driveway and headed for the door. The door swung open before he'd even reached it, and Dominic ushered them in.

"In the kitchen."

"What's going on?"

"You have to see it."

Nick's stomach swooped, and his hands twitched with the need to reach for his gun. He entered the kitchen, and a roar blasted his eardrums, jerking him to a stop. He stared at the people in front of him: Randall, Owen, Evan, Brett, Felix, Landon, Colt and Viola.

"What the fuck?"

"You need a break. We all do," Dominic said, slipping past him to join Randall. "We decided to intervene. This may not be as good as one of your parties, but it's the best we could do at short notice."

He grabbed a bottle of wine and two glasses and poured some into each before handing them to Nick and Malachi.

"Let's toast to—"

"How about giving me a heart attack?" Nick joked, though he was touched they were trying to help. It had been nothing but issue after issue since Malachi had stayed with them. Poor guy might need a breather.

"That's Malachi's job, not ours," Owen quipped, earning a blush from Malachi.

Nick chuckled and wrapped his arm around him. "Let's toast to...us. We're damn good at our jobs, and we're damn good people."

"Cheers to that."

They clinked glasses between them and drank, and then Dominic put some music on. "No work talk tonight," he said. "Talk about anything other than that."

Nick grinned and wandered over to Randall. "Hey, Randall. What's Dominic sound like when he—"

Dominic grabbed him in a chokehold, and if it hadn't been for Randall being quick off the mark, Nick's drink would've ended up on the floor. Dominic took him down, keeping a hold on him, and Nick couldn't do much about it, laughing as he was.

"All right! All right! I give in!" Nick shouted, and Dominic let go. Nick slumped on the floor beside him and glanced over, breathing heavily. After a beat, he said, "Thank you."

Dominic gave a small smile and a nod. "I know what it's like. The worry. The need to figure it out. The panic when you can't.

We'll get the son of a bitch. Eventually, we'll get him, and he won't know what hit him."

Nick breathed through his nose, trying to withhold his emotions. When he could, he grinned. "Where's the karaoke?"

"Not a chance in hell," Dominic said, climbing to his feet and reaching a hand down to drag Nick up, too.

"I'm sure your neighbours would love it. It's *Raining Men, Hallelujah!*" Nick sang, his voice cracking as he knew it would.

Dominic ignored him and turned the volume up. Giving him the middle finger, Nick smiled and headed back to Malachi, who was deep in discussion with Felix. They'd become two peas in a pod since they'd started researching together.

"I hope this isn't shop talk," he said.

"I'm just explaining to Malachi how to kill a man with a fork," Felix deadpanned.

Nick raised his eyebrows. "I would've thought that was fairly self-explanatory, but okay." He grinned.

Felix narrowed his eyes. "You don't have a leg to stand on, my friend. You weren't exactly sleeping the other night when the boss told you to relax, were you?" He tutted towards Malachi. "It's a good job you've already broken him in." He winked.

Nick scraped his teeth across his bottom lip, having no clue what he was on about, and focused on Malachi. "Are you having fun?"

"Jesus, Nick. You've been here fifteen minutes," Felix said. "Give the man a break." He walked off, shaking his head.

Nick watched him go, a little surprised at the outburst. Felix wasn't usually one for snapping at people—except for bad guys—so his slight show of temper was out of character. The man grabbed a bottle of beer and rested his hip against the counter, staring out of the back window and into the darkened garden.

"Hmm."

"I think he's stressed," Malachi said. "He was practically tearing his hair out as we worked earlier. Every avenue we tried was a dead end."

Nick sighed and slid his arm around him again, pressing his lips to his temple. "I know it's hard, but we'll figure it out. I know we will. Felix is the best of the best. He just doesn't believe in his own abilities some days."

Brett stopped beside Felix, muttering something he couldn't hear over the music, but he saw how Felix leaned towards him, and when Brett cupped his nape, Felix's eyes closed.

"Huh."

"Leave it alone, Nick," Malachi said. "That one is not for you to meddle in."

Nick gaped at him. "How dare you! I'll have you know I have an excellent track record of predicting and helping people to get together."

"Maybe so, but that one needs to be left to work alone."

"Why?" Nick was truly interested in what Malachi might've seen that he hadn't.

Malachi shifted closer, lowering his voice. "They spend most of their time together, so they've already got a rapport. They just need to first figure out that they care for each other—if they haven't already—and then admit it. If they can manage that, they might have the chance to build something new from what they already have. But at the moment, the barest wind could blow their foundations. You need to let them do their thing and not mess with those supports."

Nick stared at him. "You truly do have a way with words. It's beautiful."

Malachi flushed. "Thank you."

Despite it being the middle of the night, everyone seemed in fine spirits, and Nick realised exactly how much they all needed the break from work. Sometimes—and not to the Sutcliffes' fault—their work could be long and stressful, especially Brett's role, but they were all such good friends as well, that they all supported the others. Nick had never known a workplace like it. And he wouldn't change it for the world.

Three hours later, he was ready to sleep again, and so was Malachi.

"Thank you all for the amazing night, but we're going home to bed." He'd switched to soft drinks after his half a glass of wine at the very beginning and was confident in his ability to drive. Tucking Malachi under his shoulder, he said goodnight to everyone and led him to the car. He doubted Brett or Felix would sleep when they returned. Knowing them, they'd go straight back to work. It had surprised him that they'd even been there that night at all. But their relationship was something Nick would study from then on. He was intrigued.

"Sleep, sweetheart. I'll wake you when we get there." He closed the car door, his man already falling when Nick saw something under his window wipers. He pulled it free and unfolded the paper, expecting to see an advert for a club or something similar.

But his blood ran cold when he saw a photograph of Malachi's mum and grandma with a red target painted over the top of them.

Nick's heart tripled its rate, and he froze, unsure what move to make. Should he wake Malachi to check on them? Should he keep quiet and check on them himself? Why had he taken the guards from them once Malachi was healthy?

"Fuck, fuck, fuck," he muttered.

Malachi would never forgive him if something happened to them. He pulled out his phone and dialled Felix.

"That was quick. You back already?"

"No, I'm outside. Do you, by any chance, have eyes on Malachi's family?"

Felix paused. "No. Should I?"

"Fuck." Was it a ruse to get him to go there? To get *them* to go there?

"Talk to me, Nick," Felix said, the words not in his ear.

He glanced up and handed Felix the paper. "I don't know what to do, Felix," he whispered. "It'll destroy him if something's happened to them. Do I tell him? Do I not and check for myself? What do I do?"

Felix dragged him into a hug, then stepped back. "You do what you would've done before. You ask for help." He disappeared back inside the house, and within seconds, everyone was outside. Landon and Viola disappeared from the driveway, possibly checking for anyone around. Owen and Colt got into a car and drove off. Brett was on the phone. Dominic and Randall came over to him.

"Wake him up, Nick. Tell him. He won't trust you ever again if you keep stuff from him," Randall said.

Nick inhaled and rounded the car, opening Malachi's door again. He crouched beside him. "Malachi? Sweetheart? Wake up for me. Come on," he coaxed as Malachi slowly roused. "That's it. Open your eyes, sweetheart."

When he did, Malachi gave a dopey smile, but Nick couldn't return it. Malachi frowned and blinked a few more times. "What's wrong?" He yawned.

"I need you to do something for me, but I need you to stay calm first."

Malachi sat straighter, his gaze darting around. "What?"

"I need you to call your mum. I know it's late, but it's important."

"Why?"

Nick swallowed hard, hating the pain he was causing. "They've been targeted, and we need to make sure they're okay."

"What!" Malachi grabbed for his phone, fumbling with it. Nick put his hand over Malachi's. "No! Let me call her!"

"Malachi," Nick's voice broke, "you need to be calm; otherwise, you'll worry her."

"I'm going to worry her, anyway! I'm calling her in the middle of the night!" But he took a breath and then another one. "Okay."

"You can't tell them what's happening. I know that's hard, but we need to keep it between us for now. Can you do that?"

Malachi inhaled again and nodded.

"Owen and Colt are almost at their house," Brett said. "Once you've spoken to her, ask her to let them in so they can check the house. We'll have people guarding them all day from now on." Brett growled. "We'll find them, Malachi. I promise you."

Malachi exhaled and dialled. The longer it rang, the more he trembled, and Nick grabbed his hand between his. When it went to voicemail, Malachi's tears overflowed.

"Try again. She might need a minute to wake and answer," Randall said.

Malachi licked his lips and dialled, closing his eyes while it rang.

"Malachi? What's wrong? What's happened?" his mother said, and there was a collective sigh.

"Hey, Mum. I'm sorry for waking you. I-I know this is stupid, but I had a nightmare that something had happened to you both. I'm going to sound overprotective here, but there are two guards at the house. Could you let them check everything is okay?"

Emily exhaled softly. "Oh, Malachi. You are a worrier. Okay, yes. Let me just get something a bit more decent to wear in company, and I'll let them in."

"Thank you. Their names are Owen and Colt." He bit his lip. "Can I stay on the line until you open the door?"

Emily chuckled. "Okay."

They listened to the rustles of clothing, and Nick hoped no one was in for a nasty surprise.

Brett gave him the thumbs up to say the guards had arrived and nothing seemed amiss from the outside. Nick would withhold judgement until the interior had been checked, too.

Finally, Emily came back on. "I can see two people at the door. Who is it?" she called. There was a murmur and a click before Emily came back louder again. "They're here. Are you feeling better now, Malachi?"

"Yes. I'm so sorry, Mum. Is Grandma okay?"

"She's fine. And you don't need to be sorry. I would be more upset if you lost sleep over a worry that one phone call could alleviate."

Malachi gave a watery chuckle. "I'm sorry, anyway."

"What are you doing worrying about me when you have a man to distract you now?"

Malachi's cheeks flamed in the light of the car, and Nick chuckled. "I'm not even...going there with you."

Emily's chuckle came across loud and clear. "But at least now you're not worrying. You're thinking of your man. A much better use of your time."

Nick rose, leaving Malachi to speak with his mother, and headed to Brett, anger building like a furnace in his stomach. "I don't like that this fucker knows where we all were. He has to be either following us or someone is telling him. Could he have a tracker or something?"

"I agree. I should be grateful that they're not targeting the royal family, but I'm not. They're now going after my family," Brett growled.

Nick raised his eyebrows. Angry Brett was a sight to behold on any day of the week, but pissed-off Brett rarely happened. When it did, everyone needed to beware, especially if the aim was them. But this was next level. He practically vibrated while standing in front of Nick, and as much as he agreed with him, Brett needed to calm down.

Before he could say or do anything, Felix came up and put his hand on Brett's shoulder, leaning to whisper something in his ear. Brett shuddered and closed his eyes, visibly reigning himself in.

Now Nick knew to watch them, their interactions were as clear as a windowpane, but were they already together or just pining for each other?

"Nick!"

Malachi's voice dragged him away from his musings, and he jogged back to the car. The phone was in his lap, and tears streaked his cheeks.

"Are they okay?" He knew they were, but he asked so Malachi could say the answer aloud.

"Yeah, both are fine. Mum checked on Grandma, and she was sleeping." He sighed shakily. "What the heck is going on, Nick?"

"I don't know, sweetheart, but we'll figure it out. I promise we will." He clasped Malachi's hands, squeezing and hoping it helped. When they got back to Windsor, he'd hold him as much as he needed for him to calm down and remember his family was safe.

Nick needed to do something because whoever this asshole was, he was getting too close. He couldn't believe, after all this time, they still didn't have a clue who was pulling the strings at the top. Someone was fucking with them all, taking each guard in turn, but what was the overarching plan? To unsettle them? To kill them all? To get them out of the way and aim for the Sutcliffes? Anything was possible, but he hated not knowing. In not knowing, there were no predictions; nothing they could do to sidestep a potential risk because they couldn't see where it was coming from.

And that scared the fuck out of him.

Smiling, he said, "Come on. Let's go home."

Malachi nodded, and Nick closed the car door. He stalked over to Brett. "Tomorrow, I want everything we have. I want to see it all. Every action, every piece of evidence, every spark of an idea someone has about who and why this is happening."

Brett nodded. "I'll be right beside you going through it all. Again." He sighed and shook his head, his gaze wavering. "It'll be all hands on deck. This has gone on long enough. One piece of good news from today—they finished closing the tunnels."

Nick nodded once and headed for the car, climbing in and driving off. It was only when he parked that Nick had a thought, and as they wandered down the corridors to their suite, he messaged Brett.

NICK: *Can you get the car checked for bugs? It could be how he keeps finding us.*

BRETT: *Good idea.*

Brett's almost immediate answer soothed his anger a little. And as he settled Malachi back into bed, he held him tightly, whispering to him as they both lay there, troubled by what the future could hold. No one would hurt what was his. No one.

19

Owen

Owen and Colt checked through the house fully, except Malachi's grandma's room because she was sleeping, but no one was around. As far as Owen was concerned, whoever was doing this shit was just testing them and making them run around like headless chickens. But what else were they to do? They had to check.

"Thank you for letting us check so late at night, Mrs Sanders," Colt said. "We'll wait outside until the new guards arrive, and then they'll stay with you all the time. They'll wait outside when you're in the house, but if you go anywhere, they'll have to come with you."

Malachi's mother nodded. "I understand. Thank you for doing this to ease Malachi's mind."

Owen almost grinned. She knew it wasn't to ease his mind from a nightmare at all. She wasn't stupid. They left and climbed into Colt's car, getting comfortable for the moment.

"Do you think anyone was going to try anything?" he asked after a few minutes.

Colt sighed and stared out of the window, and Owen let him gather his thoughts. "I think they're trying to find our weak points."

Owen stared at him. "What do you mean?"

"The event, the restaurant, the bathroom, here... They're all tests to see our reactions, our resources, our timings. I could be wrong, but that's where my head keeps going."

Owen mulled it over. It made sense. "Do you think they're going to attempt a large scale attack?"

Colt shrugged. "I don't know. It could be that or it could be nothing. Maybe they're testing Malachi. I'm not sure."

"With everything that's happened over the past few months, coupled with what you've just said, it makes me think attack. Why else would they be aiming it at bodyguards?"

"Bodyguards are easily replaced, though."

Owen grinned. "I love you, too, man."

Colt rolled his eyes. "Idiot."

A car parked behind them, and they got out to greet their replacements. "Foster, Carl, how're things?"

"Good, thanks," Foster replied, clapping hands with him. "Things are hotting up, it seems. Brett didn't say much. Just asked us to come here."

Owen pursed his lips. "Unfortunately. Keep an eye on them, okay? They're family now."

Carl frowned. "How come?"

Owen glanced at Colt, grinning. "How have they not heard about Nick's mighty fall?"

"No idea. They must've been under a rock." Colt shrugged.

"We've only just got back from holiday," Carl whined.

"This is Nick's new boyfriend's family's house. And guess who the boyfriend is?" Foster and Carl shared a look, and both shrugged. "Malachi Sanders."

He watched with undisguised humour as their jaws dropped.

"The reporter?" Foster said.

"One and the same," Owen confirmed. He sobered a bit. "As much as I'm happy he's found someone, poor Malachi has been brought into this...whatever it is, and now his family has been targeted as well."

"Whoever these fuckers are, they'll get what's coming for them," Foster said.

"That they will," Colt said. He nudged Owen. "Come on. I need sleep, and I have to take you back first."

"Okay. Take care of them."

"Like we would our own family," Foster promised.

Owen and Colt sped away, each lost in their thoughts. Owen hated that whoever had targeted him, and Dominic before him, was now after Nick or Malachi. They needed to shut this down and quickly because it was pissing him right off.

20

Malachi

Malachi had slept like shit, even though he knew his family was okay. The shock of seeing them supposedly targeted by whoever it was had seeped right down to his bones. It had been real before, but that had made it hell on earth.

By the time he woke the next morning, despite their extremely late midnight rendezvous with Nick's friends, he was alert and eager to get back to research mode. The offer to get to know the royal family behind the scenes had been put on the back burner as far as he was concerned, and although he wanted to get to know them, he needed to find this person first.

Freshly showered, he found Nick on the phone in the living area, laptop balanced on his knees.

"—seems to be a link there, maybe." He made a few noises as he listened to the other person. Malachi set a cup ready to make tea when Nick finished, not wanting the boiling kettle to disturb him. "Okay, I'll add that to my list to check out. Thanks. Speak to you later." He ended the call and faced him. "Morning. I didn't wake you, did I?"

Malachi shook his head, leaning over the back of the sofa for a kiss. "I was instantly awake this morning. Eager to get on. Do you want another drink?"

"Sure. I'll never say no to coffee."

Malachi chuckled and made them a drink each before settling beside him. "Are we heading back to Sec HQ today?"

"We can, or I can get you a laptop and we can stay here. What would you prefer?"

He thought about it. It might be nice to spend some more time with Nick alone, even if they were technically working. "Here would be good, but only if it doesn't cause problems with security and me."

"It'll be fine. Have you spoken to your mum this morning?"

"No, I thought I'd let her start her day without the reminder that I woke her up and lied to her." He sighed. "She won't be happy if she finds out."

"She'd understand, but I bet she already knows. Mother's intuition and all that." Nick huffed a laugh.

"You're probably right. She'll have my guts for garters when I next visit."

Nick laughed. "I've not heard that expression for a long time."

Malachi's cheeks heated. "It's something Grandma always says. I'm sure I have lots more priceless ones in my brain somewhere."

"I can't wait to hear them," Nick said, studying him.

"What?" Malachi finally asked.

Nick shook his head, a small smile playing around his mouth. "I love that I can get to hear them. That this isn't a quick flying thing we've got. I love that we're thinking long term. At least, I am."

Malachi put his cup down and grabbed the laptop from Nick's lap, putting it on the table before straddling him. Sliding his arms around his neck, he smiled, and though his stomach was churning with the potential for being rebuked, he laid his heart out. "I am, too. This is it for me. You're it for me." He inhaled. "I love you."

Nick's eyes widened, his jaw dropping, and his gaze frantically mapped Malachi's face. "You do?"

Malachi nodded, scratching his nails through Nick's hair. "I love you, Nick Tennant. I think I probably did before I even let myself. You're a kind, generous, funny, lovable rogue, and I love you." Now Nick hadn't thrown his words back at him, Malachi felt braver.

Suddenly, Nick crushed him against him, burying his face in Malachi's neck. He trembled, and Malachi's heart grew more when he heard the muffled sniffles. Nick wasn't one to show his emotions all the time, needing to keep them inside him because of his job, and with his friends, he would let some of them out, but with Malachi...he bared it all. So many nuances about this man made him love him even more.

Nick pulled back, cupping Malachi's cheeks. "I love you." His voice broke, but it had never sounded more beautiful.

This time, Malachi's eyes filled, but he grinned. "We're such saps."

Nick smiled. "I wouldn't have it any other way."

Dropping his head, he brushed his lips across Nick's mouth, letting his eyelids close and the scent and feel of him settled into Malachi's bones. And as the kiss deepened, the taste of him was something he would never forget.

They pulled back a long few minutes later, and Nick skimmed his thumb across Malachi's bruised lips. "Quick question. Why Kai Ruffers?"

Malachi grinned. "Because I wanted to rough them up for being assholes."

"I love you."

Malachi smiled. "I love you."

Exhaling, Nick said, "Let's catch this asshole so we can live in peace and have a party, yeah?"

"Deal."

Malachi made them some more drinks while Nick ran down to Sec HQ for a laptop he could use. While he waited, he checked his emails. He'd been lax in checking them for the past couple of days because of everything that had happened, and the ones that had come before weren't anything to write home about. Nothing had ever jumped out at him as being more than nasty words.

Until now.

Malachi/Kai,

Being two-faced is not a positive personality quirk. You either love the royals or you hate them. Which is it? What would your boss say to finding out that you're messing with his articles by counteracting them under the Kai Ruffers name? That you didn't have the same opinions as Adelaide Thompson?

Would you still have a job to support your family in times of ill health?

And to be in a relationship with the very same bodyguard that protects the royals? Tut, tut, tut, Malachi.

Personally, I don't think you deserve such benefits when you don't believe in what you write. I think I might need to rectify that. Nick looks so delicious through a scope.

Hold on tight, Malachi. Your life is about to become a rollercoaster.

The moment he finished reading, he was up and out of the suite, racing down the corridors towards Sec HQ. Nick had to be okay. He had to be. He was inside Windsor Castle. No one could shoot him there, right?

Pain lanced through Malachi's chest as he pumped his legs and arms faster through the corridor, but as he rounded a corner, he crashed into someone, landing on his ass. He didn't care. He scrambled up.

"Malachi! What's wrong?" a voice shouted, but he didn't have time. The voice didn't belong to Nick, and he needed to find him, needed to make sure he was okay.

He reached Sec HQ and banged on the door with his fist. The door opened a sliver, and he started babbling immediately.

"Where…Nick? He…safe? Where's…Nick?" he panted.

"Woah, calm down, Malachi. He went to fetch a laptop from down the corridor," Felix said, holding Malachi's shoulders.

Malachi pushed away from him, leaving the room again and scanning both ways. He chose the opposite direction from where he had come and shouted for him. "Nick! Where are you?"

"Malachi, tell me what's going on?" Felix said from beside him.

"Email. Threatened Nick. Need to check…"

Nick came out from a doorway, and a sob left Malachi's throat, his knees giving out and slamming him to the floor. He was okay. He was alive. Arms came around him, and he clung to them, soaking in Nick's scent, and his heart calmed. His entire body ached, and his eyes burnt with the continuous tears seeping from them. But Nick was safe.

"Malachi, sweetheart, what's wrong?"

Malachi inhaled, clearing his throat before he looked up. Nick went to move, but Malachi clutched at him.

"Okay, we'll stay here for a minute," Nick soothed. "Can you tell me what happened?"

Malachi nodded. "I was checking my emails while I was waiting for you. You were…" His breath caught.

"Can I see?"

Malachi nodded but couldn't remember where he put his phone. He looked down at himself.

"Here. You dropped it in Sec HQ," Felix said, holding it out.

"Thanks," he murmured. He unlocked it and handed it to Nick before closing his eyes and tightening his hold again. All this up and down emotional shit was getting old. What he wouldn't give for a balanced, easy life from then onwards.

"Fucker. Can you trace this, Felix?" Nick said.

"I can try. Malachi, could I borrow your phone for a moment, please?"

Malachi nodded against Nick's chest, concentrating on his heartbeat, the one thing tethering him to that moment.

"Let's move you somewhere more comfortable than the corridor floor, yeah?" Nick said, and Malachi finally disentangled himself. Nick helped him to stand.

"I swear I'm more stable than this usually," Malachi joked.

Nick held him. "You can be as unstable as you want with me. It won't change my opinion of you."

Malachi scoffed. "Give it time."

They settled into some chairs in Sec HQ, and Malachi rubbed a hand over his face, his entire body feeling far too heavy and achy. A cup of tea was put in his hands, and Nick covered them to stop the trembling as he brought it to his mouth. The heat seeped into him, and he relaxed. Conversations were happening around him, but he couldn't make his ears work enough to dial into them, so he stopped trying, just being content that Nick was beside him, touching him.

"—Tarrant's laptop."

Malachi tuned in at the last minute. "What?"

"It was sent from Tarrant's laptop. The problem is, that laptop was in police hands the last time we checked. Either someone has managed to get their hands on it to send it, or it's someone who knows how to hack networks."

"This guy, or his accomplice, was able to delete that camera footage. Would this be a stretch for something he was capable of?" Brett asked.

Felix was already shaking his head. "If he could do that, he could do this. And that means they could be anywhere. Anyone."

Malachi didn't need to ask what that meant because the silent and stony people around him told him it was bad news. He wasn't a technophobe, but he wasn't brilliant at hacking. He could do minor things—not that he'd tell anyone that—but he had no idea how to pull something like this off. Did he know anyone who could? No one came to mind.

"Let me take you back to the room. We can get some work done while we relax." Nick stood, but Malachi shook his head.

"Can we stay here? I feel better about being around others."

Nick nodded. "Of course. Let me get that laptop—"

"I'll get it," Felix said, disappearing before Malachi could protest Nick leaving him again.

He'd have to thank him for that. Malachi wasn't sure he could stand Nick being out of his sight for a while. They moved from their seats to ones at a table, side by side. Nick sent someone to fetch his laptop from their suite, and Malachi sent him a grateful smile.

When he was finally set up on a laptop, he was feeling mostly back to normal, although he found himself glancing sideways more than once to check Nick was still there. And he was, a crease between his eyebrows as he stared at his screen, his thumb and index finger pulling at his bottom lip. Nick turned his head and shot him a wink, reaching out to put his hand on Malachi's thigh, grounding him further.

"Sorry," he whispered.

"Don't be. I know how it feels to be worried."

"I don't think my heart can take anymore worry," he admitted.

Nick leaned over, sliding his arm around his shoulders. "We can share the worry now. Sharing halves it, remember?"

Malachi rested his head on Nick's shoulder, closing his eyes and letting himself soak it in for a moment. They had work to do, so he didn't linger, but the brief contact was enough to bolster him again.

"Okay, I'm good."

"Let's do this."

He wasn't sure how long they had been working before his eyes started burning, but it was long enough for different guards to be in the room to who they had started with. His research had proved fruitless, and he was pissed.

"Don't worry about it," Nick said. "We've been at this for months and have found nothing that would help us identify them. As we mentioned before, they've been using lackeys to do their dirty work. They don't seem to have got their hands dirty themselves."

"Did we ever figure out who the guy was that asked Tarrant to deliver that message?"

"He sat with a sketch artist and produced something, but we've had no luck in finding them so far. Felix is going to send it to someone he knows who can check all the CCTV cameras with facial recognition, or something like that, anyway. I don't understand it all. But hopefully, that will give us something."

"Fingers crossed." Malachi sighed.

"Right!" Brett called. "Enough for now. Everyone go and eat. I don't want to see your faces for two hours at least, unless you are here for guarding duties. Understood?"

Guards agreed and disappeared quicker than a stink bomb could empty a room. Nick was more reluctant, but after more prodding from Brett—who almost had to ban him from the room for the next *two days* if he didn't listen—he finally packed up his stuff, threaded his fingers into Malachi's and tugged him from the room.

"I hate not being able to do anything, but we could do with a nap, I think," Malachi said, trying to make Nick feel better.

"I think we can arrange that."

They both decided a quick shower was in order, and then they snuggled, naked, in bed, Nick's fingers tracing patterns across Malachi's back. Silence descended, and Malachi could tell Nick was lost in his thoughts, just like he often was, but he wanted to do something to help distract him. Malachi used his fingertips to draw lines down his chest and stomach towards his ultimate goal.

When he reached the wiry hair surrounding his cock, he slid his fingers through it, like he would've had it been the hair on his head. Nick's cock perked up, brushing against the back of Malachi's hand as it grew. Putting Nick out of his misery, he slid his thumb and index finger around the base, using his other fingers to tease his balls. It wouldn't be enough, he knew it, but he loved the breathy sounds coming from him, the shuddering rise and fall of his chest.

Wrapping his hand completely around his shaft, Malachi stroked to the head, finding plenty of precome to slick his way back down. He started a steady rhythm, twisting around the head on every upward stroke, and Nick's grip tightened on him. Malachi kissed his chest and increased his speed. He lifted his eyes to Nick, the man gasping for air even as he reached for more.

Nick's jaw clamped shut, and Malachi stroked faster. Nick squeezed his eyes closed, clenched his stomach muscles and came, ropes of white fluid streaking his chest. Malachi marvelled at the silent climax, knowing full well he could never do that himself. But if Nick's red face was anything to go by, he shouldn't do it either.

Finally, Nick breathed again, his chest heaving, and he met Malachi's gaze. "I wasn't expecting that, but thank you."

Malachi grinned. "You don't need to thank me for that. I love watching you come." He paused. "One thing, though." Nick frowned and nodded. "Please breathe next time. You were going rather red."

Nick burst out laughing, and Malachi's heart clenched at the joyous sound. Everyone needed to hear that more often, so he made it his job to pull that sound from him as often as possible.

"Okay. I just didn't want to break the quiet cocoon we'd built."

Malachi smiled. "You can always break the silence with sex noises, Nick. Always."

Nick leaned down for a kiss, and within seconds, Malachi was panting in the aftermath of his own release, a quick and dirty orgasm that left him reeling.

"Now let's sleep," Nick said.

"Aren't we going to shower again?"

"Nope," he yawned. "Too tired."

"You'll regret that in a couple of hours."

"Probably." Nick, however, didn't move except to wrap himself around Malachi.

It took very little for him to fall asleep, even with the upset of the day, but it was probably because of the stress he'd been under, and before he slipped into sleep, he made a note to call his mum when he woke. Insomnia? What insomnia? When Nick was around, it seemed he didn't struggle with sleeping.

Two hours later, when Nick's phone alarm woke them, they unstuck themselves from each other and showered, bringing some pleasure to the bathroom as well. Malachi couldn't get enough of him. Once they were dressed and ready to attempt to get back into Sec HQ—if Brett would let them—Malachi stood and stared down at his phone. He hadn't wanted to check his emails, but he was a glutton for punishment.

For the second time that day, he wished he didn't own an email address.

"I have another email." Malachi sucked in a breath, not wanting to share it but knowing he needed to.

"What does it say?" Nick asked, coming to look over his shoulder.

Oh, my bad. Wrong brother.

21

Nick

Nick stared at the words, trying to understand what they meant, but he couldn't. What did they mean, the wrong brother? There weren't any brothers at the castle, so what were they...? His thoughts stuttered to a stop. Malachi took the phone away, but the words were burnt into his retinas.

"Nick? Sit down."

The words broke him from his fugue, and he pulled his phone from his pocket, dialling Jonah. He had two brothers. They had to be okay.

"Hey, what's up?"

"Jonah? Are you all right? Where are you?" Nick fired at him.

"Woah, bloody hell, Nick. Where's the fire? I'm in France, remember? Work sent me here last week."

Nick exhaled but didn't settle. "Keep your eyes open, Jonah. Things are happening back here, and I need you to stay safe, okay?"

"Sure thing. Eyes open."

When Nick had taken the job protecting the royals, he'd known there was a chance his family would be targeted in some way, so he'd prepared them right from the beginning. They had to make sure they were aware of their surroundings at all times, even more so since Eliza's incident.

"What's going on, Nick?"

"I can't talk right now. I have to get hold of the others. Just stay safe, yeah?"

"Sure thing."

He ended the call and dialled again. Rye's phone rang and rang until it clicked to voicemail. He hung up and tried again. And a third time. "Come on. Pick up." A fourth. "Where are you, Rye?"

Malachi rested his hand on Nick's arm when he tried dialling a fifth time. "Let's go ask Felix if he can find him."

Nick let him lead him down the corridors to Sec HQ, all the while redialling his brother. Rye would never *not* answer. Never. Images he didn't want in his head filled it anyway, and he swallowed hard, hoping they didn't come true. He couldn't lose his brother. Any of his family.

"Have you found him?" he asked Felix when they entered, but the man looked at him, bewildered.

Malachi squeezed Nick's hands. "We've not explained yet."

"I can't get hold of Rye. We got another email. We need to find him. He's not answering his phone. Where is he, Felix?"

Images bombarded him, and he cradled his head, staring at his phone. Where was he? He kept dialling, religiously lifting it to his ear to hear it connect, but Rye's voicemail was all he heard. Not the real-life, alive version of his brother. A recorded message that wasn't enough reassurance. He needed...something. Anything.

"What's wrong?" Rye's voice broke through Nick's internal dialogue.

"Rye?"

"Yes, what's happened? Why are you blowing up my phone while I'm in a meeting?"

Nick's entire body deflated, and he exhaled, barely able to breathe. "I was worried," was all he could say.

Rye sighed in his ear. "I'm fine, Nick. I'm—ahh!"

A sharp sound echoed through the phone, and Nick frowned. "What was that? It sounded like—Rye? Rye!" He stood, pressing the phone closer to his ear. "Rye!" He heard people talking and shouting down the line, but no one took the phone and told him what was going on. He stared at Malachi. "He's at work, Kai," he whispered. "He's safe at work, right?"

"Fuck."

A murmured curse hit his ears, and he glanced at Felix, who lifted his gaze to Nick.

"What is it?" he croaked.

Felix glanced at Malachi and then back at him. "There's been a shooting."

A stone settled in Nick's stomach. "Where?" He knew where.

"Rye's office. Two dead, three wounded."

Nick's knees locked to keep him upright. "Who's dead, Felix?"

Felix hesitated. "I don't know."

"WHO'S DEAD?"

"I don't know!" Felix shouted, pounding at his keyboard.

Nick turned and ran, ignoring the shouts from behind him and the pain shooting through his calf. He raced through the corridors to outside and his car. He unlocked it, climbing into the driver's seat and slamming the door, before starting the engine. Before he could drive off, the passenger door opened, and Malachi slid in, followed by the back doors, with Owen and Colt joining them. He didn't argue, just slammed his foot on the accelerator and headed for Rye's office.

He didn't hear the conversation in the car, though he knew they were talking. All he could focus on was getting to his brother.

If the panic was half of what Malachi had felt earlier that day when he was racing to find Nick or when he was worried about his family, he could understand how terrified he'd been. The not knowing was the worst thing about it all. If he knew one way or the other, maybe he could figure out how to act, what to feel.

Breaking far too many speed limits, he finally abandoned the car down the cordoned-off street leading to Rye's workplace. He went under the tape and headed for the paramedics and ambulances.

"Sir! You can't be here! You need to get back behind the tape!"

Nick ignored him, seeing gurneys being wheeled out of the door, two with blankets completely covering them. He stopped. He wasn't sure he could know now he was there.

"Nick, he's over here," Malachi said, touching his arm.

Nick blinked and focused on where Malachi pointed. He could see Rye's face. Glancing over at the other gurneys, he breathed easier. He could *see* Rye's face. Of the six gurneys, two were covered completely, and he could *see* Rye's face. Rye was wounded. Rye wasn't dead.

He went over, legs trembling with every step. "Rye?" he whispered.

Rye's eyelids were dark against his pale skin, and Nick leaned forward. A gauze dressing covered his chest, red seeping through.

"Excuse me. Who are you?" a paramedic said, pressing a hand to Nick's chest and pushing him away.

"I'm his brother," he growled, pushing right back.

She let go. "Sorry."

"How is he?"

She sighed. "He has a chest wound, but we managed to stabilise him. We're taking him to hospital now. Do you want to ride with us?"

Nick nodded and watched them lift Rye into the ambulance. He turned to Malachi. "I need to—"

Malachi nodded. "Go. I'll be there soon."

Nick refocused on Rye again, climbing in when the paramedic said he could. He settled on the seat and reached for Rye's hand, hesitating until the paramedic nodded at him. He slipped his hand under the sheet and carefully held his brother's hand, needing that connection. He wasn't allowed to die. He couldn't. All of this was Nick's fault, and he refused to risk his family any longer. The moment Rye was well, Nick was handing in his resignation. He couldn't put them through this again.

As soon as they arrived at the hospital, Rye was wheeled away, and a nurse led him to a comfortable chair in a small room away from the main waiting area. He dropped his head into his hands and rested his elbows on his knees. Calling his parents was essential, but he just needed a minute. Tears dripped down his nose, and his entire body shook with the force of his sobs, but eventually, he eased.

A tissue appeared in front of him, and he jerked back, eyes widening until he saw Malachi.

"Sorry," Malachi whispered. "I wasn't sure if you'd heard me come in."

More tears filled Nick's eyes, and he dropped to the floor, wrapping his arms around Malachi's waist, his cheeks pressed against his chest.

"It's okay, Nick. He'll be okay. He'll be okay."

The repeated mantra helped him to calm down again, and Malachi helped him to sit back on the seat. When he'd got hold of himself, he pulled out his phone. "I need to call Mum and Dad."

"They already know," Malachi said. "I called them before I came in. They should be here soon."

Nick's heart skipped a beat at the love shining from Malachi's eyes, and he pressed his lips to his. "I love you."

Malachi smiled. "I love you."

The door opened, and his parents came in, Eliza following. "How is he?" his mother asked, grabbing hold of Nick when he rose.

"He has a chest wound, but he's alive. I've not heard anything else since we arrived." His eyes filled again, and he was so sick of crying. "I'm sorry."

"It's not your fault. You don't have control over other people's actions."

"But it might be my fault—"

"Pssh," she said, waving his words away. "Doesn't matter what job you have. It doesn't give people the right to go around shooting others just because they feel like it. You know we'd never blame you because of your job."

"Well, I'm not going to have it for much longer, so you don't need to worry."

His father pinned him with his gaze. "Don't be ridiculous. You'll be a bodyguard until you're too old to move."

Nick shook his head. "I'm done. I can't let this happen again."

His father stepped closer, grabbing his nape and holding him still. "You're bloody good at what you do, Nick. Don't let anyone take that away from you."

"What? So I let them take my family instead?" His voice rose with each word.

"If that happens, it happens. But you fight every day for the right side of the coin. Quitting your job won't change how these people act, but having you keeping people safe means I can sleep at night."

Nick stared at him. Why was he not mad at him for causing Rye's injuries? Why was he not ranting and raving about Nick not taking care of his family before anything else? Other families probably would have.

He opened his mouth to argue when a doctor entered the room. "Mr and Mrs Tennant?" His parents nodded and stepped closer. "Rye is doing well after the surgery. The bullet went straight through him, but it did a little damage to his chest. We repaired everything with no problems, but now we need to let his body do the healing. He's in intensive care while we observe to make sure nothing unexpected happens, but I have no doubt he'll make a full recovery."

Nick sank onto a chair, and Malachi wrapped his arms around him. He closed his eyes and just breathed. His mind, full of what-ifs and what-nows, kept churning through everything, but he let it all bypass his conscious thoughts. He needed a mental health break right then. He heard nothing more, letting the conversation sink into the background. His mind drifted, remembering times from when Rye had been born, through his childhood, and the way he clung to Nick whenever he left to go somewhere. He couldn't lose his mini-me.

The thought made him chuckle, and Malachi asked, "Are you okay?"

Nick nodded, finally back in the room. "The son of a gun is too strong to be taken out by a bullet. He has too much to live for." He stood. "I'm sorry, but I need to go," he told his parents, the doctor having disappeared at some point. "I'm going to find who did this."

His mum hugged him. "I know you will, but I want you to rest first."

Nick shook his head. "I've rested enough lately. I need to do this. I can rest after."

She looked at Malachi. "Please take care of him? Make sure he eats and sleeps. He tends not to when he's distracted."

"I will. I'll stick right to him enough that he'll do it to make me go away." He grinned.

"I doubt that'll happen, but thank you. It was nice to meet you."

Nick threaded his fingers through Malachi's, and they headed for the door. He needed to see the police report and to find any information they had on where the shot came from, if they even had any idea at that point.

Malachi led him to the car and drove them back to Windsor without a word.

"What is it with these guys that they like shooting?" he muttered to himself, rubbing his jaw.

"What?"

Nick glanced across at him. "Whoever this guy is, or whoever these people are behind it, they like using guns. Dominic was shot, and Randall was held at gunpoint, as was May. Granted, Owen and Evan nearly got blown up, but not before Owen had been shot. And now, it's guns again. It's almost like they don't know any other way."

"Like they've been brought up around them or they've been trained to use them?"

Nick stared at him. "Military?"

"Makes sense. How they could get into places undetected. How they know people who can alter camera footage. It's all readily available to military personnel."

"But what's the point? What are they trying to do? What's the point they're trying to make?"

Malachi exhaled, pulling into Windsor Castle. "Chaos?"

Nick shook his head. "I could've gone with that if we had been all over the place and in chaos, but we're not. We're taking it as we normally would. We're stressed, of course, but not chaotic."

"To prove they can?"

Nick paused on that, but his gut was telling him no. He said as much. "With most people, we know what they're after because they make it abundantly clear, almost right from the beginning. It's almost like this is..." He froze, gaze locked on Malachi. "Cat and mouse."

"What? He's testing us? Seeing what the reaction times are?"

That didn't feel right, either. "I'm not sure. I need to talk this over with Brett."

They climbed from the car and, within minutes, were settled around a table with Brett. Nick explained his thoughts, trying to vocalise what his gut was telling him, but it wasn't easy. Brett didn't laugh him away, though. If anything, his expression grew grimmer by the second.

"The idea has merit. Military personnel would have that experience and ability. Or it could be someone who has friends with that experience. Either way, looking into that area would prove beneficial. I'll get someone on it straight away."

"We're going to keep researching what we can, and I want to see the police report," Nick said.

"It should already be in your inbox. They haven't found the location of the shooter yet. They're bringing in a professional who can figure out the trajectory."

"Same one as last time?" Nick raised his eyebrows.

Brett tilted his head. "I'm not sure. Why?"

"Aren't they trained?"

"You think it could be someone like that?"

Nick shrugged. "Why not? They'd be giving away where they'd made the shot from, but they could be convinced we'd find nothing. Getting cocky."

Brett nodded slowly. "I'll look into that, too."

Nick and Malachi settled at two computers, side by side, working through their own research areas to see what they could dig up. Nick read the police report, which, as usual, was scarce and had little to offer. What they did have, though, was something unexpected. Video footage. A witness had been recording on her phone at the time and had caught the shooting in the background. They had been a short distance away, and parked cars hid some of it, but Nick could see the impact of the bullet as it hit Rye and sent him sprawling to the ground. A lump made a home in his throat, but Malachi squeezed his shoulder, helping to dislodge it.

"We'll find them."

He spent the next few hours scouring everything he could find, rubbing his eyes more than once when things got bleary. When Malachi cleared his throat, Nick expected a reprimand. Instead, he got words he hadn't expected.

"Nick, I think this was staged."

His head shot up. "What do you mean?"

"He sent that email an hour before I read it. But the shot didn't happen until you were talking to Rye. He wanted you to hear it. He purposefully waited. How did he hear you? Was Rye's phone bugged? Yours? Mine? Did he have some satellite...whatever to let him hear your conversation with Rye?"

"It's not an impossibility," Felix interjected. "They're more common than most people believe. And easy to make if you know how and don't want anyone to know you have one."

Malachi and Nick shared a look. "Military," they chorused.

Felix nodded. "Some would know how to do it. Some are trained to know how to mock things together in case of emergency, like their radio breaking or something."

Nick frowned. "So, is he listening to *us*? Or just sometimes?"

"Let me check for any abnormalities in our frequencies. I might be able to tell if anyone is piggybacking off our signals, but it might not be so if they are using something else." Felix had moved to his computer and already started typing before he finished his words.

Nick rubbed at his eyes and then his temples, unable to stop a yawn.

"After this, we're going to bed," Malachi said. "You won't be any good to anyone without a brain rest."

Nick wanted to argue, but he couldn't. "Okay."

Malachi opened his mouth as if to counter Nick's argument and paused when there wasn't one. He narrowed his eyes. "Am I going to have to sleep on top of you to make sure you don't sneak off in the middle of the night?"

Nick chuckled. "Maybe. Would that be such a hardship?"

"I never said it would be. I was just wondering." Malachi smirked.

"You're always welcome to sleep on top of me."

Malachi's cheeks heated, but he didn't reply.

Abruptly dropping into his chair, Felix cursed. "Fuck me."

Nick rose and went to him. "What is it?"

"I should've checked. I thought we were clear..." His voice trailed off, his face paling. He turned wide eyes to Nick. "They've been piggybacking off our radios. They're likely to have heard everything."

"Have you stopped it?"

Felix nodded slowly. "I should've checked. It never occurred to me."

Nick squeezed his shoulder. "You can't do everything, Felix. And we've found it now. So where does that leave us?"

"Up shit creek," Brett said, his mouth a grim line. "I've just got off the phone from Commissioner Thomas. Tarrant Milton is dead."

Nick stared at him. "I thought we had him being watched?"

"We did."

"I'm starting to worry about any potential witnesses."

"You're not the only one."

22

Felix

Felix felt like a failure. He'd missed catching the ball too many times lately, and it was pissing him off. Maybe he wasn't cut out for the job. Maybe he should quit, and they could get someone else to do it better.

He focused on the computer screen as the conversation continued around him, the words bleeding into muted tones as his eyes scanned the data on it. Why hadn't he checked? It was something he did regularly, just as a general upkeep type of task, but he hadn't checked since... He couldn't remember the last time, which meant it had been far too long. How long had they been listening to them? Had his mistake cost them something? Was he the cause of Tarrant's death?

A hand gripped his nape, and he didn't flinch, recognising the hold and closing his eyes.

"Stop it," Brett said. "It wasn't your fault."

"Yes, it was. I should've checked."

"Yes, you should have, but then I should've told you to, as well. Things happen, and things get missed. It's not all on your shoulders, Felix."

Felix glanced at him. "It's just on yours instead, you mean?"

Brett stared back, his eyes showing a bank of stories he would never tell anyone. No matter how close they were. Not even Felix. His hand tightened.

"It's my job."

"It's mine, too."

Brett sighed and shook his head slowly. "You don't need this on you, Felix. Let me bear the weight. You need to keep going. Keep being the brilliant IT guy and bodyguard that I know you are."

A lump appeared in Felix's throat at his words. It was almost like a goodbye, but that couldn't be right. The only way Brett was leaving this place was in a coffin, and that was something he himself had said several times. He loved the Sutcliffes—they all did—but there was something about Brett's need to keep them safe that had always perked Felix's interest. He wanted to dig deep into Brett's past, but he'd once promised he wouldn't. That he would accept whatever information Brett gave him without questioning or researching for more. And Felix would keep that promise. But only if it meant he was safe. If Brett or anyone else was in danger because of something he didn't know, he would break that promise with only a second thought. It was nothing anyone else hadn't voiced before. Just not about Brett.

"I'm still here," he said instead of pouring out his thoughts.

Brett brushed his thumb against Felix's neck and then released him. "Good." He turned away. "I can't do this without you," he murmured.

Felix's heart began beating again, harder than before, but with purpose. He wouldn't let anyone down. He would find out what the fuck was going on, and they would stop it all.

These fuckers were going down.

23

Malachi

23

A
lthough Malachi had no love for Tarrant Milton, he hadn't wanted him dead, either. The whole thing was...

"Shut the fuck up, Malachi. Or should I say, Kai? You're a traitor. Someone who makes people think they are aligned, when actually they're not. What do you do, huh? Gather information about us for the royal family? It wouldn't surprise me. But now I'm told you have to pay."

Malachi gasped and jerked as the voice filled his head. He closed his eyes, frowning, trying to figure out where he'd heard the words and who had said them, but it was as if they were just beyond his reach. He didn't think he'd imagined it. The voice seemed so real, and he recognised it but couldn't put a face to it. He shook his head again and pushed it aside. Hopefully, he'd remember later.

Nick paced from wall to wall, and Malachi had seen enough. He stood. "Right, we're done for now." Nick opened his mouth to complain, but Malachi held up his hand. "We're both exhausted. Let's go."

Exhaling, Nick dropped his hands to his side and nodded. "Okay."

He'd expected more of an argument and wasn't too proud to use Nick's mother against him, but he hadn't needed to. Instead, they headed to the suite together, and before Nick could collapse on the bed, he dragged him into the bathroom.

"Shower first. It's been a long day."

Nick chuckled. "It's barely six o'clock."

"Exactly my point."

The water was amazing. It soothed the aches and pains he'd developed from sitting for so long. But most of all, a wet Nick was a delight to look at. When Nick turned to the spray, Malachi dropped to his knees and waited for him to turn around, and once he did, Malachi wasted no time in guiding his cock to his mouth. Nick groaned the moment he sucked him in, and Malachi relaxed his throat to take him deeper, not wanting to drag this out too long because he had a feeling, the moment Nick climaxed, he'd be dead on his feet. Malachi wouldn't be far behind him, but he wasn't angling for a release for himself, but Nick needed one. So much had happened over the past few days and weeks, and he needed to let it go before he exploded with it all.

He licked around the head, thrumming his tongue against the nerves beneath it, and then sank down again. He moaned when he was deep, and Nick slid his fingers into Malachi's hair, thrusting his hips gently. Malachi glanced up, and Nick's hooded gaze was on him, watching him work his dick.

"Fuck, Kai. You're everything I ever needed. Oh, fuck."

Malachi grabbed Nick's hips and encouraged him to thrust, and then focused on breathing when he could and sucking when he couldn't. Nick tightened his hold in warning, a telltale flush on his chest that had nothing to do with the temperature of the water.

"Kai..."

Malachi lifted off and wrapped a hand around him. "Paint me, Nick."

Nick's breath stuttered, and then he was coming over Malachi's face and neck. He felt an overwhelming need to rub it in, and so he did, closing his eyes and basking in the sensuality of the act.

Dropping to his knees, Nick fused their lips, and Malachi clung on, needing him as much as he needed air. Their tongues duelled, their chests heaved, and they eventually pulled apart.

"How did I get lucky enough to have you?" Nick said.

Malachi smiled, knowing he probably looked a bit dopey, but he didn't care. "Time for bed."

"You need to finish. You're as hard as a rock."

"I don't need to. I'm enjoying this."

Nick kissed him again. "Let's wash you off then, and you can sleep as you are if that's your wish."

He loved that Nick didn't make him feel like he should come. Some guys thought it was a sign of masculinity if they made someone climax, but sometimes, Malachi just enjoyed the arousal constantly spearing through him with no end in sight. It was...him. And Nick seemed to accept it without question, something no one else ever had.

He, unfortunately, washed away Nick's release, but his cock still stood proudly as they climbed into bed.

"The moment you want me to take care of that, let me know," Nick said, and Malachi's heart grew some more.

"I didn't think I could love you anymore, but I do."

"Not sure I deserve it, but I'll take it, anyway." Nick kissed his shoulder, once again the big spoon, and Malachi was asleep before he knew it.

The phone ringing woke them—yet again—and while Nick answered it, Malachi cursed their choice to bring phones into the bedroom. Maybe he could make it a rule that phones be left outside so they weren't constantly interrupting their sleep.

"Uh-huh... That's great... Yeah, I can be there in twenty minutes... Are you sure? I don't mind... Okay, I'll visit him this afternoon instead... Yes, I've slept... No, I haven't eaten yet because you woke us with your call. Not that I'm complaining."

Malachi snorted. It must be his mother. It sounded like good news, and he hoped Rye had woken up. He hadn't heard how long they expected him to sleep off the anaesthesia. Hopefully, he was awake and causing as much havoc as Nick would have.

When Nick hung up the phone, he groaned. "It's barely five in the morning." He put the phone down and snuggled back into Malachi's back. "Mum said hi."

"Hi," Malachi mumbled.

"Rye woke up. He's doing well and can remember what happened, so there's no memory loss, which is good. Mum said we can visit this afternoon because Jonah and Eliza are there at the minute."

"That's good. I doubt he'll be alone at all, so that's one less thing for you to worry about."

"He'll still have a guard—they all will—but I don't think this guy will try again. He made his point."

"I'm going to nip home today and see Mum and Grandma. I also have a couple of articles due, or Tucker will be on my back about it."

"Okay. Please take a guard with you. I don't want to worry if you're safe." Nick pressed his lips to Malachi's shoulder.

"I will." He rolled to his other side, facing him. It wasn't the right time, but he wanted to ask something random. "Can I ask a question, which I promise will never see the light of day in any of my words?"

Nick tensed but nodded slowly. "I can't guarantee I can answer, but you're welcome to ask anything."

"Is there any truth to Club Royal?"

Malachi would give Nick his dues; his poker face was spot on. But it was that poker face that gave him away. If it hadn't been true, Nick would've probably laughed it off.

"The reason I ask," he continued, gathering his courage, "was because I wanted to know if someone could give me some advice about…something who knew what they were talking about. We haven't spoken about much to do with BDSM or limits, though we touched on them, but there's something I'd like more info about."

Nick exhaled shakily. "I might know someone who could help answer your BDSM questions, though it might depend on what those questions are. Would you feel comfortable enough to share with me? You don't have to. I'm not pressuring you at all."

Malachi cupped Nick's cheeks. "I know you're not. You're the last person who would." He inhaled again. "Let me tell you a story. Once upon a time, there lived a young, reckless reporter, who loved everything royal. He was obsessed from a young age, and that obsession gave him the courage to do what he thought was right. So when he started having feelings about something that wasn't regular and 'normal,' he panicked and kept it to himself, making it into this big ogre of an idea that he couldn't let out." He inhaled shakily. "Then one day, he saw a video showing this same something as being an escape, a place he could disappear to, a place he was still safe in. But he didn't understand how. How it could work. How it could happen. How it was right. And so he left it stewing inside him, feeding it videos and images irregularly to keep it at bay. And then, this reporter met a knight, who made him feel wonderful, and they fell in love. He gave him the courage to ask about that something that was still tightly held beneath the surface."

Malachi's heart pounded once he'd finished. He couldn't say out loud what his "something" was because he wasn't sure he could explain it properly, but he knew he would have to try at some point; otherwise, he wouldn't be able to do anything.

"What's simmering beneath the surface, Kai? Will you tell me?"

Malachi licked his lips and focused on Nick's chest instead of his face. "I would like to be..." He exhaled, not sure if he could say it aloud. He winced, chewing his lips. Then he inhaled and said, "Whipped."

He couldn't look at Nick, not wanting to see whatever expression was on his face. He'd done some research on the subject, but he could never tell what was truth and what was not, so he'd never tried it, and he'd never gathered the courage to visit a club, especially with his name and face being known as it was, he'd be front page news before he'd made it two steps into the club itself.

Nick's hands cupped his cheek, but he didn't force him to look at him. He just brushed his thumb across his skin. "Thank you for telling me. I know someone who might be able to help, but I need to ask them if they're willing to, first. If you could sign an NDA and promise nothing will ever be written about it, I'm sure it would be okay. I wouldn't be much help myself because although I know something about BDSM, I'm no expert. I will ask them today."

"Thank you."

Nick hadn't answered his question with words, but Malachi could read between the lines, though he'd tell no one. Club Royal was the perfect place to hide in plain sight, and if that's what the royal family were doing, they had done an amazing job of it.

"As we are awake so early, I think we need a pick-me-up before we get ready for work. What do you think?"

Now his cheeks had calmed down, Malachi glanced at Nick, seeing the smirk on his face. "I think that sounds like a wonderful idea. What did you have in mind?"

Nick rolled them over until Malachi was beneath him, and Malachi's dick perked up immediately. He'd been half hard all night, but he hadn't minded. Delayed gratification had its time and place.

When Nick kissed him, wrapping his hands around his wrists and holding him to the bed while his hips thrust against Malachi's, grinding their cocks together, Malachi's brain went offline. Nick licked into his mouth, and Malachi chased his tongue. He lifted his head, following when Nick rose.

"Keep your hands there," Nick said, bracing himself on one hand and wrapping his other around both their shafts.

"Oh god," Malachi gasped, pushing his head back into the pillow as Nick kicked up the speed and tightened his hold. "I'm going to come if you keep that up."

"As I said, a quick pick-me-up." Nick groaned, his eyes on his movements.

Malachi tried to hold back. He tried so hard, but he couldn't. "Fuck, oh, fuck."

He tensed as ropes of come streaked from him, covering his stomach and chest, and Nick cursed, following him over the edge. Malachi's mind eventually came back online, and he stared down at Nick, who had collapsed on him at some point.

"I like your kind of pick-me-ups," he said, and Nick chuckled, the vibration flowing through him.

Nick rolled off, and Malachi immediately missed his warmth, but the shock of cool air stopped him from falling asleep again. He sat upright, staring down at the mess on him.

"I definitely need another shower."

Nick jumped off the bed, startling him. "Okay. Shower it is. I like showers."

Malachi laughed as Nick grabbed his hands and dragged him towards the bathroom. "Are you equating showers with happy times now?"

"Is that wrong?"

Malachi pretended to think about it. "Probably not."

An hour later, they finally got dressed and headed to Sec HQ for an update before Malachi had to leave. As they entered, a group of people stood in front of the screen, watching and listening to something.

"—don't know anything. I don't know why you keep saying I do. I was just asked to give the letter to Nick Tennant. I'm not a traitor. I wouldn't—"

Malachi washed his hands at the sink, staring into the mirror at his reflection. What he wouldn't give for some more time with Nick. Their relationship was still new, but he had such hopes for them. He wanted everything.

"Shit!" he muttered when the wall next to the sink moved, revealing none other than Tarrant Milton, holding a gun. "What are you doing here? And how did you get in?"

The smack to the head came from nowhere, but the butt of the gun was hard and unyielding. Malachi sank to the floor, his head spinning and nausea welling up fast and sharp.

"Shut the fuck up, Malachi. Or should I say, Kai? You're a traitor. Someone who makes people think they are aligned, when actually they're not. What do you do, huh? Gather information about us for the royal family? It wouldn't surprise me. But now I'm told you have to pay."

He was shoved to the floor, and another smack hit him, sending him into darkness.

He gasped and found himself on a chair with Nick kneeling in front of him. "It was Tarrant Milton."

Nick frowned. "What was?"

"The bathroom. Here. It was Tarrant Milton who did it."

"He's the one who hurt you?"

Malachi nodded, his breathing finally returning to normal. "I remembered what happened." He told them the details up to when he blacked out. "From there, obviously, I don't know."

"So Tarrant knew something was going on. Did he have contact with the person? Is that why he's now dead?" Brett asked the room. "Getting rid of witnesses, like you said, Nick."

"Sounds like. Wouldn't be the first time."

"Well, he wasn't the one taking the shot at your brother, so is that another lackey, or is that the top man himself?" Brett mused.

"Does it matter? He still needs to be found," Nick snapped.

Malachi put his hand on Nick's, squeezing. "Of course he does, Nick, but it's not Brett's fault."

Nick inhaled and exhaled. "Sorry."

Brett waved him away.

"What were you watching?" Malachi asked.

"Tarrant's police interviews. We were seeing if we could figure out his role, if he had one. But it seems he did. Can you send us whatever information or emails he sent you so we can get them analysed?"

"Sure. I'll do that before I go." He stood, and Nick steadied him. "I'll be okay. You get to work." He looked at Nick's mouth, wanting to kiss him, but not wanting to do it in front of everyone, but Nick took the initiative, dragging him in for a kiss, leaving him breathless, but for a good reason that time.

"Take a guard."

Malachi shook his head. "I'll be—"

"Taking a guard. Yes, I know," Nick interrupted.

Malachi sighed. "Fine."

Brett called over to them from across the room. "Darius will look after him."

The man in question came up and introduced himself. "Hey, I'm Darius." He held out his hand.

"Nice to meet you," Malachi said, shaking his hand.

"Look after him," Nick ordered.

Darius placed his hand over his chest. "With my life."

As much as Malachi understood the sentiment of those words, he also hated them. He didn't want someone else to die in order for him to survive, and the worst thing was, it happened every day. It was what Nick did. He stood in front of others to make sure they survived, even if it meant he died. Every time Nick left him to go to work, it might be the last time he saw him alive. It certainly brought clarity to what was important in life.

"I love you," he said to Nick, kissing him once more before heading for the door, with Darius following.

"I love you."

Despite the slim chance they would be the last words Nick said to him, they warmed his heart, and he sent another smile over his shoulder before the door closed. As they walked down the corridor towards the suite, he asked Darius, "How do you do it?"

Darius frowned. "Do what?"

"Leave the people who love you behind when, each day, you know you might not be coming back?"

Darius swallowed hard, and his gaze went straight ahead. "I don't know what others do, but I make sure I love that person as much as I can while I'm with them. And then, as awful as it sounds, I put his voice, his laugh, his scent deep down inside me and lock it away until I finish that shift. And when I make home again, I let it out and love him all the more for it."

And didn't that make Malachi feel like shit? He hadn't thought of it from the bodyguard's point of view. "I'm sorry."

"Don't be." Darius smiled at him. "There are ups and downs to every job."

And those words brought clarity to Malachi like nothing else had, and he knew what he had to do.

24

Nick

"You have a shift later. Are you okay to do it?" Brett asked. "I can get someone else to cover."

"I'm good. I need to get back to my routine. I don't need to babysit Malachi anymore, surely?"

Brett's mouth twitched. "I thought you liked babysitting Malachi."

Nick scrunched up a piece of paper and threw it at him. "I don't need to. He's mine."

Brett shook his head. "You're all loved up. The lot of you." He returned to the chair behind his desk. "Have you thought of what you're doing for George's birthday? You've only got just over a week."

Nick grinned. "I'm all set. The only thing I need is security, which I'm sure won't be a problem, as you're the man for that."

Brett sighed. "Where is it?"

"Check your emails. I sent a detailed email." He winked.

"I dread to think *how* detailed."

"Very detailed." He glanced around the room, seeing Felix hunched over his computer. Nick nodded towards him. "Is he okay?"

Brett exhaled and worked his jaw. "He's beating himself up about the piggybacking thing. He's got it in his head that he could've stopped things from happening if he'd found it earlier."

"Well, that's ridiculous. Whoever it is would've found another way of causing chaos."

"We know that, but he's not listening to reason right now."

Nick sighed. "We're all climbing the walls because of this. It's no one's fault." Brett raised an eyebrow, and Nick chuckled. "Fine. It's not my fault, either."

"Glad to hear it. Do you know where you're going with the king today?"

Nick frowned. "It's the military barracks, isn't it?" His eyes widened. "Military."

Brett nodded solemnly. "Keep your eyes open, and stay safe."

"Will do."

He headed for the exit, dropping by the weapons store to make sure he had everything he needed for his shift, and then strode down the corridor to the king's office. Grinning when he saw Dominic sitting outside, he threw his hands wide.

"What did you do?"

Dominic sighed. "He's mad because I accidentally threw away the meal he made for us."

Nick frowned. "How can you accidentally throw away a meal?"

"It was in a tub in the fridge, but it didn't have a date on it or anything. When I opened it, it looked green! I thought it had gone off. So I threw it out." He winced. "Apparently, it was supposed to be that colour."

Nick rolled his lips, containing his laughter, but only just. "Okay. Understandable mistake."

"Yes! Exactly. Maybe you can tell him that so I can come back in? He won't even get me coffee."

At that, Nick did laugh. "Oh, you poor baby. I'll save you."

He patted Dominic's shoulder and headed inside to Randall's office. He nodded at Emmy, who sat outside the king's office door. Randall lifted his gaze to him, his frown lifting into a smile when he saw him. He rounded the desk and hugged him. "Hey, Nick. How are you doing? How's Malachi? How's Rye?"

"We're all doing okay. I'm going to see Rye this afternoon after my shift."

"Well, send him our love, okay? We'll get everyone together once he's on the mend."

"He'll like that." Nick thumbed over his shoulder. "He in the doghouse?"

Randall's mouth twisted. "I spent ages on that meal." He sighed. "But I did forget to label it. I suppose I should forgive him, but he should've asked."

Nick nodded. "He should've and you should've, but it's just food. Maybe you can make him make it next time. Or even better, make him make it for everyone."

Randall brightened. "That's an idea."

He quietly said sorry to Dominic, but he wasn't concerned about them. "I'm going to grab him a coffee."

Randall waved him away. "I'll do it. You get on with what you're doing."

"I'll swap with him and send him in then."

"I'll bring you a drink, too."

"You're an angel."

"I thought I heard you," the king said, exiting his office. He hugged Nick, catching him off guard. "Thank you for the painting. It's perfect."

Nick's cheeks heated, but inside he was ecstatic that he hadn't made a mistake. "I'm glad. I wasn't sure if it was too much."

"Not even a little." Andrew smiled and headed back to his office, brushing against his cheek.

"Good job," Randall said, and Nick refocused on him and Dominic's problem.

Whenever Dominic was on shift, he would sit outside Andrew's door so he could spend time with Randall, and anyone else would sit outside in the corridor. No one minded, for the most part. It was only when they were in need of social interaction that it was a struggle, but they knew to speak up at those points, and Dominic never minded swapping.

He exited the office again and clapped Dominic on the back. "You better get in there. He's making you coffee."

Dominic's eyes widened. "Seriously?"

Nick nodded and grinned. "Go on. Just remember me in your will."

Dominic hugged him and then entered the office to Nick's laughter. He settled into the comfortable chair they'd added to the corridor. It couldn't be too comfortable because it would be too easy to fall asleep, but it was enough to stop them having numb asses at the end of it. Unlike the king's office chairs. He was truly grateful to not need to use those.

"Here you go." Dominic handed him his coffee.

"Thanks."

Then he was left to his own devices. Emmy said goodbye as she left, but the corridor was quiet. Maybe he needed to request that music could be played. Instead, he focused on his phone, checking his emails and catching up with anything he needed to before taking the tablet Emmy had given him and completing the reports he'd been neglecting. Sitting there was relaxing compared to what he had been through recently, and he took several long minutes to let everything flow through his head and just breathe.

They would find out who it was. They always did. But sometimes it took time. And it didn't always feel like that time was on their side.

Dominic stuck his head out of the door. "He's almost ready."

Nick nodded and downed his coffee, handing the empty cup to him. "Okay. Ready when you are."

"Colt and Viola should be on their way."

"We're just having the four of us?"

Dominic nodded, though his expression was grim. "Landon and Emmy are off shift. I wish he'd increase us to eight again because then we could have five or six at a time, but he still refuses."

Nick could understand it, but it would make their lives easier if there were more eyes on him when he visited places. "We'll be fine. We need to keep our eyes open, though."

"Why?"

"We're visiting a military base."

"They wouldn't dare try anything there, would they?"

Nick shrugged. "They're not getting desperate, but who knows? They can easily take us by surprise for any reason."

"I sometimes hate this job." Dominic grimaced. "No, that's not true. I love this job. I just hate the people who hate us."

"I agree with that."

Dominic disappeared again, and Nick readied himself for their visit. He had no idea if the asshole was going to try anything, especially after the most recent shooting, but he wasn't going to take that to heart. He'd assume something was going to happen until it didn't.

He adjusted his earpiece, and when Colt and Viola arrived, he let Dominic know, and the king exited. He greeted them all, and then they all headed for the car. Though how Andrew could face getting into a car after what happened to the late queen, he didn't know—car bombs were no joke. If something like that happened to him, he doubted he would even be able to look at one, let alone sit in one.

As he sat in the front of the car ferrying the king, his mind wandered, thinking over everything that had been happening. For some reason, pieces of the jigsaw began clicking into a different pattern. Why was everyone around him being targeted and not him? With Dominic, he'd been shot. With Owen, he'd been shot and blown up. With him, everything was focused on Malachi, Malachi's family and Nick's family. Nothing remotely focused on him directly. Why? Why was that time different? What had changed the pattern?

It was a question he couldn't figure out the answer to, so he pushed it aside to think about later. He couldn't be distracted when he was working. As they pulled up to the military base, a shiver went down his spine. He doubted they would be unlucky enough to visit the very base of the person doing this, but knowing Nick's luck... Regardless, the person or people were probably out of the military already.

Someone came out from a building and strode in their direction, so Nick climbed out to greet them. When they came closer, Nick had to stop his jaw from dropping.

"Good morning. I'm Lieutenant Colonel Venus Cage. It's nice to have you here."

Nick licked his lips, wanting to ask the obvious question, but he didn't. Instead, he took her hand and smiled. "Thank you for having us."

While she had been greeting him, Dominic had climbed out of the car with the king not far behind.

"Lieutenant Colonel Cage, it's nice to see you again. Brett sends his regards."

She chuckled. "I doubt that, but thank you for your optimism." She waved her hand towards the building. "Shall we?"

"Lead the way," Andrew said.

They fell into their usual formation while Andrew and Brett's sister—whom Nick still couldn't believe he hadn't known about—spoke about the topics they wanted to cover during the visit. Nick tuned out but kept his eyes on their surroundings. Being within an army base was both the safest and most dangerous place. The safest because they had more weapons than they could ever need to protect the king should someone attempt to attack, but the most dangerous because they had more weapons than anywhere else in the country. If someone decided to take them out, they would have an almost unlimited supply. But hopefully, if that did happen, there would be enough allies to help them.

Several people waited for them inside, and Andrew was introduced to them. Nick checked them out, looking at their body language, facial expressions, word choices and other ticks to see if they were a threat. No one seemed to be—or they could be good at hiding. He glanced at Dominic, who caught his gaze and shook his head minutely; he couldn't see any threats, either. It relaxed him a bit, but not enough to drop his guard completely.

"Shall we move on?" the Lieutenant Colonel said. There was no denying that she was his sister; they looked like twins. Why had Brett never mentioned her? Was there bad blood between them?

They went down a narrow corridor, barely two people side by side, and entered a much larger room filled with people and equipment, all talking amongst themselves or into microphones.

"This is our base of communications. It should have eight people working at all times on a shift rota, but due to lower numbers of sign-ups, we struggle to man all stations on all shifts. Obviously, we do our best, but with illnesses, holidays, etc, we don't always make it. It's not impossible to make it work with six, but any lower and we'd struggle."

"What do you need help with?" Andrew asked.

"Getting people in. We have a variety of specialisms, but even then, people just don't want what they believe the military is." She chuckled. "Lots of people shouting and giving orders are what they think, but we're so much more."

They continued the conversation, throwing out ideas about how they could make it appear to be a good career path, but Nick wasn't convinced. He never had been, which was why he went into protection instead of the Army.

The visit continued, and they got a tour of the "nice" part of the base, stopping and watching the exercise session where they had to crawl under nets and climb huge wooden structures. It was more work than Nick ever wanted to do, but he couldn't argue with the need. He exercised enough to keep his job and energy levels, but if he didn't have to, he wouldn't.

"Maybe we should have a competition one day," Andrew remarked. "My protection detail against your soldiers."

Venus chuckled. "One day maybe. When things have settled down for you. Is there anywhere else you'd like to view?" She led them towards where the car waited, almost as if she wanted them gone. He could understand why. Having a royal on the base made them a target, and if something happened while they were there, it would cause chaos.

"I think I've seen plenty. You're doing a wonderful job, Venus. Thank you for taking the time out of your day to show us around."

"You're always welcome, Your Majesty."

Nick glanced at her, her tone seeming different, but she had an open and smiling expression. She shook hands with the king, and as he entered the car, she met Nick's gaze.

"Thank you for protecting him. He needs the best, and I'm told you're it." She paused. "Your team, I mean."

"We do our best, which is all anyone could hope for," Nick replied.

He didn't quite understand the undercurrent of the conversation, but he smiled and nodded her way before climbing into the car. She watched them leave, standing almost to attention the entire time. What had happened between her and Brett? Were they estranged? If so, why? He doubted he would get any information from Brett, but he wished he could offer some sort of support to him. Brett wouldn't take it. He'd brush it off.

After they got back to Windsor and the king settled back into his office, Nick went through the details of Prince George's birthday party with Randall. The king's personal assistant was a little overwhelmed with the ideas he kept throwing at him, but he rallied. By the end, Nick would even say he seemed giddy at the prospect.

"I love the idea, and I know George will, but will everyone else?" Randall asked.

"It doesn't matter about everyone else. It's George's birthday, so it should be all about him and what he likes. He'll love it."

Randall nodded. "He truly will."

Nick gave a thumbs up just as the door opened and Landon came in to relieve him of his duty. "On that note, I'm going home."

"You might want to nip to your suite first. I put some boxes in there that are for you."

"Thanks! See you later!"

"Not if I see you first," Landon remarked.

Nick chuckled and strode down the corridor. Despite he and Malachi having not been in there since that morning, he swore he could still smell their joint scents in the air when he entered. It probably wasn't true, but he liked the idea of it. The boxes were hard to miss. They must be the supplies he'd ordered for the party, so he picked them up, balancing the three on top of each other, and headed for the door.

But he paused when he saw a piece of paper on the coffee table. He put the boxes on the sofa and picked it up.

I can't do this anymore, Nick. What I want from you isn't something I can have, so I need to stop this before I hurt you more. We're from different worlds. Why I ever thought we could fit was beyond me. I was deluding myself. But now you're free to love who you want. I wish you all the best.

Malachi

Nick read the words again, and then one more time before he flew out of the room to Sec HQ.

"Where's Kai?"

"I haven't seen him. Why?" Felix asked.

"Can we locate him?"

"Again, why?"

"He left me a Dear John note."

Felix's face crumpled. "God, I'm sorry, man."

Nick grinned. "I'm not. It wasn't him. Find Kai. Make sure he's okay, and then we can look at this and figure shit out." He waved the note. "Because whoever wrote this thinks I haven't read every word Kai has ever written. They finally made a big fucking mistake."

And they were going to use it to find the fucker.

25

Malachi

After Malachi had sent the Tarrant emails to Felix, he collected his belongings and gave a fond smile of farewell to the suite. He doubted they would use it again, especially as they both had homes they could visit each other in.

Exiting the suite, he found Darius waiting for him. "Thank you for this."

"It's no problem at all. Happy to help. So, what's the plan?"

Malachi sighed. "I need to visit my boss first, and then we can go to Grandma's house. After that, I guess it'll be home."

"Simple. I like it."

Malachi snorted, and they headed for the car. Darius drove—because of course he did—and they headed for the Windsor Chronicle office building. His stomach churned at the thought of what he was going to do, but it needed to be done. He had no choice now, and though the future scared him, working for Tucker had become a no-go any longer. It was time he stood on his own two feet and listened to his heart instead of his head.

On the trip up in the lift, Darius asked if he was okay.

"I'm just about to quit my job, and I expect some hurtful words and pushback. I'm a little stressed."

Darius clasped a hand on his shoulder. "I'll be with you in the room. All will be well."

"Thanks."

He felt like he was walking to his doom when the doors opened onto the busy office floor, and with the looks some of them gave him, he knew his time had come, no matter the decision he'd come to on his own. He knocked on Tucker's door.

"Enter."

Malachi headed inside, Darius following him and closing the door behind them.

"Well, if it isn't the quintessential royal backer," Tucker said with a smile. "Or should I call you Kai?"

"You have no right to call me anything. As of this moment, I no longer work for you." He sounded a lot more confident than he felt.

Tucker snorted. "You have to follow the process the same as everyone. One month's notice."

"Actually, I don't. My contract states, as I found out when I requested someone to check it, that it's a rolling monthly contract which can be ended at any point *without* notice. Remember? You put that in yourself, in case you wanted to get rid of me. Well, it works both ways."

Tucker's face grew a darker shade of red with every word, and Malachi took great pleasure in it. He had Felix to thank for the information. He wasn't under the impression that Tucker would let him go without a fight, though.

"You have commitments to uphold."

"No, I have whatever you deem necessary for me to write. That's not the same thing. And as I said, I no longer work for you."

Tucker stood, placing his hands on the desk and leaning forward. It was a pose he often took to make him feel superior and whoever was on the other side of the desk feel inferior. It used to work, but then Nick showed him what life could be like if he just stopped being scared of what-ifs.

"You still owe me three articles."

Malachi tilted his head. "Check your email."

As much as he'd hated it, he'd written the three articles Tucker had mentioned because he had said he would do them. He hadn't liked it, but it was the only argument Tucker had, and Malachi didn't want any chance of making things worse. So, he'd caved and written them. And he'd only thrown up once instead of three times.

"Good luck."

He turned and walked out, enjoying the approving smile and nod from Darius—not that he needed it, but it felt good anyway.

"Don't think your name is going on these!" Tucker shouted.

He didn't reply. Stopping at his desk, he grabbed what few belongings he had dared leave in the place full of Rottweilers and headed out. When he got to the street, he exhaled.

"You don't need to hear it, I'm sure, but well done. That was nicely played."

"I've spent far too long in his clutches to not know how he works. As much as I hate the idea of writing those final articles—well, all of them really—it was the only way he would've left me alone."

They climbed back into the car and aimed for Malachi's grandma's house. "You remind me of Jason."

Malachi frowned, not recalling the name. "Who's Jason?"

Darius smiled. "My boyfriend. He had a tough time with it, but recently, he was able to cut himself free from his awful family. It's how we met, actually." He shook his head and grinned. "I'll never forget the sight of him when he faced his father the final time. But more so when he got custody of his siblings. I've never seen him happier."

Malachi gasped. "Prince George's best friend! I heard about that. I promise I didn't write about that, though."

Darius waved him off. "It happened, but we came out the other side, and you will, too. Maybe I can introduce you at the party."

"I'd like that."

When they arrived at his grandma's house, Malachi was eager to tell them his news. He knocked and entered straightaway. "Mum! Grandma!"

"In the kitchen, dear," his grandma said.

Malachi strode into the room, coming to a stop beside where she was making herself a cup of tea. "I did it, Grandma. I don't work there anymore."

Sally peered at him, her gaze roaming across his face until a smile grew across hers. "Really?" He nodded, and she hugged him. "I'm so glad. That job was killing you. Ich liebe dich, Kai."

"I love you, too, Abuela." He pulled back. "Where's Mum?"

"She's at the supermarket with that bodyguard. I can't remember his name. They all look the same."

A chuckle from behind them reminded him that Darius was still with him. "Speaking of... Grandma, this is Darius. Darius, my grandmother, Sally."

"Very nice to meet you, ma'am." He put his hand on his chest and bowed his head to her.

Sally looked him up and down. "He's almost as nice as your Nick."

Malachi and Darius laughed. "He's also taken, so no getting ideas, Grandma."

"Where is your bodyguard, ma'am?" Darius asked. "Aren't you supposed to have someone staying here and accompanying your daughter?"

Sally waved towards the front of the house. "He needed the bathroom."

Darius frowned. "Okay. I'll check in with him while you chat." He glanced at Malachi and mouthed, "Stay in here."

Malachi's stomach twisted. Why was Darius worried? Bodyguards had to go to the bathroom during a shift, didn't they? Trying not to worry, he carried Sally's cup to the table and helped her into the chair, even though she didn't need it; he liked helping her, and she liked letting him. Half of his brain was on his conversation with his grandma, but the other half was on Darius.

When Darius returned, he appeared calm. "Jacobs is back outside again now."

Malachi frowned. "I didn't know there was a guard called Jacobs. Is he new?" Malachi asked.

Darius froze. "His credentials checked out," he said carefully. They stared at one another for a long moment before Darius pulled his phone from his pocket and dialled, heading back into the hallway.

"What's wrong, dear?"

Malachi tried to smile, but his grandma would see through it; she always did. "We don't recognise your guard. We're just checking up to make sure you're safe."

Sally nodded and sipped her tea. Malachi filled the silence by telling her about the events at the Windsor Chronicle. She beamed when he told her what he'd said.

"I always knew you could do it, and I'm so glad you're free now. It was too heavy a burden for you to carry."

Darius came back in, grim-faced. "They've no idea who he was, and he's disappeared. The guard who was supposed to be on duty is called Foster. Carl is with your mother."

"So where is Foster?" Malachi asked.

"That's what I'm going to find out, but first, I need to get you into a safe room of the house, which I'm afraid is the bathroom, as it has the smallest window for anyone to get through."

Sally huffed as they helped her to the small room. "The dignity of hiding in a bathroom," she complained when she settled on the closed toilet seat. "I wish we had one of those large bathrooms with armchairs and rugs that you get in hotels. Much more comfortable."

"Lock this door and don't let anyone in." Darius handed him a small gun. "Brett told me you know how to use this." Malachi nodded. "Shoot anyone who tries to get in."

"Anyone?"

"Anyone. If it's a royal bodyguard, we'll identify ourselves properly and give you the code word." Darius lowered his voice, leaning closer. "Ratatouille."

Malachi couldn't help the laughter. "Intriguing."

Darius winked. "There's a story behind it. I'll gladly tell you once this is over."

"Deal."

Darius left, and Malachi locked the bathroom door. There wasn't enough room to pace, so he sat on the edge of the bathtub and jiggled his leg.

"Everything will be fine, Kai. Don't you worry. Tell me, how is that young man of yours?"

Malachi couldn't help but smile. "He's good. Working hard, as always."

"At least you can write about happier things now."

"That's true."

She gazed at him, her eyes seeing too much. "You love him."

His cheeks heated, but he didn't deny it. "I do. Very much."

"I can see it." She waved a hand around her face. "Less stress, more happiness."

"It's more than I could have hoped for."

"I knew you'd find it when you needed it. It's usually when it happens. When you least expect it but most need it."

He smiled at her again. "Very true."

A knock sounded, and he tensed. "Ratatouille. It's Darius. It's all clear."

Malachi unlocked and opened the door. "Did you find him?"

Darius nodded, a grim expression on his face. His gaze went past him to Malachi's grandmother. "We should have a guard here shortly. Carl is with your mother, and they're on their way back from the supermarket. They shouldn't be long."

Malachi's brain went through all the possibilities, but his heart knew Foster was dead. Someone had killed him and taken his place. But why? To mess with them, or had he and Darius turned up at just the right minute before Jacobs had done something to his family? His stomach rebelled at the idea, churning and twisting enough that he wasn't sure he could keep anything down. But as was his grandma's way, she invited them to sit down for a cup of tea and went about her day as if she hadn't been in danger.

"So, Darius, tell me about you."

And that was how Malachi came to know the entire Darius and Jason story, plus more information than Darius probably had intended to share, but it was his grandma. She'd be good at interrogations.

Malachi would be the first to admit that when the new guard turned up and it wasn't Nick, he was disappointed, but he couldn't keep expecting him to drop everything and run to him when there was a problem. He had his own job to do.

His brain was rebelling, though. So much had happened in such a short amount of time that he was clutching at so many balloon strings, trying to keep them from floating away. By the time his mother returned and they'd talked a little, Malachi was done.

"I have to go, but I'll be back again soon. Now I'm working for myself, I can choose my hours." He grinned, half-hearted as it might've been.

As they drove away, Darius said, "I'd like to try something if you agree."

"What?"

"I'm trying to figure out if this person knows where you are. I want to take you to a place you would never dream of visiting yourself. Can you think of somewhere?"

"The river boats. I hate the idea and avoid them where possible. Even watching them freaks me out."

"Okay. Try not to freak out on me while we're there, though, yeah?"

Malachi chuckled. "I'll do my best. Are you going to tell anyone?"

Darius sighed. "I'll admit to being reluctant to because any communication with them could be intercepted. I know Felix found they were hearing our radios and he stopped it, but they could have others. But I also know, you must be running out of people you deem safe and secure. If you'd prefer me to tell someone, I can."

"No, it's okay. If Brett trusts you, I trust you."

Darius sent him a smile, and they dropped into silence. He parked the car, and Malachi shivered as the cool breeze, wafting from the river, reached him.

"What made you not like boats?" Darius asked as they settled on a bench near to, but not close enough to view, the edge of the water.

Malachi shook his head and rubbed his hands together, not enjoying recalling the event. "I fell off one when I was younger and almost drowned."

"Holy shit, that would do it." Darius whistled. "I completely understand that."

Malachi filled his lungs with salty air and closed his eyes. "It's funny because I'm fine at the beach. But there's something about rivers. A sense of claustrophobia, maybe. I don't know."

"Phobias are weird things."

"How will you know if they've found us?"

Darius sighed. "They already have. Have you had any technical issues recently where you've had to get your laptop fixed, or your tablet, or your phone? Anything like that?"

Malachi frowned, thinking back. "How recently are you thinking?"

Darius shrugged. "Just the most recent."

"Well, my phone had issues around four months ago, I think it was. I had to get a replacement through my insurance."

"Do you have all your phone data saved somewhere else as well as on your phone? Phone numbers and whatnot?"

"I think so. Why?"

"Can I have your phone, please?"

Malachi gave it over without a second thought, and when Darius threw it in the river, he certainly didn't feel the need to check if it was okay by going closer. He just watched it sail over the edge and disappear. He sighed. "I guess I need to contact my insurance again," he muttered.

"Sorry. Can you think of another place where you might not usually visit to test my theory?"

Malachi blew out a breath. "The cemetery? I find it rather creepy."

Darius's mouth kicked up at the corners. "You're not the only one. Oh, how I wish you were reluctant to go to a coffee shop."

They laughed as they headed back to the car before climbing in and Darius leading them to a cemetery further afield from the closest. It didn't matter that the place was in a beautiful setting. It still seemed creepy. But as they wandered through the graves, Darius sighed.

"I think we have a winner."

"What do you mean?"

"No one is here yet, so I think they had bugged your phone. That's how they were keeping track of you. And then the radios were keeping tabs on us."

Malachi sighed. "I'm so sick of this. I don't know how you can all stand the whiplash you get. Don't get me wrong, I know chasing a story isn't all bells and whistles, but it's better than the mountains and valleys we've been through recently."

Darius squeezed his shoulder, turning them back towards the car. "Let's get back now. Nick is probably wondering where you are, and since we've lost our tail, we might even be able to stop for coffee on the way."

Malachi fell silent during the trip, unable to stop the melancholy from weighing down his shoulders. First, he had to deal with Tucker, and then what happened at Grandma's house, and now being followed. All of a sudden, it was too much.

Nick raced into the car park when they pulled up and opened Malachi's door before he could.

"Hey, how are you doing?"

Malachi closed his eyes. "I'm tired, Nick."

Nick cupped his cheek, and Malachi nuzzled against it. "I know, sweetheart. We're almost there, though. I'm sure of it."

Malachi blinked and climbed out, wrapping himself around him. "Why do you say that?" he murmured.

"Because you broke up with me."

Malachi jerked back, almost colliding his head with Nick's chin. "What? No, I didn't!"

Nick grinned. "I know. But I've never been more glad about it. They fucked up."

"Why?"

Nick led him into the castle, his arm around his shoulders. "They were very careful with their writing. It sounded just like you would've done had you written it. The problem is, they signed it Malachi, and I know you want to go by Kai now. And also, although we haven't talked in detail, I know you know that I can help you. That letter said you didn't think I could. If I hadn't been secure in us, sweetheart, I would've fallen for it. They needed us separated or on the outs. Didn't work how they thought."

Darius brought them all up to speed when they reached Sec HQ.

"What concerns me," Brett said, "is that your phone was replaced four months ago." When no one responded, he shook his head. "You weren't even on our radar for a visit here until two months ago. What made them choose you?"

Nick paced, raking his fingers through his hair. "You're telling me, this asshole staged everything? Knowing how we would react to certain triggers."

Brett gave a grim nod. "Looks like it."

Nick stared at him. "He set up the initial attack at the charity dinner just to set the ball rolling, knowing the royal family would do whatever it took to make it up to Kai. From then, it was just tweaking the plan with other events to push us where they wanted us."

"We're puppets to his show," Malachi said.

"But what's the finale?" Felix asked.

"I don't think I want to find out," Malachi said. "How did that letter even get into our suite?"

"A household staff member hand-delivered it. He doesn't know where it came from, only that it was amongst the letters they had to distribute when he started working this morning."

Malachi dropped his head into his hands. "I would ask how he knew I was leaving, but he would've heard it on my phone."

Brett nodded, and Malachi stood. "I'm sorry, but I'm done for today. I just...can't."

"Go get some rest. Both of you. We're still waiting for some information, and we probably won't have it until tomorrow, anyway. Sleep."

Malachi would've loved to sleep for several days. His mind was completely fried. Information overload had nothing on him. It was a little easier to cope with Nick by his side, but he was done.

Tomorrow was another day, and hopefully, one they would all survive.

26

Brett

Brett kept his façade in place as Darius delivered the news of Foster's death over the phone. Another bodyguard lost, and there'd be another, too, because there was no chance that Carl would continue working when his husband had just died. It had always played on his mind when Foster and Carl had requested having the same protectee. Usually, Brett wouldn't have allowed it, but Carl and Foster had been willing to decline the jobs unless they did. They'd argued that they would never see each other if they were with different people, and Brett couldn't deny the truth. Against his better judgement, he'd agreed. It had only taken two years for him to regret his decision, but at least Carl hadn't been present when it happened. Small mercies.

He sat in his squeaky chair and rested his forehead in his hand, trying to rub away the tension. When he lifted his head, he caught Felix's concerned gaze. The man saw too much.

Looking away, Brett tried to hide the news, at least for a little longer. The puzzle pieces were slowly clicking into place, and they were revealing a picture he didn't like the look of. He didn't want to be right, but it was looking more and more likely.

"What's wrong?" Felix asked, and Brett sighed quietly, both wanting and not wanting Felix beside him.

He'd run out of time. "Can you get everyone together, please?"

Felix stared at him, and he saw the moment realisation hit him. "Who?"

Brett swallowed and stood, crowding closer to him and lowering his voice. "Foster."

Felix closed his eyes and lowered his head, his forehead brushing Brett's chest. He couldn't resist and placed his hand on his nape. He wanted to do more, but he couldn't. Too much was at stake.

"I'll get everyone," Felix said, clearing his throat.

"Thanks."

When everyone, except for those currently guarding, was settled in Sec HQ, he broke the news of losing another of their own. Several asked about Carl, and Brett didn't have an answer for them. He didn't know what the future would hold for their friend, but they would be with him every step of the way. They spent several minutes cursing and calling out those who would do such a thing to them and then calmed and held a minute's silence for their fallen comrade.

Brett would hold it for a lot longer. He had no choice. Far too many people relied on him, and if certain information got out...well, there would be too many casualties.

Most of the guards filed back out once they were done. He would break the news to anyone who hadn't been there as and when he saw them. It was the risk they all took by taking the job. They could leave the house that morning and never return. Or they could spend years doing the job and never have an incident. It was...painfully unfair. But he wouldn't change it for the world.

Protecting the Sutcliffes was what he'd been born to do, and he would do it until he had no choice but to stop.

A short time later, when he was completing the never-ending pile of paperwork, Felix said his name. The devastation on his face was plain to see, and Brett glanced around the room, realising they were alone. He stood, dragged Felix towards him and held him as tightly as he could as Felix cried.

He wanted to join him, but he needed to stay strong. If he broke, there would be no putting him back together again.

27

Nick

Nick could see Malachi had reached his limit. He had nothing more to give, and rightly so. The following day, he seemed much more himself, and they headed back to Sec HQ—they apparently lived there now. Nick wanted to go through all the information they had about this guy again to make sure they hadn't missed anything.

"But where's my blast from the past?" he said, and Brett frowned.

"What do you mean?"

"Dominic had Addams, someone he had met during his past. Owen had reminders of his sister, something from his past. Where's that connection to me?"

"Maybe it's nothing to do with you this time?" Felix mused.

"But it is for everyone else. We were wondering before if this had anything to do with it being because Dominic and Owen were friends, or because they were bodyguards. Well, it's happening to me now, so I'm assuming it's bodyguards. I didn't know them before I started working here. Have we missed something, or has he changed his MO?"

"There isn't anything else connecting the three of you, is there?" Brett asked. They shook their heads. "So, the connection is either the royal family or bodyguards in general, do you agree?"

"Maybe he hates the royal family, and that's where the connection is with Malachi," Colt said from behind them. "You mentioned a note saying he was two-faced and not telling the truth about his feelings? Maybe he's annoyed because he thought he found an ally in Malachi but realised he'd been duped, and that was why he's focused on him."

Nick glanced at his lover. "Have you had any new connections or sources lately?"

Malachi exhaled. "I get new sources weekly sometimes. Let me grab my laptop."

While he did that, Nick turned back to Brett. "So, we're thinking this is someone with a hatred for the royal family?" Brett nodded slowly but didn't seem convinced. "Where's your head at Brett?"

Brett crossed his arms over his chest and leaned his ass on the desk. He stared at the floor, and everyone let him think it through as he usually did before voicing his thoughts. During that time, Malachi came back, settling beside him with his laptop.

Brett sighed. "It makes sense, but if the plan had been to remove bodyguards to get to the royal family, it failed dismally. It always would. Because when one guard goes, another takes his place. What is he going to do? Take out a hundred, a thousand guards before he even has the chance at the Sutcliffes? As much as I hate to state the obvious, there are easier ways to get to them, as many others have proven."

"So, if we take the royal family out of the equation, that leaves the bodyguards. But why go after us? Is it someone who has an issue with us or a disgruntled former employee?" Felix asked.

Brett scoffed. "There are far too many disgruntled employees, unfortunately. It goes with the territory."

"You must have a list, though."

"Oh, I do, but I've been through it a hundred times. Those that stood out all have alibis and confirmed proof that they aren't involved."

"Could they be hiring someone? That would give them an alibi, but not an alibi for the one actively involved," Felix said.

Nick watched the back and forth between them, Felix having come to stand closer to Brett, and now that he knew there might be something between them, it was plain to see. The look in Felix's eyes as he spoke to their boss was unmistakable.

"I suppose it's possible. I'll look into them again."

"Remember to add in the military aspect, too," Malachi said.

"A lot of bodyguards have military experience..." Brett trailed off and then turned and faced the board they had set up with information, much like what the police did on TV shows. "But none of you," he muttered.

Nick rose. "What do you mean?"

Brett pointed at him. "You don't have military experience, you have regular security experience. Owen doesn't have military experience. Dominic doesn't have military experience. Who else doesn't among us?"

It was a rhetorical question because Brett was the one with that information. He leaned over his laptop and typed away at it for a moment before lifting his head, his gaze immediately going to Felix. "Only two others."

"Who?" Nick asked when his boss fell silent.

Felix answered. "Me and Brett," he whispered.

"I thought you had been in the Army?" Nick asked Brett.

Brett shook his head. "It was expected that I would because my entire family has been at some point, but the family business wasn't for me."

Maybe that was the underlying tension between him and his sister.

"Do you think we're next?" Felix asked.

Brett didn't answer, which was answer enough. Nick stood. "Okay, let's go through this again with fresh eyes. This is someone who seems to target those who haven't been in the military but holds a role where they might think we should have. Someone who knows our pasts or has access to it, and the people who were involved at the time. Someone with technical abilities or access to people with those abilities. Someone who's cocky and willing to take risks."

"That's a long list of people," Owen said, entering the conversation.

"But is it, really?" Nick said. "It might seem like it if you take each one separately, but putting them all together narrows the field a lot."

"Anyone in the military could have all of this," Owen said.

"Yes, but where's the link to us?"

Everyone fell silent, undoubtedly trying to find the connection.

"Malachi, any luck on your sources," Brett said suddenly.

Malachi nodded. "I'll email you a list of those that have come to me or that I've found in the last few months. There's actually not as many recently."

"Were you using Tarrant Milton as a source?" Brett asked, while studying the screen.

"Yes. He'd happily email me his theories about who should be the rightful king and whatever. It was fantastical at times, but it made for good stories." He winced. "Sorry."

"Don't worry about it. We've known for long enough that you weren't writing for yourself."

Nick blinked. "Just how long did you know?"

Brett managed a small smile. "Long enough to realise you were blinded by your attraction." He shook his head. "Almost a year."

Malachi gasped. "That long?"

"You weren't doing anything harmful that others weren't doing, so it didn't matter. And you were counteracting your words on the other side. It made no difference to us. We would've made it our business had something come of it, but we weren't concerned."

"I can't believe that." Malachi covered his mouth. "I thought I'd managed to keep them separate."

"You did. It was only Felix who managed to link them, so thank him."

Felix flushed. "I was trying to figure out why Nick was so obsessed with you, and the string I followed went a lot deeper than I expected." He shrugged.

"Well, you're not the only one who knows now," Dominic said, pointing at the laptop he was using. He spun it around.

REPORTER REVEALED AS A SHEEP!

It has recently come to our attention that a reporter at this very paper has been a sheep in wolf's clothing. While we believed Malachi Sanders to be on our side of the story when it came to the unnecessary role of the royal family, it turns out he is one of them.

Malachi, also known as Kai Ruffers, has been sabotaging our paper for far too long, and it's time to bring that shadiness to light.

Now everyone knows not to believe a word he says, we can get back to telling the truth about how things should be, and what the royal family is doing to ruin and corrupt our country.

By Adelaide Thompson, Windsor Chronicle.

"Well, I suppose it could've been worse," Malachi said, rubbing his face. "I shouldn't be surprised they took her on."

Nick took his hand. "You'll have people flocking to your other name now."

"Maybe not for the right reasons, though."

"They'll soon tire of it."

His words were pointless because he knew, as well as Malachi did, that people could be tenacious. But he wanted to get that look off Malachi's face.

"Felix, can you work on getting a program to work through the parameters we're looking at for our guy? Use all the info we've been through today, especially Nick's break down and cross reference it with Malachi's list. I'm not sure what use it will be, but give it a try."

"Yes, boss." Felix headed to his desk, where several monitors were set up, and started tapping away at the keyboard, already entrenched in his cyber world.

"Brett, did we ever get any more information about Tarrant and how or why he died?" Malachi asked.

"He was poisoned. His water had been tampered with. He went back to the cell after the interrogation, and they found him a couple of hours later." He shook his head. "As for why, there's only speculation that it was because he held information about whoever is behind this. Especially as he was the one to attack you here. He had to know more than he was telling."

"As much as I didn't agree with the guy, I still feel bad he died," Malachi said. "Sometimes, I don't think enough people stand up for what they believe in, but it is a double-edged sword."

"The program is still running, but I have a couple of people who've already popped up," Felix said. "Robert Duncan and," he stared at Darius, "Ian Jacobs."

Darius nodded, firming his lips. "Yeah, that's him. How did I fall for it?"

"How do kids get away with their fake ID cards? Damn things are good now."

"It wasn't your fault, Darius," Brett said. "I should've told you who would be there. That's on me."

"But he went by his last name. We don't."

"Some of our ex-military does, though," Felix said. "Not everyone has got into the hang of first names for themselves. Like Colt." He nodded towards the guy, who waved a hand, eyes still on the screen, and said, "Paul Colt, at your service. Besides, look at the sketch Tarrant did. Take off the beard, and it's a match. It's like he was playing with us."

"What's his story, then, Felix?" Brett asked, moving closer.

"Honourably discharged last year after an accident left him with back pain and numbness. Based at..." Felix stared at Brett. "Based at Transport Squadron Royal Logistics Corps, Morden."

"That's where we went the other day," Nick said. "Where your..." He trailed off.

"Is it a coincidence that the king visited the same squadron Jacobs was part of?" Brett asked, ignoring Nick's unsaid words. "It's been on his calendar for a while."

"How long?" Malachi asked. "Four months?" he said with meaning.

Nick latched on to it. "Did this all start when it was confirmed that the king was visiting that specific squadron? If that was the catalyst, and Malachi was the second ignition, where are they planning to end it?"

"It's usually confirmed between three to four months out," Brett confirmed.

"It was just before Douglas and Mav's wedding, so around mid-March," Felix confirmed. "When did you get your phone fixed, Kai?"

Malachi shrugged and swiped through it. Nick waited for the inevitable confirmation. "I have the receipt. It was 18 March."

"We have a winner," Felix muttered. "Jacobs had been discharged from the hospital two weeks prior."

"Let's not jump to conclusions just yet," Brett said. "Jacobs could also just be another pawn here. A fall guy like Tarrant. See who else pops up on your list and look into all of them. If we find something, we need the evidence to be perfect."

"Yes, boss." Felix turned back to his computer.

"Everyone else, go back to work. There's not much more we can do now."

Nick didn't wait for Brett to be sure, and he grabbed Malachi's hand and dragged him from the room. They'd had so little time together since it all started—since they started—and he was sick of other people dictating their timeline. He was taking Malachi to his home, and they weren't going to leave until they had no choice. It wasn't even a physical thing for him. He would be ecstatic to sit on the sofa and cuddle, but they just needed time to...be.

"Not that I have a problem with you dragging me off to places unknown, but where *are* we going?"

"My house. I think a takeaway and a movie sound like heaven. What do you think?"

"Hmm, wonderful. What about Rye?"

"I called earlier. He's happy we're okay and told me to bugger off."

Nick held the passenger car door open while Malachi climbed in, closing it behind him, and then headed around it to get in himself. He handed him his phone. "I know you haven't got the new one Felix gave you set up yet, so use mine and call a takeaway. I don't mind which."

Malachi tapped a few times on his phone while Nick worked his way through the streets, but then he put it to his ear.

"Hola, Nick. Long time, no speak."

Nick grinned. He could hear Carlos through the phone, even without it being on speakerphone.

"Oh, um, sorry. It's, um, Mala—it's Kai. Um, Nick's...boyfriend?"

He hadn't meant it as a question, but Carlos was known to latch onto anything to keep the conversation going. He loved talking to people and getting to know them. He said it made the service they provided more special, and Nick couldn't disagree. They had the best tapas.

"Ooh, Nick has a boyfriend? Nice to speak to you, Kai. If Nick has entrusted you to phone in his order, he certainly holds you in high esteem. What can I get you?"

Malachi stared at him, eyes wide. Nick glanced at him and nodded, trusting him and promising himself he'd eat whatever Malachi decided on for him, even if he didn't like it.

"Could we have the tapas buffet, please? I do have a peanut allergy, though."

"Good choice. Anything else?"

Malachi ordered some drinks and said goodbye. "Please tell me you like tapas."

Nick grinned. "You just found another way to my heart, gorgeous. I love tapas."

He found himself a little nervous as they approached his door. Malachi's opinion held a lot of weight, and he hoped he liked the place. If nothing else, he had to love the TV—everyone loved the TV.

Nick busied himself in the kitchen area while Malachi looked around because, if he went with him, he'd probably harass him for his thoughts. He grabbed some plates and two glasses of water, putting them on the breakfast bar, and flicked the kettle on for a hot drink.

"Holy shit! How big?" he heard from the distance, and he grinned.

"I love this place," Malachi said, settling at the bar and resting his head in his palm. "It's surprisingly quiet. I was expecting noise from the neighbours."

"I'm lucky. We have some great tenants here at the moment, and they're all conscientious about noise and things like that."

"That's fantastic, but no parties for you, then." Malachi grinned.

Nick held up his hand. "Woah, don't go that far. We have parties, we just make sure we invite everyone, and then we don't need to worry about the noise."

Malachi snorted. "Trust you to think of a way around it."

"I live to please." He groaned. "I do need to get the finishing touches to George's party done, though."

Malachi gaped at him. "You told Brett it was all sorted!"

"It is. Mostly."

"You are going to be in so much trouble. What do you have left to do?"

Nick sipped his coffee and went through his list. "I need hundreds of balloons inflating. I also need the cake."

"You haven't got a cake yet?"

Nick held up his hand. "I did have a cake sorted, and then the people cancelled on me. I tried to find someone else, but then all this happened."

Malachi shook his head and picked up Nick's phone, which he'd given him the passcode for. He pressed the screen a few times and held it to his ear.

"Hey, Mum. How are you?"

Nick put his drink down and waved his hands. "No," he whispered. "It's too much to ask."

"Yeah, I was wondering, do you have time to make one of your amazing chocolate cakes? It would need to feed around..." He glanced at Nick.

Nick put his head in his hands and mumbled, "Fifty."

"Around fifty people? Yeah... We're on a bit of a time crunch. We need it for the weekend." He smiled and chuckled. "How did you guess? Are you sure? Brilliant, thanks, Mum." He spoke for a few more minutes and then hung up. "There you go. One less thing to worry about. As for balloons, do not ask me. I hate blowing them up."

The doorbell rang, and Malachi rose. "I'll get it. It's time I meet this Carlos."

He disappeared around the corner, and Nick listened to the door open and the mumble of conversation. He grabbed the cutlery and some napkins and placed them in some semblance of order on the breakfast bar.

"Nick," Malachi called.

He headed for the door, wondering what Carlos needed from him, but as soon as he rounded the doorway, he froze. Takeaway containers and food covered the floor, and Malachi stood with his back against the wall with the barrel of a gun pressed against his forehead. A gun which had a certain military man they had been looking for since he'd disappeared at Malachi's grandma's house on the other end of it.

"Jacobs, what are you doing?" he asked as calmly as he could when he was too far away from his own weapons to do any good. The scent of the tapas was extraordinarily strong, and it turned his stomach right then.

Jacobs stared at him, his hand on the butt of the gun never wavering, his eyes empty of any life. "My job. I may not be fit for public military service, but I can still do a damn good job when I need to."

"I can imagine you do. What job have you come here to do?" He didn't want to know, but any extra time he could get was a bonus. There was no way of telling Brett there was a problem, but if Jacobs had killed or hurt Carlos, someone might find him and call the police.

"You both need to die. It's what the plan says."

He said it without emotion, and Nick's heart seized. There would be no getting out of this for either of them.

"Now, who's first?"

28

Malachi

Malachi locked his knees to stop from sinking to the ground because he didn't want Jacobs to pull the trigger, thinking he was trying to get away. But something he had said sparked the researcher in him. There was "a plan." If that was the case, even if that plan was to kill them both, they might be able to keep him talking for a bit before they got to the finale.

"Will you tell me what happened to make them think you weren't fit for duty?" he asked, his voice wobbling.

Jacobs met his gaze, and a chill went down his spine. That was a man who had nothing left to lose. The stare lasted a second longer than most would, making Malachi stop breathing before Jacobs raised his eyebrows. "Why do you care?" The gun remained at his forehead, steady as anything.

Malachi understood the undertone of the question, and he had two choices. He could tell the truth, or he could lie. The truth might get him angry, or it could make him soften slightly because he was truthful. If Jacobs realised he lied, it could set them up for disaster.

He went for the truth. "I don't. But there are plenty of people who would. If you want to tell me your story, I could write it down."

"You won't be alive to publish it, though," Jacobs said, the matter-of-fact tone spreading even more fear through him.

Malachi swallowed. "I can publish it before," he croaked.

Jacobs glanced over at Nick when he stepped to the side, the gun moving against his forehead, and his breath hitched. The man reached behind him and something jangled. Jacobs threw the item at Nick, who caught it reflexively.

"Lock yourself to the radiator. Where I can see you."

Nick opened his mouth to argue but met Malachi's gaze and snapped his mouth shut again. Shoulders lowered, Nick did as he was told, and the clicks of the handcuffs being snapped into place sent Malachi's heart rate through the roof. They had to do something, but what?

The gun lowered from his head, and he held his breath until Jacobs stepped back. "Where's your laptop?"

Malachi straightened, an idea forming. "In my bag." He gestured to the backpack on the breakfast bar.

"Take it out. But remember, I know tech stuff, so don't mess with me. This will be aimed at you the entire time," he said, waving the gun.

"I won't try anything."

Malachi shuffled over to his bag, pulled his laptop free and rested it on the bar before opening the lid. He logged in, as usual, and settled onto the stool, grateful he could sit. He glanced at Nick, who stood, slightly hunched, next to the window. Nick smiled and nodded, and it made Malachi feel easier about the situation. Not that it was a great situation, but at least he'd managed to give them a little more time.

Jacobs sat beside him, facing Nick, but able to see Malachi, too. He tilted the screen a little lower.

"Make sure I can see the screen," Jacobs said.

"Sorry, is that okay? I need it lower or the reflection from the window stops me from seeing it."

Jacobs stared at the laptop, which he wouldn't be able to see properly from where he was, and nodded slowly. "Make it good."

Malachi nodded and hovered his fingers over the keys. "You tell me in your own words, and I'll write it down."

Jacobs went quiet, seemingly contemplating where to start. "My entire family is in the Army. Generation after generation signed up with no clue what it would do to them. Or to the ones left behind. Mum was never the same when Dad died. He had been captured and tortured, but eventually rescued, but it was too late. Even though she was still in the army, she wasn't really there, not even with her family.

"The Army *became* my life. I lived for it, breathed for it, pretty much died for it, and when they deemed me unfit because of something that happened during an event they have now swept under the rug, they have the audacity to say, 'It's how it's done.'" He shook his head. "Finding a new purpose was hard at first, but when I was approached by those who had received the same treatment I had, it was easy to join. It makes sense, what they say."

"What do they say?" Malachi dared to ask.

Jacobs gave him that cold, flat stare again. "That we are vessels to provide the truth."

"What truth?"

"That only the strong survive. And only the Army can make you strong."

Malachi raised his eyebrows. Despite their current predicament, he found himself intrigued. "Even though they deemed you unfit?"

"They had no choice. I was no longer the strongest. But I worked hard and fought for my place. And I'm back where I should be."

"Which is where?" Nick asked, and Jacobs looked at him. Malachi used the opportunity to open another window and send an email, brief but to the point.

"The Army. They can't acknowledge me in the same format as before, but my superiors are happy with my ethics." He glanced back at Malachi. "I want people to understand that they need to work hard and work smart. It's the only way to survive in this world."

"And where do we come into that?" Nick asked, and Malachi wished he hadn't brought attention back to them.

"You haven't had the required training. You refuse to follow the rules. You're weak but pretend to be strong. It doesn't work that way."

"What about those people who haven't been trained by the Army but are just as strong as those who have?" Nick continued.

Jacobs shook his head before he'd finished his question. "It doesn't work that way," he repeated. "Only the Army can train you how you need to be to live in this treacherous world. You need to know how to look after yourself and others, how to locate and identify those of a weaker standing, and how to dispose of them. How else can we survive? We also need to show others how close we can get without anyone knowing. Which is what we did to you and your grandmother."

Malachi's throat dried up at the fanatical words, despite the outwardly calm demeanour of their kidnapper. He had no idea of how they could make him change his mind, or how to subdue him. They needed help, and fast. Hopefully, Felix had got his message quickly enough that they were on their way.

"Do you have sniper training?"

Jacobs tilted his head, staring at him in that almost unseeing way. "We all need it."

"Is there anything else you want to add?" Malachi asked.

"Only that the trap is set, and all the flies will soon meet their match."

Malachi typed those final words, asked a couple more questions about the article itself, to bide more time, and then added a few things before hovering over the publish button.

"Ready?"

Jacobs tilted his head. "I will admit to enjoying the back-and-forth we've had. You're smart. Both of you. But you'd need the proper training before you'd survive."

"Is that something we could get?" Nick asked. "Could we be rehabilitated?"

Jacobs shook his head. "Maybe before the kill order, but not after. It's too late."

"I am weak," Malachi said suddenly. He lifted his gaze to Jacobs. "Will you make it quick?"

Jacobs nodded. "We do not prolong the agony of those who need rebirth. Every execution is quick and painless."

"How many executions have you done?" Nick said.

"Too many people didn't have the strength."

"It weighs heavily, doesn't it?" Nick said. "Too much blood on your hands that it's hard to tell when they're clean."

Jacobs tilted his head again. "You shouldn't understand," he muttered. "If you didn't have the strength, how would you know that?"

Malachi's attention veered to the cupboard behind Jacobs. A red light wavered against the wood, and he breathed a relieved sigh. The red dot split into five, then one disappeared, then another, and Malachi realised it was a countdown. He glanced over at Nick quickly, who dipped his head once in acknowledgement of seeing them, and Malachi refocused again. Two dots merged into one, and when that disappeared, he threw himself to the floor and covered his head. He expected a shattering of glass, a thump as Jacobs fell to the floor, anything but the silence that reigned.

Then his hearing kicked back in, and Nick was shouting his name. "Malachi? Kai! Kai, answer me! Are you okay?"

Malachi groaned and rose, rubbing his hip where he'd bashed it going down. He raced over to Nick. "Are *you* okay?"

"Fuck, how did they know?" He looked through the window, squinting.

"I managed to send Felix an email."

Nick stared at him for a moment. "You're going to give me a heart attack every day, aren't you?"

Malachi grinned. "Maybe." He kissed him. "Let's get you unlocked." He went to turn, but Nick said his name again, the cuffs rattling when he reached for him and was stopped.

"Stay with me, sweetheart. You don't need to see that. I can wait for reinforcements as long as I need to with you by my side."

Reinforcements hadn't taken long, and someone brought the keys over. By the time Nick was out of the cuffs—with red, painful gouges in his skin from where he'd tried to get free—someone had draped a cover over Jacobs, shielding Malachi from the vision of him dead. He wasn't sure if he needed to see it, but he acquiesced when Nick said he didn't.

Nick slid his arm around his shoulders and steered him towards the bedroom. After encouraging him to sit on the bed, Nick crouched in front of him. "How are you feeling?"

Malachi exhaled, long and loud. "Less shaky than I was. I've got a headache, though."

Nick brushed his fingertips across his forehead, and Malachi could feel a bruise already forming. Having a gun-shaped bruise on his forehead was going to look wonderful. He shook his head, silently reprimanding himself, because at least he was alive. At least *they* were alive.

"Talk to me, sweetheart," Nick said, squeezing his hands. "What's going through that clever brain of yours?"

Malachi scoffed. "I'm not feeling particularly clever. I didn't even check the peephole before I opened the door. That was stupid."

"Should you have checked the peephole? Yes. Would the result have been different? No, I doubt it because Jacobs would have found his way into the place some other way. And if he'd found a different way in, we'd be dead because he would've shot us on sight due to the amount of noise he would've probably had to make. You actually saved us." Nick smiled. "How the heck did you get that email out?"

"When you started asking him questions, and he looked at you, I switched to email and sent one. It only said—"

"Nick's home. Hostages," Felix said, entering the room with a grim smile. "Best email I've ever received. How are you feeling, Kai?"

"Shaken, but I'll be fine. Who was the sniper? I'd like to thank them for the countdown."

Brett entered behind Felix. "Someone who prefers to remain anonymous. But I'll pass on your thanks."

"It's okay," Felix mumbled, glancing at Brett before looking at them.

"Felix..."

Felix smiled and shook his head. "It's about time I stopped hiding, Brett. That sniper would be me."

Nick stood, stared at Felix and said, "All those times...?" Felix tensed but nodded. Nick pulled the man in for a hug, and the expression on Felix's face was nothing short of flabbergasted. "I can't thank you enough for every time you've done it. I can imagine how difficult you found it. Why...? Never mind. It doesn't matter. *Thank you.*"

Felix nodded. "You're welcome." He pulled away and smiled at Malachi. "Chin up, yeah?"

Malachi nodded back. "Thank you."

The strain on Felix's face was easy to see, and Brett could see it, too, by the deepening lines on his face as he studied the man. Malachi probably had as many questions for Felix as Nick did, but in the end, it was nobody's business but his. It was obviously something he didn't want to talk about, and they would respect that.

Felix left with a wave, and Brett watched him before turning back to them. "I saw what you wrote on the laptop. Is that really what he was saying?"

"He was almost fanatical. Brainwashed. It's like he had no concept of why someone wouldn't want to go into the army." He shrugged.

Brett closed his eyes, resting his head back against the doorframe in an uncharacteristic show of tiredness. "Some people don't understand, no matter how many times you try to explain it." He pushed off the doorframe. "Get some rest. I want you at Sec HQ tomorrow morning, bright and breezy."

"We'll be at Malachi's if you need us."

Brett nodded and disappeared. Malachi exhaled again.

"Is it over?" he asked.

"I hope so," Nick said. "This seemed like the last point in their plan for us. After all, we were supposed to die. What else could've happened to us after that?"

Malachi grimaced. "That thought is for if I ever turn to writing horror fiction or fantasy." He shivered. "Which I doubt I will."

Nick chuckled and wrapped his arms around him again. "Let's go."

The journey was a blur, but when they finally closed the door to Malachi's home, his knees gave out, and he sank to the floor. Nick picked him up as if he weighed nothing and carried him to the bedroom, setting him on the bed. When he went to pull back, Malachi grabbed him.

"No."

Nick seemed to understand what Malachi was trying to say, which was a good thing because his brain couldn't find the words. A funny thing, as words were his life.

"It's okay. We're safe now."

Nick kept mumbling to him, who knew for how long, but eventually, Malachi came back to himself, stiff and aching, but not in the pleasant way he wished it was.

"Ah, there he is," Nick mumbled as Malachi moved his head to look at him. They were lying on the bed with Malachi almost on top of Nick. "My amazing, gorgeous boyfriend."

"I don't feel so amazing. A man lost his life because of me."

Nick cupped his jaw. "No. A man lost his life because of *him*. He chose that life. He chose to kill."

"But should he have died for it?"

Nick sighed. "I know what you're saying, Kai. As much as it pains me to say, some people are more dangerous alive and incarcerated. That doesn't mean we should be judge, jury and executioner. It just means that, as horrible as it is, sometimes we don't have a choice."

"I know. I really do. It's just a little close to home right now."

Nick tightened his hold. "I know."

Malachi soaked in the warmth of Nick's body, trying to keep it for himself. "How long was I out?"

"About an hour."

Malachi reared back. "Oh god! Sorry. You must need to move by now."

Nick pulled him back down again. "There's nowhere I'd rather be than wrapped around you." His stomach chose that moment to growl, and he chuckled. "We probably should eat, though."

Malachi huffed a laugh. "I should probably feed the beast before he eats me."

"That idea has merit."

It took Malachi a moment to catch on, and then he swiped at Nick's hands, laughing as he tried to get away. "Food first!"

Nick paused. "Fine."

Malachi climbed off him. "I'll make us some soup and toasties to tide us over."

"I can order takeaway."

"No!" Malachi froze, having not expected such a vehement response. He stared at Nick, who patiently gazed back. "It might take a while before I can do that again."

Nick nodded. "Whatever you want."

"I forgot to ask, did they find Carlos?"

"Yeah. He's fine. He was knocked out but alive. A few bumps and bruises, but he's good."

Malachi exhaled. "That's good. I would have hated being the reason he died, too."

Nick grabbed his arm as he went to leave the room and swung him around to face him. He cupped his cheeks. "You are not the reason. If anyone was, it was me. But why are we beating ourselves up about something *they* did? It was *their* fault. *They* came after us. *They* chose to hurt us. A man died because of choices we had to make, but if *they* hadn't made those choices before us, we wouldn't have had to make them."

The words finally pierced his brain, and his shoulders lowered. "You're right. It might take me a while to truly believe it, but I know you're right."

"Good. We have time to help you believe it." Nick dropped a kiss on his lips. "Now, let's get those toasties." His stomach grumbled again.

"We might need a whole loaf of bread for the number of toasties you'll need to fill that hole."

"I can think of other holes that could be filled." Nick waggled his eyebrows, and Malachi laughed. A real laugh he hadn't thought he'd be able to do so soon.

Malachi kissed him, deepening it when the taste of Nick flooded his mouth. He wrapped his arms around his neck and took everything he could. Reminding himself of what he had. At least until Nick's stomach complained again. He broke the kiss, laughing.

"Fine! I'll feed you!" He pushed away and headed for the kitchen. Everything would be okay. It would. It just might take some adjustments on his part. Maybe he should talk to someone. A counsellor or someone. He just had to keep reminding himself that he was alive, Nick was alive, and the threat was gone.

And as they settled down to eat, he could almost believe it.

29

Nick

Three days later, Nick was ready to sleep, but he still had more to do. They'd received no more threats, nothing else to assume someone was after them again, but he was still on edge. As was Malachi. He would be forever grateful that Timothy had offered to speak with him as he had done countless others before. It was potentially a conflict of interest, but neither he nor Malachi cared about that. Malachi just needed to get it off his chest and understand where he was with his emotions and thoughts.

And while all that had been happening, Nick had been adding the finishing touches to George's party, and now it had finally arrived, he was worried it wasn't good enough. All his parties were made with love from him, but they weren't always suitable for everyone. And throwing a party for a prince was something he had never done before.

In the end, he went with his instincts, and when George entered the room, he threw his hands in the air with a shout and ran for the inflatable bouncy castle.

Timothy and Eddie laughed, the latter folded in two as tears slid down his cheeks.

"Oh, my god. You couldn't have picked anything more suited. Nice work," Timothy said.

Nick grinned. "You haven't seen room number two yet."

"I dread to think."

"It's amazing. I might do that for my own birthday."

"Eddie! Come in! Quick! It's awesome!"

Eddie laughed again and patted Nick on the shoulder. "Thank you." He ran off in search of his husband.

Nick loved that even though they weren't officially married—stupid laws that say more than one person couldn't get married—they still referred to each other as husbands after their ceremony the previous year. And he couldn't remember seeing them happier. That Nick had made George's day was the best thanks he could ever have had.

Arms slid around his waist, and he glanced to the side. "I honestly thought you were going to run out of time, but you pulled it off," Malachi said with a kiss on his cheek.

"I always keep my promises."

"That you do," Malachi murmured, and Nick shivered at the reminder of his words.

Over the past few days, they had spent many an hour reminding and reassuring each other that they were fine and they were still alive. There wasn't a patch of skin that didn't have Malachi's touch tattooed on it, and more than once, Nick had wondered about getting a new literal tattoo. Enough that when he'd woken that morning, he'd bitten the bullet and contacted Life in Ink, a tattoo business that dealt with celebrities and rich people. It wasn't that he wanted the fame of using them, but the knowledge they *did* adhere to their NDAs was a plus in their column—and the fact that other royals had used them. He'd happily pay whatever their rates were to ensure he didn't end up on the front page of the media and pull the royal family down with him. Plus, Malachi knew nothing about it. It would be a surprise.

He let George have his fun for an hour before he got his attention and brought him to a door leading off from the room they were in.

"One more surprise, Your Highness." Nick waved towards the door.

George frowned at him and then headed for the door. When he opened it, several balloons floated out, and he chuckled. "It's balloons," he said, glancing back, unsure.

Nick nodded. "Thousands of balloons, Your Highness."

"A balloon room?" George asked, eyes wide.

Nick nodded, and George whooped and raced into the room, fighting his way through the multi-coloured balloons. It had taken hundreds of volunteers hours of work to blow up enough balloons to fill the room from top to bottom, but it was worth it. The balls of air floated from the room the further George pushed his way in until they couldn't see him. They could hear him, though.

"I don't know how you do it, but you always seem to know what we truly want as a party," Kean said, stopping beside him.

Nick chuckled. "I base it on what you would've liked as a child and go from there. Being brought up in the royal family might've shown what you couldn't have, and I wanted to bring back the chance. Besides, everyone loves inflatables and balloons. What could I do wrong?"

Kean squeezed his shoulders. "Don't belittle the talent you have, Nick. Knowing people is what makes you excellent at your job. And I will never take that for granted. Enjoy yourself. You deserve it as much as my brother does." He nodded, leaving Nick a little emotional.

"He's not wrong," a voice said, and Nick turned. "You do deserve it. That and more," King Andrew said. "You've been through hell and back these past few weeks, and yet you've made sure you turned up for work and did your job, even when you were unsure if you would survive. You put your life on the line for me, and then go home and put your life on the line for yourself and Malachi. I can imagine the amount of stress you've been under, and I just want to acknowledge that you are one of the best men I know. And if you ever need anything, anything at all, you let me know."

Nick tried to talk, and it took a few swallows before he could. "Thank you, Your Majesty."

Andrew winced. "Andrew, please?" He put his hands together in prayer.

Nick huffed a laugh. "Against my will, thank you, Andrew."

Andrew lifted his fists into the air. "Someone said it! Finally! Someone called me Andrew!"

Nick's cheeks heated as everyone started clapping and cheering. Andrew dragged him in for a hug and whispered, "You've made my day now, too. Thank you, Nick. For everything."

He pulled back, and Nick smiled. "You are very welcome...Your Majesty."

Andrew groaned and palmed his face. "Once is better than none." He stepped away and then back again, leaning close. "Malachi has clearance for Club Royal, just so you know. The details were included in the original NDA he signed." He winked and headed over to Kean, who was fangirling over Malachi again.

Darius and his boyfriend, Jason, sidled up. "He seems to have settled in with everyone well," Darius said, nodding towards Malachi.

Nick smiled, and he was aware how sappy he probably looked. "He has. Like he was born for it." Malachi glanced over at him at that moment, and Nick waved him over. When Malachi had made his excuses, he slipped beneath Nick's arm and kissed his cheek.

"Hey, you." He glanced at Darius. "Hey, Darius."

Darius nodded. "Malachi, this is Jason, my boyfriend. I told you far too much about us all, so it's only fair I introduce you."

Malachi chuckled. "That's what happens when you get talking to my grandmother." He held out his hand to Jason. "Nice to meet you."

They spent an enjoyable day filling up on food, drink, music and company, and Nick had several requests for birthday parties, but he couldn't fit them all in, so he decided to keep them to close family and friends, which naturally included the royal family. Unfortunately, that meant he had to start planning the next one, Patrick's, which was in two weeks' time.

When he finally made it back home with a sleepy Malachi, he had a fully booked party calendar, and Malachi, Felix and Jason had a coffee date-that-wasn't-a-date. Nick would admit to being worried about that trio.

As sleepy as Malachi seemed when they entered his house, he soon perked up as they climbed the stairs for bed. They had yet to make it back to Nick's apartment. Well, Nick had, but Malachi couldn't yet face it, which he could completely understand. Sometime soon, he would broach the subject of selling the apartment and buying a new one to make the memories easier for him. But they weren't at that stage yet.

Malachi slid his arms around Nick's neck, fusing their lips the moment they closed the bedroom door. "I feel like I haven't touched you in days."

Nick chuckled. "Definitely not days. More like hours."

"Don't care. I need you. Get naked and on the bed. Now."

Nick paused, the king's voice coming back to him. "Actually, I have something you might want to see. Do you fancy a quick trip out again? It won't take long."

Malachi narrowed his eyes. "Sure?"

Nick smiled. "I promise, you'll like it."

Malachi lifted his fingernails to his mouth but hesitated, a reminder they were trying to break him from the habit of biting them. He nodded, and Nick took his hands and led him back down the stairs and into the car. Malachi asked where they were going several times during the journey, but Nick wouldn't tell him. He wanted him to see it first.

When he parked in the underground parking and took Malachi's hand, leading him to the lift, he kissed the back of his hand. "Calm down. It's all good."

"Where are we, Nick?" But the knowledge was in his eyes.

Nick smiled. "You know where we are, Kai."

Malachi's breath caught as the doors opened to the tastefully decorated foyer of Club Royal. Malachi gripped him tighter.

"Should I be here?" he squeaked, belying his excitement.

Nick nodded. "You have clearance. You already signed the NDA, that included this place."

"Oh, my god. I can't believe this is real. I can't believe I was right. That so many people are right, but can find no one to corroborate it." He glanced at Nick. "Not that I would now, but wow."

Nick chuckled. "You definitely can't write about it. But you may find what you're looking for here." And that was the main reason he wanted to bring him. Malachi still hadn't broached the subject again with him, and if this made it easier for him to figure out what he needed, then Nick would bring him back as often as he had to.

Malachi tightened his hold again as they headed for the reception desk.

"Good evening, Clarice."

The fabulous receptionist and all-round amazing person who could do and get anything and everything they could possibly need smiled at them. "Good evening, Nick. I'm glad to see you. I was wondering when I would meet your beau."

Chuckling, Nick gestured to Malachi. "This is Kai. Kai, this is Clarice. If you are ever in any need, Clarice is the person to go to. She's fantastic."

Clarice waved him away, though he saw the praise pleased her. "Would you like to put your thumb on the sensor, Kai? I need to add your print to our database so it can open the doors for you." He did. "Thank you. I see you've already signed the NDA, that's great. Now, we just need a lock of hair and a drop of blood, and we'll be done." Malachi gaped at her, and she chuckled. "I'm kidding, Kai. You're all done."

Malachi huffed a laugh, some of the tension leaving him. "I wouldn't have put it past this place to need those things."

"It's something I keep campaigning for," Clarice said with a wink. "Go on through whenever you're ready."

"Who is on duty tonight?" Nick asked.

"Princes Christian, Patrick and Albert, and Princex Alice."

Nick chuckled at Malachi's expression. "Thank you, Clarice. Have a wonderful evening."

"You, too."

He led Malachi to the double doors behind the reception desk but paused. "Are you ready?"

"Yes. No. Yes. Maybe."

Nick cupped his cheeks, something that seemed to calm Malachi. "Breathe."

Malachi did and then nodded. "I'm ready."

"Press your thumb to the sensor to make sure it works." Malachi did, and the door clicked. "Let's go."

He pushed through the door and into the main bar. Leading Malachi over to the bar, he explained a few things about drinking and how, if someone had any amount of alcohol, they weren't allowed to play. He also introduced him to Oliver, the resident bartender who spent most of his hours here or in the club with his husband, Griffin, and their partner, Xan.

"Are you ready for reveal number two? The club itself?" Nick asked.

Malachi inhaled and let it out slowly. "Yes."

Nick led him to the door. "It's louder in here."

He wasn't underestimating the noise volume either. The music blared through the speakers, but even that wasn't enough to stop the sounds of pleasure from ricocheting around the room.

"Holy crap," Malachi muttered, and the only reason he heard it was because of how close they were standing.

"This is just the beginning."

He led him around slowly, telling him about the different things they saw or heard. Malachi had some experience with BDSM, which was something he had wondered about, but Malachi had never confirmed. Hopefully, Malachi would trust him enough one day to let him know what it was he was unsure about.

Malachi pulled him to a stop when Prince Christian came towards them. "Good evening. How are you doing?"

"We're good, thanks. Is everything going okay here?" Nick asked.

Christian nodded. "All quiet on the club front." He glanced at Malachi. "Enjoying your first visit?"

"Yes," he squeaked, and Nick smiled. He was so cute.

"I'm looking for Kieren. I wasn't sure if he was going to be here with Patrick working, but if not him, then someone else with similar needs."

Christian didn't change his expression at all, which Nick was grateful for. He thought it would take a while for Malachi to be comfortable talking about BDSM in hearing range of others, and though he'd been open with Nick to a degree, he didn't think he would be willing to openly discuss it with anyone.

"Actually, Kieren is here. He's in the pet play room, talking with Robert.

Nick smiled. "Thanks. We'll go take a look."

Christian nodded. "See you later." He strode off.

Malachi gaped and stared at Nick. "I have no idea what's going on here."

"Let me tell a little story..." he said, repeating the words Malachi had used when he told Nick *his* story. He knew from previous experience that the royals didn't mind their BDSM choices being explained to others in the lifestyle, and so Nick went through the royals and what they enjoyed. Freddie and Damon with their medical play, Douglas and Mav with their sensation play, and George, Timothy and Eddie with their bondage and impact. Henry and Robert with their pet play, Patrick and Kieren with their impact play, and Christian and Oscar with their Daddy and little. He could've gone further, but he'd made his point. Everyone liked different things, and that was okay.

"Why Kieren?"

Nick frowned. "What do you mean?"

"Why do you think Kieren can help me?"

He waved towards the room they were coming up to. "He's into impact play, which is not whipping as such, but it's still impact. He might be able to help you understand something, especially as he's not long found his own way here. If he can't, we'll find someone who can. There are plenty of choices here."

They entered the large room, decorated with every pet play piece of equipment anyone could want. He located Kieren and Robert and pulled Malachi onto a sofa next to them.

"Hey, you two," Robert said. "How're things?"

"Good, thanks," Nick said. "When you have a moment, Kieren, can we have a word? No rush, though." Malachi buried his face in Nick's chest, and Nick's mouth twitched.

"Sure. We were just chatting anyway. Is this something for here or somewhere else?"

Nick was glad Kieren understood the undertones of his words. They'd been friends for a long time, especially as Kieren had been a bodyguard for Patrick before becoming his husband the previous month. He still was a bodyguard in some ways, but he had his own guards now as well.

"Somewhere we can chat without being overheard?"

Kieren nodded. "Follow me." They left the pet play area and headed down the corridor, entering the medical play room. "This isn't booked out, so we can use it for now." He closed the curtains and made sure no one could see inside.

Nick turned to Malachi. "I'll leave you to talk. I'll be close by, though, okay?"

Malachi shook his head. "Stay."

"I think this first conversation needs to be you and Kieren. You need to feel free to say whatever you want without thinking about what I might think about it. Once you've had this initial conversation, you can talk it through with me or ask Kieren to help. Whatever works. But this is for you. Okay?" He cupped Malachi's cheeks again.

Malachi smiled. "I love you so damn much."

Nick kissed the smile off his face and then let him go. "Talk. I'll be in the pet play area with Robert if you need me."

"I'll always need you."

Nick grinned. "And that is damn good to hear." He kissed him again and left, closing the door behind him and hearing the lock engage.

Feeling like he'd left Malachi to deal with it alone but knowing it was the right thing, he strode for Robert, hoping he was still there. He was.

"Everything okay?"

Nick nodded. "They need to talk."

Robert clasped his shoulder. "You did a good thing. Leaving him alone."

"I know." He exhaled. "I kinda feel like I threw him to the lions, though."

Robert snorted. "I'll tell Kieren you called him a lion."

"I've called him worse to his face."

They laughed, and it eased some of the tension in him. They chatted about nothing in particular, interacting with the puppies, kittens, cubs and more when they approached them, throwing the balls for them and whatever else they wanted. Nick had been told it was a relaxing experience in the pet area, but he'd never experienced it for himself until then. They were right. How anyone could get mad at such cute animals was beyond him.

Arms slid around his shoulders, and he startled, making Malachi laugh in his ear. "It's me."

Nick covered his hands with his own. "You okay?"

"Absolutely perfect. Thank you for that."

"You're welcome. What do you want to do now?"

Malachi nipped his ear. "I want to go home and fuck you."

Nick swallowed. "That can be arranged," he croaked. He stood, dislodging Malachi's arms. "We're going! See you later!"

Laughter followed their retreat, but he didn't care. What Malachi wanted, Malachi got, and if he needed him, who was he to disagree with the boss?

30

Malachi

The conversation with Kieren hadn't got Malachi hot and bothered but seeing Nick playing with the pets had. He had such a good heart, and it was often taken for granted. Malachi felt a visceral need to show him how much he cared, especially after what he'd done for him with Kieren.

Talking with him had helped tremendously, and though he wasn't ready to explore it yet, he had no qualms about doing it at the club any longer. Kieren had settled those nerves with an explanation of what he'd experienced. If Malachi hadn't already known the royal family were the best people on the planet, he would've been won over by that.

But for the moment, he was more than content with what he had with Nick, and if that ever changed, he knew he would be able to talk to him about it.

He still liked control, though.

"Naked. Bed. Now," he said as soon as they entered the house.

"Yes, Sir."

Nick ran up the stairs, and Malachi stared after him, watching the muscles in his legs and ass, despite being covered up. He couldn't wait to get his hands on him. Following at a more sedate pace and giving him time to do as he was told, Malachi thought back to his life just two months ago, when he believed Nick hated him and he would never be free from Tucker's clutches. What a difference a short time could make. He still had concerns about his mother's or grandmother's health, but losing his soul to a job just for the health benefits was a good way to an early grave. But he was here, and things were definitely looking up.

He leaned against the doorframe, crossing his arms over his chest and dragging his gaze across Nick's exposed skin. The darkness of the tattoos stood out against the tanned skin, and the prominent veins running across his arms, legs and cock were like a map he could use—and maybe would.

"Hands around the headboard," he ordered, licking his lips as Nick's body stretched to obey.

He pushed off the doorframe and wandered closer, stopping beside the bed and meeting Nick's needy gaze. Hopefully, he would love what Malachi had in mind for him. Reaching for the bedside table, he pulled out the supplies, plus something else, hiding it so Nick couldn't see. After the past few days, they both knew each other's bodies like they knew their own, so it didn't take him long to nestle between his legs and start prepping him.

Malachi's cock was hard behind his zip, and he couldn't wait to get it out and buried inside Nick's ass. While he stretched him with the first finger, he stroked his shaft, keeping him on the edge. He added a second and then a third finger, and then Nick pleaded with him.

"You. Please, you."

Malachi unzipped his trousers and pulled his cock free, lubing it quickly. He didn't take the time to undress, just lined himself up and slid home with groans from them both. When he was deep inside, he paused.

"Wrap your legs around me."

As soon as he did, Malachi grabbed the new toy he'd bought online. He squirted some lube onto Nick's cock, smirking at the deep lines on his face as he tried to figure out what was happening, and then slid the cock sleeve onto his dick.

"Holy fuck!" he hissed.

"Move your hips, sweetheart. Fuck yourself on me and the sleeve."

It took him a few seconds to figure out the rhythm, but soon enough, he was dropping onto Malachi's cock and thrusting forward into the sleeve. His fingers were white on the headboard, his muscles bulging with every movement. Malachi could feel himself drawing closer and closer to the edge.

"That's it. Take yourself over the edge, Nick."

Nick increased his speed, and Malachi barely kept hold of the sleeve, but then Nick groaned and worked his way through his climax, the pure, painful pleasure of an orgasm flowing across his face. Chest heaving, Nick slumped to the bed, though his hands remained around the headboard.

Malachi was on the edge. "Nick, keep moving."

Nick opened his eyes and stared at him, licking his lips before continuing his previous movements. Malachi inhaled through his nose as his climax barrelled forward. Three more thrusts, and he flew, gripping Nick's hips as he took over and slammed deeper, coaxing every bit of his orgasm from him. Resting back on his heels, he dropped his head back, wincing when he slid free from Nick's ass.

He peered down at him after a few seconds. "You can let go now, Nick."

Nick unpeeled his hands from the headboard and fisted and stretched them repeatedly. "Ouch."

"Maybe I need to swap it out for some cylindrical ones, rather than square."

Nick's stomach muscles clenched, and he rose, encircling Malachi in his arms. "It's fine. I love you."

Malachi sighed, never tired of hearing that. "I love you."

"Mum, please. I'm fine. You don't need to worry about me looking a mess. It's just them. They won't mind! I only donated blood. It's not all over me."

Emily huffed. "Just them, he says. They're important, Malachi! We have to give a good impression."

Malachi smiled. "I think your chocolate cake at Prince George's party was enough of a good impression. More than one person said it was the best they'd tasted, and even Oscar said he'd love to have it in his coffee shop."

Emily flushed, and she busied herself with putting her light jacket on. "Okay. Well, we're as decent as we're going to get. We better not keep them waiting."

Malachi withheld his comment and held the door open for her and his grandmother. Nick waited by the car, opening the doors and helping them in. Sally took the passenger front seat, like he knew she would, and Malachi settled behind Nick. It meant he could meet his gaze in the rearview mirror, too. Nick had offered to take them to dinner, but the king had offered to host them instead, giving Malachi's and Nick's families the chance to meet them properly.

Sally asked plenty of questions of them on the journey, even questions she'd asked several times before. It was her way of settling her nerves because the royal family had been a big part of *her* life, too. She had grown up with them as much as he had, and it was where his love had come from.

Parking at Windsor Castle was easy enough, and then he and Nick escorted them into the building. The moment they entered, Sally gasped, holding onto Malachi's arm as she looked above her.

"It's so big! The pictures don't do it justice."

"I thought the same when I first came here," Malachi said.

"Mrs Hopkins, Mrs Sanders, I'm so glad to meet you. Malachi has told me a lot about you." Andrew stood before them, and Sally gripped Malachi's hand. "I would love to escort you to dinner if you would let me."

Emily smiled and curtsied. "It's very nice to meet you in person, Your Majesty. Thank you for the escort. Mum?"

Sally visibly pulled herself together. "I would like to say one thing before we go." Malachi winced, wondering what was going to come out of her mouth.

"Of course."

"I'm so dreadfully sorry about your father, your mother and your wife. You've had a life filled with grief and yet you're determined to pull every ounce of happiness from it as you can. I wish I had the same perseverance."

Andrew's expression softened further. "Thank you for your kind words. It hasn't been without a lot of soul-searching and help from my family that I managed to do so. I hope we can help you do the same."

Sally waved her hand. "I'm too old to change my ways now, but thank you for the offer."

Andrew waved his hand towards the corridor. "Shall we?"

Emily asked some questions about the decoration as they walked, and Sally listened intently. Malachi dropped back and walked beside Nick.

"It seems to be going well," he whispered.

Nick smiled. "They already love each other because of what we've told them, so I doubt there will be any problems. The main thing will be keeping an eye on your grandmother and making sure she doesn't go walkabout." He winked.

Sally glanced over her shoulder and narrowed her eyes at Nick, and he tensed.

"Did I forget to mention that she had supersonic hearing?" Nick glared at him. "Yes."

Malachi laughed and slipped his arm around Nick's, resting his head on his shoulder while they walked. Reaching the royal family's dining room, Andrew held the door for the women, and Nick grabbed it so the king could enter, and then they followed. The rest of the Sutcliffes rose from their chairs, and Sally gasped, her hand covering her mouth. Malachi stepped to her side.

"Are you okay?" he whispered.

She smiled, though it was a little shaky. "I'm just so glad to see the entire family so happy. It's different seeing it on the TV, but in person, it makes everything much clearer." She wiped her eyes, and he led her to the table where Andrew and Emily waited.

Andrew went around the table, stopping at each person and introducing them, even though Malachi's family knew who they were. Then he led them to the chairs next to his and settled them in. Malachi and Nick took the seats at the other end.

"How long before they have to extend the tables again?" he asked.

Nick chuckled. "No idea, but soon, even this room will be too small."

"Unless you add a 'children's' table," Malachi joked.

"Who would be on it?" Nick asked, his face alight with humour.

"George," three voices said at once.

Malachi looked around Nick to see Oscar, Eddie and Kieren grinning at him. He snorted, covering his mouth before it became too loud. He glanced at the top of the table and received a glare from his grandmother, and he straightened and looked down at his plate, his mouth still twitching.

"That told you," Nick whispered.

"It wasn't just to me," Malachi replied, and Nick glanced up the table before snapping his head back again, eyes wide.

"How does she do that?"

"Magic," Malachi whispered. "It's passed down, generation after generation."

"What's your magic power, then?"

Malachi raised his eyebrows. "If you have to ask, I'm not doing it right."

He kept a straight face for several seconds before Nick's flush cracked his composure, and he burst out laughing.

"You'll pay for that," Nick murmured.

A jingling bell announced Malachi's entrance into Book Drunk. The scent of coffee and cake assaulted his nose in the most pleasant of ways, and his stomach rumbled. It was his own fault. He wanted to save his appetite for the coffee shop instead of eating at home with Nick. Plus, he'd been eager to get going that morning, and the choice to meet Felix and Jason at eleven o'clock in the morning was far too late by his standards.

He'd grown close to Felix in the weeks he'd been at Windsor Castle and with Nick. They hadn't had anything to do with each other before that, only in passing at events occasionally. But since his almost assault had taken him into the realm of royalty further than he could have ever imagined, Felix had been talking to him, messaging and calling him to check up on him.

In that time, they'd become friends. Malachi might even go so far as to say best friends, if that could happen in such a short time.

And when Darius had introduced him to Jason, they had hit it off completely, and their surprising trio had been born. Their first coffee date had turned into four hours of chat, laughter, food and drink, and they'd made it a weekly deal from then on.

Nick had been a little uneasy about the three of them getting together, to begin with. Malachi sensed he thought he was being replaced, but once he showed Nick how much he needed him—four hours was nothing to them—he hadn't been worried after that.

And there they were. Felix and Jason were already at what he was coming to think of as "their" table, deep in conversation. Deciding not to interrupt, he went straight to the counter to order their drinks.

"Hey, Oscar. How are you?"

Oscar beamed at him. "Never been better. You?"

"Good, thanks."

"Are you wanting your usual?"

"Yes, please. Have they already ordered?" he asked. Oscar shook his head. "Can I get theirs as well, then, please?"

"No worries. I'll bring it all over once it's done."

"Thanks, Oscar." He held out his card and raised his eyebrows, and Oscar sighed.

"Fine." Oscar rang up their order and huffed as he held out the card reader. The man had a penchant for allowing the royal family and their families, spouses and all, to have free food and drink, but Malachi had been concerned about him tanking his business by doing that so much, especially with how many of them there were, so he'd demanded to pay. It had been a battle of wills in the beginning, but eventually, Malachi had his way. Oscar did get him back a bit because he always made sure to add a hefty discount—but at least he was still making money instead of losing it, so he'd call that a win.

Malachi winked at him and headed for the table. "Have you stopped gossiping yet?" he asked as he settled beside Felix.

Felix nudged him with his elbow. "We don't gossip. We—"

"Deconstruct. Yes, I know, but it's still gossiping no matter what label you put on it," he said with a grin.

"You should talk," Jason said, coming to Felix's defence. "Who was it who brought us the information about The Ports?"

Malachi chuckled. They weren't wrong. "Well, when I get given an exclusive scoop on the lead guitarist, what more could I do?" He held out his hands.

Oscar chose that moment to bring over their drinks, and he must've caught the tail end of his words. "That exclusive was epic! I can't believe they gave you that. Who would've thought? I wonder if Dennis Carter is regretting it now with how much more publicity he's got?"

"I honestly didn't think it could've got bigger, but somehow it has," Malachi said. "But I suppose when he was proven to be in a relationship with a man who died, it was always going to be a story, no matter what he did. At least he was able to get his own version out there for all to see. Poor guy is broken."

"I would be, too," Jason said.

They all shared a moment of silence. It had been a difficult article to write, but it had been a good one. Dennis had been able to get everything onto the page without giving too much of his life—and other people's lives—away. Oscar squeezed his shoulder and left, leaving them to their chat.

"What's the dirt on Randall's party, then?" Felix asked, leaning closer.

Malachi chuckled. "There is no way in hell I'm giving you that information," he said. "It's worth more than my life."

Felix groaned. "Come on! It's not even a week until his party. You can tell me. I won't tell a soul."

Malachi stared at him, eyebrows raised. Just stared because he'd found that Felix got a little uncomfortable when friends met him head-on about something. Give him an interrogation environment with someone who was against him, and Felix could hold his tongue with the best of them, but give him a friend, trying to pry information out of him, and he caved after a while.

"Oh, fucking hell. Fine. Dominic bet me that you wouldn't cave, and I said you would."

Malachi gasped and palmed his chest. "You have so little faith in me. I'm heartbroken." He pretended to wipe a tear from his eye. "And I thought you loved me." He fake sobbed into his hand, covering his eyes with the other.

Felix nudged him hard enough to scrape his chair across the floor, and Malachi laughed. "Shut up. I just wanted to win the money. Dominic is far too good at predicting stuff. I would love to get one over on him at least once."

"What's in the pot?"

"One thousand."

"A thousand?" Malachi gaped. "A thousand pounds?" Felix nodded. "Where the hell do you get that amount of money to play with? Jeez." He paused, an idea percolating in his head. "What are the terms of this bet?"

"Whoever gets you to spill details gets the money. If no one does, Dominic gets it," Jason said.

Malachi tilted his head. "And that's it. No other rules or fine print?" Felix shook his head, and Malachi grinned. "So, there's nothing to say I can't give you a little piece of the puzzle because, theoretically, I will have given you some of it. I don't need to ruin the surprise, but I can give you *something*."

The smile that stretched across Felix's face was nothing short of a sunbeam, and Jason chuckled, shaking his head.

"You're both as bad as each other," he said.

"Half for you and half for me?" Malachi said, holding out his hand to Felix.

"Deal."

They shook.

31

Nick

N ick watched his family interacting with Malachi's family and smiled. He hadn't been wrong when he said they would get along, but having so many people in one room, in addition to the royal family and everyone else, it became a huge undertaking for him to create a party for Randall and yet make sure everyone was having fun, too.

He saw Malachi shaking hands with Felix, a huge grin on his face, and shook his head. Wheeling and dealing was something his boyfriend had just started doing, and he placed the blame solely on Felix for corrupting him.

Malachi came over, counting out money. When he stopped in front of Nick, he handed out a few notes. "It's only fair," he said, and Nick took it, knowing Malachi wouldn't have it any other way.

"You're a menace. All three of you are," he said, chuckling at Dominic's stormy expression.

"Well, what can I say? If you don't make the rules without wiggle room, then you should expect to be fleeced." He laughed.

"Working with Felix to find a loophole was mean."

Malachi shrugged. "Maybe it'll teach Dominic a lesson."

"Even though he was on your side?"

Malachi winced a little at that. "Yeah, maybe I'll have to make it up to him somehow."

"You think?" He pulled him in for a hug and pressed his lips to his temple. "He'll forgive you, don't worry about it."

"I hope so."

"How is your family getting on?"

Malachi sighed and glanced over at where his sisters were chatting with Princes Douglas and Mav. "Good. A little surprised they turned up," he murmured.

As if they had known they were being talked about, his sisters glanced over at him. Nick could see their expressions change, and they must've made their excuses because Douglas nodded his head and they headed towards him and Malachi.

Malachi straightened.

"Hey. Thanks for inviting us," Christine said with a smile.

"I wondered how you seemed to find time in your 'busy' schedule when it comes to a royal invitation, yet you can't find the time when it comes to family. Funny that," Malachi said, and Nick was proud of him for standing up to them for once—and for his restraint in not knocking them sideways for being assholes.

Christine and Zara glanced at each other and then back. "You're right," Zara said. "It's just that, since...Mum, it's been hard. I know it's hard for everyone, but..." She shook her head. "I'll do better."

"I will, too," Christine said.

"You will," Malachi replied. "Because it can't just be on me any longer. It's not fair."

"We thought you didn't mind!" Christine said.

Malachi snorted. "Of course I don't mind. They're family. But I shouldn't have to carry the weight of it *all* by myself. You're more than capable of helping out. Especially at Christmas."

Zara cleared her throat. "I will make sure I'm there this year. We can't have you cooking and doing everything on your birthday now, can we?"

"Why? I've done it for the past four years."

Nick tightened his hold and pressed his lips to his temple again, murmuring, "Back off a little, sweetheart. They're trying."

Malachi sighed. "Thank you. That would be great. Mum and Grandma would love you to be there."

The sisters smiled, though it didn't quite reach their eyes, and then they headed to their mother, who was surrounded by Andrew, Kean and Kendal. They appeared mesmerised by whatever she was talking about.

"I should've taken it easier on them."

"No. You did right. But they know they did wrong, so it doesn't need to keep going. See if they do actually change their behaviour, and if not, broach it again."

"Who made you so wise?"

"Your grandmother," Nick deadpanned.

They laughed, receiving a far few stares in the process, but nothing held his attention more than the man he loved with his head thrown back and happiness on his face. It made everything worthwhile.

Malachi

One year later

Malachi inhaled deeply as he waited in the changing room at Club Royal. It had been a long year, one filled with grief, happiness, sadness, humour and…training. A few weeks after he'd had the initial conversation with Kieren, he'd sat down with Nick and talked through everything. He'd been surprised to find out that Nick had some news for him. He'd arranged for the princes to train him in impact play and whipping so he could be the one to do it, instead of being apart from it. It wouldn't be something he would be able to do straight away, but then Malachi wasn't ready to do it right away, either. So, after a long discussion over several days, they decided to wait until Nick was fully trained before Malachi experienced whipping. It made things easier on Malachi, too. As much as he trusted the princes, he didn't think he would be able to relax enough to enjoy it.

Their sex life was nothing to be ashamed of, though, especially with his new favourite thing—phone sex! Nick had persuaded him to try one night, and after the initial uncomfortable feeling, it had been…orgasmic.

But tonight was the night. Nick had been trained fully, and Malachi had been present when he'd whipped several people over the past few weeks. Nerves abounded, but he wanted this. For himself and for Nick. Nick was excited about being able to do this for him, and he refused to let him down. He could cancel. No one would care, but he wanted this.

Kieren entered the changing room and smiled. "He's ready whenever you are."

Malachi inhaled again, letting it out through his nose. "I'm ready. I'm a lot nervous, but I'm ready."

"It's scary the first time, but you can take it as slow as you need to, and if it doesn't feel right, you can try again another day. There's no right or wrong here."

"I know. I suppose I don't want to let *myself* down. I've wanted this for so long, but to be here now, it's a big thing." Malachi wrung his hands.

"It is. It really is."

He liked that Kieren wasn't giving him false platitudes. Everything he said was correct, and even though he knew it already, it helped that someone else was saying it.

"Thanks. I'm ready." His voice was stronger this time.

Kieren grinned. "Okay, then."

They wandered through the club, both smiling and greeting people they knew, something Malachi never believed he'd get to, and came to a stop in front of the door Nick was behind.

"You good?" Kieren asked.

Malachi smiled, actually feeling it. "Yes, I am."

Kieren knocked on the door and waited until Nick opened it before waving and leaving them alone. Malachi entered the room, meeting Freddie's gaze while Nick locked the door behind them. He stepped into Nick's arms and clung to him, inhaling his scent.

"We don't have to do this."

Malachi pulled back. "I want to. I really do. I'm just nervous as I would be if I was going on a rollercoaster ride for the first time." He glanced at Freddie and smiled. "Thank you for being here."

They had decided—well, Nick had requested—that having Freddie in the room would help with any potential incidents and would make them both feel better. And he'd agreed immediately when they'd approached him about it.

"Are you ready?" Nick asked.

"Yes."

Nick led him over to the St Andrew's Cross they'd arranged for the room. It had been discussed as to the best way to experience the first whipping, and Freddie had said that being restrained and therefore not able to move would make things easier on Nick and Malachi because it would reduce the chance of injuries.

Malachi removed his shorts, leaving him in a jock, and stepped up to the cross. Nick fastened him to it, trailing his fingers over his skin as he did. He glanced at Freddie, but the prince was reading a book and not looking at him.

"Have you decided on your safe word?"

"The traffic lights."

"Good. As a reminder, if you are unsure, you need to say yellow or red immediately and don't wait for me to ask. Okay?"

"Yes, Sir."

"If you're ready, I will start with your warm-up."

"I'm ready, Sir." Malachi breathed, calming his racing heart.

"I'm going to rub some body disinfectant into your skin to protect you."

"Thank you, Sir."

The liquid was cool, to begin with, but as Nick rubbed in circular motions across his back and ass cheeks, it began to warm. Once he had finished with that, he continued the circles with his hands, heating the skin more, and then, after explaining the next step, he began with small taps on his ass. When Nick decreed him sufficiently warmed, he then rubbed the tails of the whip along his skin, getting him used to the sensation, though he knew it would be much different when it turned into a whip.

Malachi lost track of time during the warm-up, and he enjoyed the sensation of Nick's hands on him, and the difference between that and the whip itself was easy to decipher. His mind floated, his body humming as the sensations floated through him.

"Are you ready for more?" Nick asked.

"Yes, Sir," Malachi said, eager to feel the bite.

"I'll do five strokes to begin with. Count for me."

There was a brief lull where Malachi tensed, expecting to be whipped, but it never came, and as he relaxed when it still never happened, it finally did. The sting took his breath away for a second, and then he inhaled again as the heat spread through his body.

"One," he whispered. Another sting, and his breath hitched again. "Two." Another. "Three. Four. Five."

Then Nick was in front of him, cupping his jaw. There was a slight pressure on his wrist, but he ignored it in favour of staring at his boyfriend. He smiled, his head spinning a little.

"How are you feeling, Kai?" Nick asked.

"Loopy." He grinned, and Nick smiled.

"Do you hurt anywhere?"

"Nope. Feels good."

"What colour are you?" Nick asked.

Malachi blinked. "Green, Sir."

"Glad to hear it." Nick dropped a kiss on his lips and brushed his fingers across his cheek. "Do you want more?"

"Yes, please, Sir."

"Okay, we'll do five more strokes. You don't have to count this time."

Malachi didn't tense, enjoying the sting of every stroke, and when Nick stood in front of him again, he couldn't help but tell him, "I love you so damn much."

Nick smiled, lighting up the room. "I love you, too. Let's get you down, okay?"

"Yes, Sir."

Malachi's entire body buzzed, and there was a low-level hum in his brain, but as Nick laid him down on something soft, he closed his eyes.

"Kai, wake up, sweetheart."

"Hmm?"

"I'm going to clean your back, okay?"

"Okay." He floated until whatever stuff Nick used touched his skin. He hissed. "Ooh."

"Sorry, sweetheart. It'll feel much better soon. Let the cream do its job."

Malachi breathed through the sting—a different type of sting this time—and eventually, it eased and began to feel nice.

Something warm surrounded him, and he dropped into a doze, still able to hear the sounds around him, but not reacting to them.

When he pulled himself from his slumber, he snuggled into his pillow, realising it was Nick's chest. He blinked, peering up at Nick, and smiled. "Hey."

"Hey, you." He reached down and lifted something—a bottle and a straw. Malachi sucked greedily.

"I needed that, thanks."

"You're welcome. How are you?"

He checked in with himself. A slight ache to his back and ass, but other than that, he felt great. He told Nick as much.

"I'm glad. Freddie checked my work and said it was perfect, but I couldn't relax until you were awake. I didn't want to hurt you badly."

"You didn't. I promise. It feels good."

Nick smiled and the tension released from his body. "We can stay here as long as we want, Freddie said."

"Good. I'm enjoying snuggling with you."

He closed his eyes and drifted off again, his hand resting on the newest tattoo decorating his lover's body. A phoenix to remind them that no matter what they went through, they could always reform brighter than before. Nick would protect him, and he would protect Nick. After all, a relationship needs compromise, right?

Want to know Darius and Jason's story? Check out the free book you get when you sign up to my newsletter below!

Read on for a teaser of the book description for Protecting his Life, the final book in the Guarding Royalty series.

Would you like to read my books before anyone else? You can sign up to Steamy Delights, a membership subscription service, and gain early access to chapters from my work-in-progresses, exclusive bonus content and more. I have four tiers available: Contemporary, Kink & Daddy, Taboo & Dark and Club Royal Bonus. See which one grabs your fancy.

https://reamstories.com/elouiseeast

Protecting Jason

FREE!

Jason doesn't have the strength to fight his stepfather for a happy life, so, to stop the man from turning his fists and words to his younger siblings, he takes the brunt of his anger himself. He vows to get those children away from him as soon as possible. Then, when there is one bruise too many for his best friend's eyes, they come up with a plan for a fake boyfriend for Jason—someone who's really a bodyguard.

Darius doesn't get asked to the royal family's domain often, but he doesn't say no when he is. Being asked to be a fake boyfriend is far from usual, but he's happy to do it if it means he gets to spend time—and protect—the man he can't stop staring at. When things don't quite go the way Jason hopes, Darius offers another option. One that might backfire. But with Darius at his side, Jason finds more strength than he ever thought possible.

And maybe, he might've found the one person who could give him his happily ever after.

This is an MM bodyguard romance that spans both the Club Royal and Guarding Royalty series.

Get this book FREE here: https://elouiseeast.com/newsletter

Protecting his Life

When he loses everything, what does he have left?

Brett has a highly stressful job, but he loves it and the people he works for. His family, however, have made their feelings clear about his career choice. The people who depend on him have been targeted by someone trying to take them out, but so far, they've kept one step ahead. But now, as clues point towards someone closer to home, he turns to the one person who has never let him down.

Felix has been in love with his boss since the day he started working for him. It's unrequited, but Felix can't help but torture himself every day. He doesn't have any intention of leaving. At least until someone physically removes him from the vicinity, and when all hope is lost, he clings to the memories of Brett and the whispers of what-ifs.

When one of their own is taken, they'll take down anyone to get them back.

Protecting his Life is a kinky, friends to lovers romance with a security boss who doesn't believe anyone would want

him with his past and a cheerful computer genius who wants anything and everything his boss will give him.

Books by Elouise East

Guarding Royalty
Protecting his Past
Protecting his Heart
Protecting his Secrets
Protecting his Life

Club Royal
Royal Firsts
Rogue Royal
Secretive Royal
Grieving Royal
Disowned Royal
Trained Royal
Awakened Royal
Commanding Royal

Illuminate Matchmaking
Ignite
Blaze

Kindle
Scorch

Boys, Daddies, Snuggles & More
Need Him
Trust Him

Daddy
Love Me, Daddy
Soothe Me, Daddy
Spoil Me, Daddy
The Complete Daddy Series

Love in Flames
Fight Fire with Fire
Out of the Frying Pan
Smokescreen
Breathing Fire
Love in Flames Collection

Crush
Love Conquers
Instant Desire
Primary Seduction
Deep Down
A Crush for Christmas
Life Support
Covert Strength
Love Scene
Lawful Attraction
Crush Collection Volume 1
Crush Collection Volume 2
Crush Collection Volume 3

Just A Little Crush
First Kiss
He's Behind You
A Special Love

Standalone
Treehouse Whispers
Star-Crossed
Protecting the Thief
Sizzling Chauffeur
A Home for Barney
Mattie

<u>Elouise R East (taboo)</u>
Dark & Divergent
Forbidden Temptation
Too Many Secrets: A Life of Secrets
Too Many Secrets: The Lake House
Secrets in his Eyes

Collide
When Fantasies Collide
When Dreams Collide
When Pleasures Collide
When Cravings Collide
When Hungers Collide

Dark
Defying Sanity
Stronger Together

About Elouise East

E louise East writes sweet and steamy connections in gay romance. She also touches on taboo stories under the name Elouise R East.

Books that tell the stories where friendship and family are the focal point - be it blood family or chosen - are very important to her. That's why she includes a variety of personalities, talents, ages, situations and abilities as she believes a story or character needs. She wants her characters to be real, to be relatable, to be free to have whatever views they tell her they have. And trust her, most of the time, she does not have *any* say in the matter!

Her characters come to life on the page for her as well as her readers. Their stories unfold in front of her as she writes, and she has very little input into how they want to be shown. Just like real life, the lives of her characters change with every choice, every interaction and every conversation. And she wouldn't have it any other way.

She writes books that are emotionally realistic, even if liberties are taken with other aspects of the stories. She doesn't know any other way to write. It comes from deep inside.

Who is she? A single parent to two children living in the UK. An avid reader who still tries to devour every book she can get her hands on. A student of learning about any subject that takes her fancy. An author of books she would read herself. And a romantic at heart who loves anything cheesy.

Who's joining her on her journey?

Stalk her here… ;-)

Website : https://elouiseeast.com

Newsletter : https://elouiseeast.com/newsletter

All links : https://elouiseeast.com/links